SO-AHH-552

Line of SCRIMMAGE

MARIE FORCE

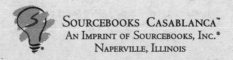

SOURCEBOOKS CASABLANCA™
AN IMPRINT OF SOURCEBOOKS, INC.®
NAPERVILLE, ILLINOIS

Copyright © 2008 by Marie Force
Cover and internal design © 2008 by Sourcebooks, Inc.
Cover photo © iStockphoto.com/Mark Stout, Getty Images

Sourcebooks and the colophon are registered trademarks of Sourcebooks, Inc.

All rights reserved. No part of this book may be reproduced in any form
or by any electronic or mechanical means including information storage
and retrieval systems—except in the case of brief quotations embodied in
critical articles or reviews—without permission in writing from its
publisher, Sourcebooks, Inc.

The characters and events portrayed in this book are fictitious or are used
fictitiously. Any similarity to real persons, living or dead, is purely coin-
cidental and not intended by the author.

All brand names and product names used in this book are trademarks,
registered trademarks, or trade names of their respective holders. Sourcebooks, Inc., is not associated with any product or vendor in this book.

Published by Sourcebooks Casablanca, an imprint of Sourcebooks, Inc.
P.O. Box 4410, Naperville, Illinois 60567-4410
(630) 961-3900
FAX: (630) 961-2168
www.sourcebooks.com

Library of Congress Cataloging-in-Publication Data

Force, Marie.
  Line of scrimmage / Marie Force.
   . p. cm.
  ISBN-13: 978-1-4022-1424-0
  ISBN-10: 1-4022-1424-3
  1. Marriage—Fiction. 2. Football stories. I. Title.
PS3606.O7L56 2008
813'.6—dc22
                        2008013934

Printed and bound in the United States of America
      OPM 10 9 8 7 6 5 4 3 2 1

For my parents,
George and Barbara Sullivan,
who always said I could,
and for Dan, Emily, and Jake,
who stood by me while I did

Chapter 1

IF THERE WAS ONE THING SUSANNAH SANDERSON—SOON to be Susannah Merrill—excelled at, it was setting an elegant table. Along with sparkling crystal and gold on silver flatware, there were dainty tapered candles perched in sterling candlesticks. A floral centerpiece in buttery yellows and golds complemented the main attraction: her grandmother's Limoges china. Susannah often said that in a fire she'd grab the photo album from her debutante ball and as much of Grandma Sally's china as she could carry.

Not every dinner party warranted the use of the china with the pale flowers and strip of fourteen-carat gold around the edge. But entertaining her fiancé and his parents certainly qualified as a china-worthy event.

Susannah glanced at Henry, and he smiled with approval as he took a bite of the succulent leg of lamb she had prepared with just a touch of mint.

"This is absolutely delicious, honey," Henrietta Merrill said to her future daughter-in-law.

"You're a lucky man, son," Martin Merrill added. "There's nothing quite like being married to a beautiful woman who can cook."

Henry reached for Susannah's hand, his love for her apparent in his worshiping gaze. "I know, Dad."

When a strand of his salt and pepper hair fell across his forehead, Susannah had to resist the urge to brush it back from his handsome face. Henry wouldn't approve of such an overt display of affection in front of his parents. The paisley bow tie he wore with his starched light blue shirt was a little crooked, but it only made him more adorable to her. He filled her with such an over-whelming sense of safety and tranquility—two things that had been sorely lacking in her life until Henry had returned to it. In just one month she would be his wife, and she'd have that safety and tranquility forever. Susannah couldn't wait.

Almost as if he could read her thoughts, Henry squeezed her hand and then released it to reach for his wine glass.

"Have you found your mother-of-the-groom dress yet, Mrs. Merrill?" Susannah asked. Henry's parents were spending the month before the wedding with their son in Denver.

"Just yesterday at Nordstrom. It's a lovely pale green silk."

Susannah forced herself not to cringe. The color would be horrible with the deep reds she had chosen for the late February wedding. "I'm glad you found some-thing you're happy with."

"Now tell me," Henrietta said with a twinkle in her eye. "What's with this 'Mrs. Merrill' business?"

"Sorry," Susannah said with a small laugh. "Old habits die hard. I've been calling you Mrs. Merrill since Henry and I dated in high school."

"Well, now you're going to be his wife, so I thought we'd agreed to dispense with the formali-ties, hadn't we?"

"Of course . . . Mother."

Henrietta's portly face lit up with a warm smile.

After Susannah served her famous chocolate mousse, her future in-laws lingered over coffee—decaf so Martin would be able to sleep.

Susannah was startled to hear a chime echo through the house, indicating the front door had opened.

"Were you expecting someone, honey?" Henry asked.

"No." She pushed back her chair but froze halfway up, flinching when she heard first one boot and then another drop onto the marble floor in the foyer. Only one person had ever dropped his boots in her foyer . . . *It couldn't be. Could it? Oh, God, please no* . . . "Excuse me," Susannah stammered to her guests as she rushed from the dining room, through the kitchen, and into the foyer, stopping short at the sight of her ex-husband, Ryan.

"*What are you doing here?*" she asked in an exaggerated whisper.

He was bent in half putting something into the shabby duffel bag that sat at his feet. When he slowly stood up to his full six-foot, four inches, his signature Stetson shaded half his face. One deep dimple appeared when he smiled at her. "Hello, darlin'," he said in the lazy Texas drawl that used to stop her heart. But now, like everything else about him, it left her cold.

"What are you *doing* here?" she asked again.

"I'm home," he said with a casual lift of his broad shoulders. He shrugged off a beat-up calfskin jacket and tossed it at the coat stand.

Susannah wasn't surprised when the coat snagged a hook and draped itself over the antique brass stand.

"What do you mean *home?*" she hissed. "This isn't your home."

"See, that's where you're wrong." He made a big show of checking his watch. "For ten more days I own the place."

"This house is *mine,*" she whispered. "You need to get your stuff and get out of here. *Right now.*" She reached for his coat and yelped when his hand clamped around her wrist.

Bringing his face to within inches of hers, he grinned and asked, "Why are we whispering?"

"Because I have guests." She made a futile attempt to break free of the grip he had on her arm. "And you're not welcome here."

He sniffed at the air like a dog on the scent of a bone. "Do I smell lamb?" He ran his tongue over his bottom lip. "You know I love your lamb. I hope you saved some for me."

Realizing the movement of his tongue on his lip had captured her attention, Susannah tore her eyes away. "I don't know what kind of game you think you're playing, Ryan Sanderson, but you need to pick up your stuff and *get out,*" Susannah said in an increasingly more urgent tone as she struggled once again to break free of him.

But instead of letting her go, he brought her left hand up to his face, his brown eyes zeroing in on her engagement ring. "Is that the best old Henry could do? Not exactly the rock you got from me, is it?"

"It doesn't come with any of the headaches I got from you, either. Now, let me go and *get out!*"

"*Let go of her!*" Henry roared from behind Susannah. "This *instant!*"

Ryan snorted. "Or else what?"

Susannah wished the marble floor would open up and swallow her whole. "Henry, honey, go back to your parents. Everything's fine. Ryan was just leaving."

"The hell I was. I just got home. Is this any way for a wife to greet her husband?" Ryan asked, adding in that exaggerated drawl of his, "Got yourself another man while I was off fighting the wars, did ya, darlin'? You didn't even send a Dear John."

With desperation, Susannah glanced up at Ryan. The half of his face that wasn't hidden by the big hat was set into a stubborn expression that told her he was determined to get his way. This was *not* good. "Henry, please. Go back in with your parents and give me a moment," Susannah pleaded with her fiancé, who shot daggers at her ex-husband—or, well, her soon-to-be ex-husband. "*Please*."

"Only if he takes his hands off you," Henry said. His ears turned bright red as he clearly struggled to keep his rage in check.

Ryan released Susannah's arm. "Happy now, lover boy?"

"I'll be happy when you get the hell out of here and go back to whatever rock you crawled out from under."

"*Ohh*," Ryan said with a dramatic shiver. "I'm scared. You're *so* intimidating in that bow tie."

"That's enough, Ryan," Susannah snapped. With a weak smile for Henry, she nodded toward the dining room.

After one last long, cold stare for Ryan, Henry turned and left them.

"He's a real tiger, that one," Ryan said with a growl. "I'll bet he tears it up in bed."

"What do you want, Ryan?"

"In a word? You."

"Well, you can't have me. So this visit—while unexpected—has been nice." She spun on her heel and walked away from him. "You know the way out."

"Not so fast. I'm not going anywhere. This is my house. I bought it and everything in it."

Susannah whipped around to face him. "And you gave it all to me in the divorce!"

"Which, I might remind you, is not final for ten more days. Now, I'm a pretty reasonable guy, and believe it or not, I'm not looking to start trouble for you and lover boy. So let me make this easy for all of us, okay?"

Wary, Susannah nodded. "That would be best."

"We've got ten more days as Mister and Missus, and we're going to spend them together."

Susannah started to protest, but Ryan held up his hand to stop her. "Every minute of every day for the next ten days."

"You're out of your mind! There's no way I'm spending ten *minutes* with you, let alone ten *days. No way.*"

"You always had such a soft spot for the McMansion." He sent his eyes on a journey through the spacious foyer, the sweeping staircase, and the formal living room. "It took us long enough to hammer out a settlement the first time. A renegotiation would tie things up for months, and in light of your *engagement,* I'm thinking that might be a little inconvenient for you . . . "

"You *wouldn't!*" Susannah fumed, but even as she said it she knew he would. Her stomach knotted with tension as she thought of the wedding and all her plans with Henry.

Ryan crossed the marble foyer to her. His scent, a woodsy mixture that always reminded Susannah of the mountains, was as familiar to her as anything in her life. "Watch me," he said so quietly she might not have heard it if he hadn't been standing so close to her.

Her blue eyes filled with tears. "Why are you doing this?"

He reached out to touch her shoulder-length blond hair. "We made a mistake."

"*How can you say that?*" She slapped his hand away. "Our marriage was a nightmare. The divorce was the best thing we ever did."

He shook his head. "It wasn't a nightmare. Not always. Remember the first few years, Susie?"

"Don't call me that. That's not my name, and you know I hate it."

"You didn't used to hate it. Remember when we made love and I'd call you Susie? Do you ever think about how hot it was between us?"

"No! I never think of you. *Ever.*" She pushed him away, and he gasped. "What? What's wrong with you?"

Struggling to catch his breath, Ryan said, "Nothing." But his lips were white with pain.

Susannah reached up to remove his hat and recoiled when she revealed the side of his face the hat had hidden. "*Oh my God!* What happened to your face?"

"Sack gone bad on Sunday. Shoulder pads to the ribs, helmet to the face. Three busted ribs, but fortunately the mug is just badly bruised. Won't hurt my endorsement deals."

"Well, thank God for that," she said sarcastically. His face was so black and blue Susannah had to resist the urge to reach up and caress his cheek. She couldn't help but ask, "What about your helmet? How could this have happened?"

"The dude hit me so hard, it didn't do me much good," he said, shaking his head before his grin returned. "We won, though. They didn't knock me out of the game until late in the fourth quarter when we'd already sewn it up."

"Great," she said without an ounce of enthusiasm. If she never heard another word about the Denver Mavericks, it would be too soon.

"The *Super Bowl*, baby," he said with the cocky grin that was all Ryan. "That makes three in five years in case you were counting."

"I wasn't but congratulations. Now, please leave. I mean it, Ryan. This trip down memory lane was interesting, and I'm sorry you're hurt, but there's nothing left for us to talk about."

"I beg to differ." He hooked his arm around her neck and dragged her to him, flinching when she made contact with his injured ribs. Tipping his head, his lips found hers in a kiss that was hot and fast.

Susannah tried to protest, and he took advantage of her open mouth to send his tongue on a plunging, pillaging mission.

When he finally pulled back from her, Susannah could only stare at him.

"How could you forget *that*, darlin'?" he asked softly.

She shoved him and didn't care about the flash of naked pain that crossed his handsome face. Whether it was the hit to his ego or his ribs that caused it, she didn't know and didn't care.

"*Don't touch me!* Do you hear me? I'm *engaged* to another man. You had your chance with me, and you blew it. You come in here like a big conquering hero jock and think that crap is going to work on me. I've heard it all before, Ryan, so you can save it. I've asked you nicely to leave. If you don't go, I'll call the police."

He snickered and combed his fingers through his dirty blond hair. "And what do you think they're going to do to the guy who just brought home *another* Super Bowl trophy?" Reaching into the pocket of his faded, form-fitting Levis, he withdrew his cell phone and held it out to her. "Give them a call. Be my guest."

"*Ugh!*" she growled with frustration, knowing he was right. The cops wouldn't do a damned thing but fawn over him the way everyone always did.

"If you're going to be pig-headed about this, I guess that leaves me no choice." He casually scrolled through the numbers on his cell phone. When he found what he was looking for, he pressed the send button.

"Who are you calling?"

"My divorce attorney. Putting the brakes on things."

She snatched the phone out of his hand and turned it off.

He raised an eyebrow, and his battered face lit up with amusement. "Does that mean we have a deal?"

"And just what am I supposed to tell Henry?"

"I don't give a flying fuck."

"Lovely, Ryan. That's just lovely. You're as rude and crude as ever."

"And you're still hot for me," he said with a smug smile. "*Damn,* that just pisses you off, doesn't it?"

"I know your over-inflated ego will find this hard to believe, but I'm not even lukewarm for you."

"Whatever you say, baby," he said, wincing as he bent to pick up his worn Mavericks duffel bag. He took the Stetson from her, tossed it at the coat rack—where it landed with spot-on perfection—and started up the stairs.

"What do you think you're *doing?*" Susannah asked with mounting desperation.

"Going to bed. Feel free to join me when you ditch lover boy. Oh, and if you're feeling generous, you can bring me some ice for my ribs."

"When pigs fly."

"If that's how long it takes, I can wait. The season's over, and I've got nothing but time."

Helplessly, she watched as he trudged up the stairs and disappeared down the hallway. She stood there for a long time trying to figure out what to do until Henry finally came to find her.

"Did you get rid of him?" he asked.

With a glance at the top of the stairs, she said, "Um, not exactly."

Chapter 2

"WHAT?"

"Shhh," Susannah said. In that moment, she realized arousal wasn't the only emotion that made Henry's ears turn red.

"This is *outrageous!* He can*not* stay here."

"Keep your voice down," she hissed. "This foyer echoes through the house. He'll hear every word you say, and so will your parents."

"I don't care. I want him out of here."

Susannah nibbled on her thumbnail as anxiety coursed through her. "I don't think that's going to happen. Not tonight anyway."

"So what am I supposed to do? Just leave you here with your ex-husband?"

"Technically, he's not my ex-husband. Yet."

Henry tugged at his bow tie, which seemed to be choking him all of a sudden.

"Let's go back in with your parents." Susannah slid her hand into the crook of his arm. "We'll talk about this later."

"Yes, we certainly will."

Ryan eased himself onto the bed and winced when the mattress sagged under his weight. Pain ricocheted through his body. He unbuttoned his shirt and grimaced as he eased it over his shoulders. The simple act of swinging his legs onto the bed and resting against the pile of pillows caused him to break out in a cold sweat. He took shallow breaths in and out until the blast of pain had passed. By the time it did, though, his heart pounded and his stomach roiled with nausea.

Downplaying the injury in front of Susie had used up what was left of his energy after he checked himself out of the hospital that morning—against medical advice—to fly home from New Orleans on the private plane the team had sent for him. Aware he was running out of time to stop a divorce he didn't want, Ryan had been desperate to get home to Susie. The rest of the team had arrived home two days earlier to find their adoring fans waiting for them at the airport. Ryan had been sorry to miss the party on the plane and the celebration at the airport, but he'd been through it before—twice, in fact—so he would survive missing it this time.

He had been banged up plenty of times in the twenty years since he started playing football as a sixth grader. During his junior year at Florida, he dislocated his elbow—fortunately not his throwing arm—in a game against Florida State. The Mavs had been playing the Bears when he tore a ligament in his left knee three years ago. That had hurt like a son of a bitch and knocked him out for half a season. But he had never broken a rib, let alone three of them, and on a scale of one to ten, the pain of broken ribs was a twelve. His face didn't feel too great, either, and his head had been throbbing for days.

He wanted to cry when he realized his pain pills were in the duffel bag across the room. He hoped Susie would come up to fight with him, so he could cajole her into getting them for him.

Ryan hated being so helpless, but luckily he bounced back fast from injuries. He already felt a lot better than he had when it first happened. He'd had his eyes locked on his friend Bernie in the end zone and hadn't seen the hulking defensive end coming. The ball had just left Ryan's hand when *boom!* He saw stars as he lay on the field gasping for air and wracked with pain in his head and chest.

Eight hours passed in a pain-induced fog before Ryan thought to ask if Bernie had caught the ball. Of course he had, and the touchdown added six insurance points to the score. After also learning he had been named Super Bowl MVP—again—he found out one of the broken ribs had almost punctured his lung and the hit to his face had given him a concussion.

Ryan winced when he pictured his less-than-glorious exit from the NFL—on a stretcher of all things. No one knew yet that he had played in his last game. He made the decision weeks before the Super Bowl and was waiting to announce it until after the team had its moment of celebration. No way would Ryan allow his personal announcement to detract from the attention his teammates deserved after their big victory.

A sneeze startled him, and he was unable to stop it in time. The new blast of pain ripped through him and brought tears to his eyes. He had discovered in the last three days that sneezing was the most painful thing in the world when your ribs are broken.

Unfortunately, his allergies had picked this week to act up for the first time in months. Tomorrow he would call the team doctor to get a shot for the allergies—anything to stop the sneezing.

When he managed to catch his breath, Ryan lay still to listen to the voices at the bottom of the stairs.

"Everything was lovely, Susannah," Henrietta said, offering her cheek to Susannah.

Susannah kissed the plump cheek. "Thank you . . . Mother."

"Let's talk this week about the final wedding plans," Henrietta added.

Susannah nodded as she kissed Martin goodbye. They had managed to avoid telling Henry's parents that her ex-husband was in the house.

"I'll be out in a minute," Henry said to his parents, handing the car keys to his father.

Susannah knew he wanted them gone so he could confront her about Ryan. She wanted to beg them to stay.

"Take your time, son," Martin said with a wink.

The moment the door closed behind them, Henry pounced. "I'm going up to talk to him."

Susannah grabbed his arm. "That's not a good idea."

"Let me handle this, Susannah. I *need* to handle it."

"You can't," she insisted. "He's not listening to reason. I know him. When he gets like this, all you can do is wait him out until he changes his mind. You have to trust me on this."

"I *do* trust you. It's *him* I don't trust."

They looked up when they heard Ryan at the top of the stairs.

Susannah gasped when she saw he was wearing only boxer shorts. The half of his face that wasn't battered was pale and pinched with pain. Above and below the tape on his ribs were evil-looking bruises that stretched from his waist to his shoulder. As he came down the stairs, she noticed his usual cocky stride was gone. That he was so obviously in agony made her heart hurt for him, despite her aggravation over his sudden reappearance after more than a year of separation. She watched as Henry's eyes skirted over Ryan's broad shoulders, his sculpted chest and abs, his narrow hips.

Henry swallowed. Hard.

Even banged up, Ryan Sanderson was the sexiest man Susannah had ever seen—and he knew it. From the look on Henry's face, he knew it, too. He was daunted by Ryan's imposing physique, which was exactly what Ryan had hoped to achieve by coming down there in his underwear.

"Is there a problem, darlin'?" Ryan asked as he reached the bottom of the stairs.

"You need to leave," Henry stammered. "It's completely inappropriate for you to just show up here and to walk around like . . . like *that*."

With an innocent look on his face, Ryan scratched his belly just above the waistband of his red plaid boxers. "Like what?"

"Half naked."

Ryan snorted. "I don't know what you consider to be naked, but I'd say I'm about three-quarters naked. Susie can tell you I prefer being *au natural*. I only kept the shorts on because we have company. Despite your low opinion of me, I'm not a *total* Neanderthal."

"That's enough, Ryan," Susannah snapped.

"I just came down for a glass of water, so I can take my pain pills," Ryan said. "Don't let me interrupt."

"You are *not* staying here with my fiancée," Henry said in a burst of courageous indignation.

"She may be your fiancée, but she's still *my* wife. So I hate to point out the obvious, padna, but I think I trumped your ace."

Henry fumed, and his ears turned bright red.

"Here's how this is going to go," Ryan said. "I want a few days alone with my wife with no annoying distractions—"

"That's *not* going to happen," Henry retorted.

"Yes, it is, or there'll be no divorce and thus no wedding. You following me here?"

"You can't do this!" Henry cried.

"I believe I already have." Ryan left them in the foyer and went into the kitchen.

When they were alone, Henry reached for Susannah's hand. "Come with me," he pleaded. "Come home with me."

"I can't," she whispered. "I have to pacify him, so he won't make trouble with the divorce. It's the only hope we have."

"What am I supposed to do while you're playing house with your ex-husband?"

"Wait and be patient."

"I've been doing that for more than eleven years. How much patience do you expect me to have?"

"It's ten more days. After all this time, surely you can give me ten more days." She cradled his face with her hands. "Can't you?"

His expression stony, Henry said, "You're asking an awful lot of me, Susannah. I know what that egomaniacal bastard put you through. How do you expect me to just walk out that door and leave you here with him?"

Ryan came back into the foyer carrying a glass of water. "Still here, Henry?" he asked, lifting that cocky eyebrow.

Henry fixed his eyes on Susannah. "I was just leaving."

"I'll be waiting for you upstairs, darlin'," Ryan said as he started up the stairs.

"Sanderson!" Henry called. "If you lay one finger on her, I'll kill you. Do you hear me?"

"You'd have to catch me first," Ryan said with a snicker.

Susannah stopped Henry from replying. "Let it go," she said softly. "He's all talk."

"I mean it, Susannah," Henry said, holding her tight against him. "If he touches you, I'll kill him."

"He won't get the chance."

"See that he doesn't."

Susannah took a step back from him. "I don't care for the insinuation."

"And *I* don't care for your ex-husband showing up less than a month before our wedding and staking his claim on you like a cowboy from a cheesy western."

"I think you'd better go now, before one of us says something we'll regret."

"*Don't you see what he's doing?* He's *already* causing trouble between us."

"He can only cause trouble between us if we let him." Susannah leaned in to kiss him. What she intended to be a quick goodbye kiss became much more when Henry hauled her to him and left her with a thorough, possessive kiss.

"Call me if you need me." He looked up to the top of the stairs. "If anything happens—"

"It won't."

With great reluctance, he nodded and left.

As Susannah watched him walk to his Toyota sedan, she saw him pause to study the brand new black Cadillac Escalade in the driveway. Apparently, Ryan had been named Super Bowl MVP—again. She touched her fingers to lips that still tingled from the most passionate kiss she'd ever received from Henry. Long after he drove away, Susannah rested her forehead against the cool glass of the storm door. *Ten days alone with Ryan Sanderson. I'll never survive it. I barely survived the first go-round with him. What in the world am I going to do?*

Susannah took her time cleaning up the dining room and kitchen. She washed and dried the crystal, returned the flatware to its mahogany box, and hand-washed Grandma Sally's china. When there was nothing left to wash, dry, or polish, she wiped her hands on a dishtowel and hung it up. She locked the back door and turned off the lights before she crept up the stairs to find the light on in the master bedroom. *Oh, he has some nerve!*

As she stood in the hallway working up the fortitude to face him again, she heard him sneeze three times in rapid succession. He cried out in pain, and Susannah rushed into the room. His eyes were closed, his skin sallow and flushed, and he was gasping for air.

"Oh, God, Ryan," she sighed. "You should be in the hospital."

"I'm okay," he said between shallow breaths. "It's the goddamned allergies. Something in New Orleans stirred them up."

Susannah went into the bathroom and returned with two Claritin pills, which she handed to him.

"Still keep that stuff in the house?"

"They're yours," she said with a shrug. "I never threw them out." She picked up his glass of water from the bedside table and handed it to him.

"Thanks." He gave the glass back to her and closed his eyes.

"What are you doing here, Ryan? Really?"

"I told you," he said with a weak sigh.

"Were you expecting a warm welcome home?"

"Not particularly. All I know for sure is I still love you, and I think maybe you still love me."

Susannah was bent in half picking up his jeans from the floor. She straightened and looked at him in amazement. "I don't," she said, folding the pants and setting them on the foot of the bed.

Ryan sneezed again and wrapped his arms around his middle to defend against the pain.

"I'll get you some ice," she said, anxious to get away from the sight of him suffering. The Ryan she knew was never this helpless. Even when he had torn his ACL, he had been up and about the day after he'd had surgery to fix it. She hadn't ever seen him flattened like this and was unnerved by it. When she returned with the ice, Ryan reached for her hand.

"Stay with me, Susie," he said, his almond-shaped brown eyes locked on hers as she laid the ice bag over the tape on his ribs.

Those eyes, that fabulous, sexy mouth, the shaggy hair that would've looked messy on most other men, the dimples . . . It was more than Susannah could bear. Anger flashed through her. *How like him to reappear like this and stir up old feelings in me just as I'm about to move on with my life—with another man.* She couldn't let him get away with it. "I can't," she said. "I won't."

"What do you think is going to happen? I can barely move." He took a shallow breath and tightened his hold on her hand. "Stay. Please."

She studied his battered face for a long moment before she pulled her hand free.

"Susie . . . " he said to her retreating back. "I need you."

Susannah went into the bathroom and closed the door. Her heart raced with anxiety and sympathy and—*damn it*—desire. He was right. She wanted him as much as ever. She wanted to lay down with him, put her arms around him, and offer whatever comfort she could. But nothing with Ryan was ever that simple. That it was still possible for her to feel sympathy and desire for him amazed and disturbed her. She changed into pink flannel pajamas, washed the makeup off her face, and applied the moisturizer she used every night without fail.

Studying her face in the mirror, she contemplated the creamy complexion she went to great lengths to keep out of the sun that shone three hundred days a year in Denver. Her blue eyes were a little too far apart for her liking, but Ryan always said they were the eyes of an innocent girl. She ran a finger down the bridge of the straight, patrician nose she considered her best feature. A few of her Junior League friends had spent small fortunes for noses that looked like hers. Dabbing balm onto lips that formed a perfect bow, she wished for the thousandth time that her lower lip wasn't quite so full. All in all it was an attractive face—albeit not her sister's stunningly beautiful face. But it was better than most. She brushed her blond hair until it was shiny and smooth and then reached for her toothbrush.

By the time she emerged from the bathroom, Ryan had fallen into a restless sleep. Susannah sighed as she studied him, remembering the first time she'd ever seen him. She had been with a group of girlfriends at the Purple Porpoise in Gainesville. When Ryan came in with a bunch of football players, Susannah's friends had dissolved into whispering, giggling fools. They were struck dumb when Ryan stopped at their table, his eyes singling out Susannah.

"How's it going?" he asked.

Ignoring the jab from one of her friends, Susannah said, "Fine."

"Ryan Sanderson," he said, extending his hand to her.

"Susannah Freeman."

He kept her hand in his as his mouth twisted with amusement. "Nice to meet you, Susannah Freeman."

Right about then she noticed everything in the restaurant had come to a halt and all eyes were focused on her. Her face had grown hot with embarrassment. She pulled her hand back and reached for her soda.

"I'll see you around, Susannah Freeman."

She managed a small nod before he walked away.

"*Oh my God,*" one of her friends said. "That was *Ryan Sanderson.*"

"Yes, I heard him say that," Susannah said.

"He's the starting quarterback for the Gators."

"Oh." Susannah glanced over her shoulder for another look at him. "What's a quarterback?" When he winked at her, she quickly turned away. As she acknowledged something about him made her nervous, she became aware that her friends were staring at her with their mouths hanging open. "What?" she asked them.

Susannah smiled at the memory. Since that day she had learned more than she'd ever wanted to know about football—and Ryan Sanderson. He shivered in his sleep, so she reached for the blanket at the foot of the bed, removed the ice bag, and carefully spread the blanket over him. She took the ice into the bathroom and dumped it in the sink. When she returned, she flipped on a night-light, so he wouldn't injure himself further if he woke up disoriented.

His eyes opened, and he held out his hand to her. "Stay with me, Susie."

"I can't. You know I can't."

"I might need something during the night, and I seriously can't move right now. Please?"

Drawn to his suffering, she turned off the bedside light, walked around to the other side of the bed, and got under the covers. As she lay down, she told herself it meant nothing. She would do the same thing for anyone who was hurt and in need of help.

When she was settled, he reached for her.

Susannah laced her fingers through his, reminding herself yet again that it was only because he was so badly hurt that she was even talking to him, let alone holding his hand and sleeping with him. Well, she wasn't *technically* sleeping with him. Most of the king-sized bed was between them, and he wasn't under the covers with her.

"Thank you," he whispered.

"We're going to talk about this tomorrow. You can't stay here, Ryan."

He turned his head so he could see her in the faint glow of the nightlight. "Ten days, Susie." His voice was hoarse with pain and what might have been emotion. "If you still want the divorce after that, I won't stand in the way. I'll leave you and Henry alone. I promise."

"*Do you?* Do you promise you won't pop in again like this to remind Henry that my ex-husband is a bigger, stronger, wildly popular, ridiculously wealthy superstar?"

He grinned. "You forgot fabulously sexy."

Susannah did not want to laugh but couldn't stop the gurgle from escaping. "You're impossible."

"I meant what I said earlier." He squeezed her hand. "I love you, Susie. I always have, and I always will."

Her heart fluttered in her chest, but she was determined not to let him charm his way past her defenses. "Those are just words, and they don't mean anything to me anymore. Not after all that's happened."

"I've changed," he insisted. "I'm not the same guy who was stupid enough to let the best thing that's ever happened to him slip away. All I'm asking for is ten days."

Ten days, she thought. *If I don't do this, will I always wonder what might have happened? No, I know what'll happen. We'll be fighting in two days, if it takes that long. Henry will never forgive me if I spend this time with*

Ryan. But how can Henry—or anyone—know what this man has meant to me for all of my adult life? Or how he hurt me. I can't let myself forget about that. I just can't. Susannah sighed. *But since I've already given him more than ten years, what's ten more days to ensure I'll finally be free of him?*

"All right," she said softly, even as she admitted to herself that she might never be truly free of him. "Ten days. Not one minute more. And when it's over, I'll still want the divorce, and I'll expect you to keep your promise to leave me—and Henry—alone."

She saw none of the usual cockiness she had come to expect from him when he got his way. Instead, his eyes and expression were solemn. "You won't be sorry."

Chapter 3

THE PHONE RANG AT EIGHT THIRTY THE NEXT MORNING. Susannah heard it but couldn't work up the energy to open her eyes and answer it—until she felt something hairy brush against her face. Her eyes flew open to find Ryan's chest serving as her pillow. Her leg was tossed over his and her arm was stretched across his belly, just below the tape on his ribs. His arm was tight around her, his lips pressed to her forehead. In the moment before she began to struggle free of him, she noticed he was hugely aroused.

He grunted with pain when she pushed him away.

"What are you *doing?*"

"Holding you," he said with a big yawn.

"I should've known I couldn't trust you," she fumed.

"Hey, don't blame me! You'll notice I'm exactly where I was when we went to bed. You're the one who trespassed."

"I did *not!*" She was mortified to think she might have reached for him in her sleep.

"Um, you did, too. I was over here minding my own business . . . "

She sprung out of bed. "Oh, *shut up!*"

He watched with amusement as she stormed around the room. "You're so damned beautiful when you're pissed off. You always were."

"You should know. You made it your goal in life to piss me off."

"Is that what you think?"

The phone rang again.

"Are you going to get that?" he asked.

With a withering look at him, she snatched the portable phone from its cradle.

"Good morning, Susie. It's Duke Simmons."

"Hello, Duke," she said to the Mavs coach.

"How's our boy doing?"

"*Your* boy is just fine." She glanced at Ryan, and he grinned at her. "I'll give him the phone."

"Thank you, sweetheart."

Susannah handed the phone to Ryan and went into the bathroom, slamming the door behind her.

"Morning, Coach," Ryan said, combing his fingers through his unruly hair.

"How you doing, Sandy?"

"A little better today," Ryan said, relieved to realize it was true. "How about you? Has it sunk in yet?"

"Three times in five years," Duke said, the amazement clear in his voice. "Hard to believe, isn't it?"

"Sure is. Are they tossing the D word around?"

"Like crazy. But if this team isn't a dynasty, I don't know what is. The reporters are like rabid dogs wanting a piece of you. Do you mind if I update them on your condition today?"

"Not at all. Just say I'm recovering at home and will be skipping the parade and everything because of my injuries."

"Are you sure you want to do that? We could work something out . . . "

"I'm not going to be paraded through the streets of Denver looking like the freaking crypt keeper."

Duke laughed. "Probably a good call. You'd break the heart of every woman in the city if they see your pretty face all banged up."

"Fuck you," Ryan said, but there was laughter in his voice. Duke Simmons was the father Ryan never had, and there was nothing he wouldn't do for the guy. His heart ached when he thought about the conversation he needed to have with his coach. But not today. Not when Duke was still basking in the glow of the Super Bowl victory that cemented his standing as the greatest living football coach.

Still chuckling, Duke said, "Is there anything we can do for you, Sandy?"

"Can you send Doc over to the house with something for the allergies? The sneezing is killing me."

"No problem. I'll have him there right after the parade. So you and Susie, huh? Back together?"

"Working on it."

"That's good. I'm glad to hear it. The two of you breaking up . . . well that was a damned shame."

"Never should've happened," Ryan agreed. "Listen, I'm going to be laying low with her for a few days, so keep the media away, will you?"

"Consider it done. Your teammates, on the other hand—"

"That's all right. They can call me."

"Oh, Rodney Johnson wants to talk to you, too. Okay if I give him this number? He's all done in over the job he did on you."

Ryan smiled. The NFL's most fervently religious player was responsible for the broken ribs and concussion. "Yeah, give him the number."

"You know where I am if there's anything you need, right?"

"Sure do. Congratulations again, Coach."

"Couldn't have done it without you, man."

"Thanks for calling." Ryan turned off the phone and held it against his chest. He would miss having the support and camaraderie that came with belonging to a team. Most of his life he'd had teammates and coaches surrounding him, and he knew that loss would leave a void when he retired.

Retired.

Ryan sighed. Thirty-two and retired. He could've played for a few more years and was confident his skills and abilities would've held out. In fact, he had been planning to sign on for three more years when his friend, Dan Trippler, had been unceremoniously dumped as the starting quarterback for the Buccaneers. A couple of bad games, a few interceptions and turnovers, and suddenly the star of the team was relegated to second string.

Ryan wasn't going to stick around long enough to let that happen to him. He would rather go out on top than wait for age, wear, and tear to catch up with him. With a Heisman Trophy and three Super Bowl rings to his name, he certainly had nothing left to prove and had secured his place in the Hall of Fame a long time ago. He had vast business interests that, along with his wife, were now going to get his full attention.

Susannah emerged from the bathroom dressed in a black pantsuit and a pale pink silk blouse. "How did Duke know you were here?"

"They wouldn't let me off the plane until I told them I'd be here with you."

"You were pretty damned confident I'd let you in, weren't you?"

He shrugged and then winced as he shifted to find a comfortable position. "Where are you going?"

"I have a meeting at the Downtown Athletic Club for the Black and White Ball."

"How long will you be gone?"

"A little while," she said as she put on the diamond earrings he had given her as a wedding gift. He was pleased she still wore them.

"Are you going to see Henry while you're out?"

"That's none of your business."

"I disagree."

"You can strong-arm your way into this house, but you will *not* tell me who I can see and what I can—or *cannot*—do."

"Why do you have to make this so difficult, Susie?" he asked with a deep sigh.

She turned to him, incredulous. "Are you *serious?* You're upsetting my whole life by blackmailing me into spending ten days with you. You've got some nerve to say *I'm* making things difficult."

"Blackmail is such an ugly word."

"What would you call it?"

He ignored that and said, "I want to know when you'll be back."

"A couple of hours," she said with a sigh of her own.
"I'll be waiting."

Shaking her head, she left the bedroom.

Ryan watched her go and was filled with an emotion
that was all new to him—fear. He was afraid he'd waited
too long to try to get her back. Maybe she meant it when
she said she didn't love him anymore. But still, in the
instant before she remembered all the reasons she
wanted to divorce him, he had seen a spark of something
in her eyes when she awakened in his arms. What it was,
he couldn't say, but it was enough. For now. He sat up
with great difficulty. When he caught his breath, he went
into the bathroom to shower and shave.

By the time he was dressed in jeans and a Mavs
T-shirt, he was weak with exhaustion and furious that
he had to sit on the bed for several minutes to marshal
the energy to go downstairs. In the kitchen, he made
coffee and toast. He was determined to get through the
day without the pain pills that left him muzzy and
fatigued. Four days had passed since his injury, and he
was already fed up with being weak and helpless. He
had learned from experience, though, that the more he
lay around the longer it would take to regain his strength.

He took a second cup of coffee into the den and sat
down slowly on the sofa. His head pounded from the
activity, but it was a less intense pain than the day before.
Even at the end of his career, he was still blessed with a
body that bounced back fast from injuries that would've
sidelined a lesser man for weeks.

Reaching for the remote, he turned on one of the local
stations to watch his teammates being paraded through

downtown Denver. He smiled when he saw Bernie, Coach Simmons, and all the guys making their way through streets lined with fans dressed in the purple-and-yellow team colors. Bernie hoisted the Lombardi trophy over his head as the flatbed they were riding on drove past a young woman holding a sign that said, "WE LOVE YOU RYAN—DENVER'S MVP!!!" Ryan smiled and was sad to be missing a moment he had worked so hard for all season. He listened to the congratulatory speeches from the governor, the mayor, and Coach Simmons, all of whom mentioned Ryan's contributions to the winning effort.

"Ryan is recovering at home and sends his thanks to the fans who've supported us all season," Coach said.

Ryan laughed when his teammates commandeered one of the cameras and shouted messages to their fallen quarterback. "Idiots," he muttered, even though he was touched by their exuberance.

When the local coverage of the victory parade ended an hour later, Ryan flipped through the channels for something to watch while he waited for Susie to get home. Since there was nothing on but soap operas and talk shows, he scrolled through the TiVo listing to see if Susie had any good movies in there. He was startled to find the Super Bowl on the list. His face lit up with a big smile. "Well, I'll be damned," he whispered. "You *do* care, darlin'." Discovering she had recorded his game infused him with hope. *Why would she bother if she didn't care about me anymore? She must not have watched it, though, because she seemed surprised last night by how banged up I am. If I get the chance, I'll have to ask her about it.*

He fast-forwarded through the game, stopping to watch his four touchdown drives in the first half and enjoying the effusive praise he'd received from the commentators. "Has the NFL ever seen another quarterback quite like Ryan Sanderson?" one of them, a retired player, asked. "Not that I can think of, Jim," the other replied. "His talent is dazzling."

Hmm, dazzling, Ryan thought. *I like that.* He skipped the over-the-top halftime show and the uneventful third quarter—during which the 49ers scored their only touchdown—and was well into the fourth quarter when he braced himself to view the hit that caused his injuries.

Watching in slow motion, he paid close attention to the guards and tackles who were supposed to protect him from a defensive line he could now see had been in a blitz formation. Ryan's center, Marcus "Darling" Darlington, had managed to hold off Rodney Johnson until the monstrous defensive end stormed past Darling, crashing straight into Ryan's side. He winced as he watched Rodney's helmet smash into his, causing his head to snap back violently.

Ryan rubbed his sore neck as he watched the play a second time. The last thing he remembered was the referee's bright yellow penalty flag landing on the field. The team's trainers and doctor rushed onto the field, followed by Coach Simmons and the offensive line coach. After a few tense minutes during which the commentators had nervously speculated about Ryan's failure to move, the trainers removed him from the field on a stretcher. Coach leaned down to say something to him. Then Ryan raised a hand to the crowd as he left the field. He had no memory of doing that or of the fans going wild at the gesture.

The phone rang, and Ryan moved carefully to reach for it. "Hello?"

"Um, yes, hello. This is Rodney Johnson. How are you feeling?"

"Like I got run over by the biggest, baddest defensive end in the NFL," Ryan said with a chuckle. "Funny you should call right now, I was just watching the playback."

"Listen, man, I'm really sorry . . . "

"For what? Doing your job?"

"I did it too well this time. I didn't mean to break your ribs and stuff."

"You did a number on my handsome face, too."

Rodney snorted with laughter. "I'm sure that's a bigger problem for you than the ribs."

"You know it. I appreciate the call, Rodney, but you shouldn't give it another thought. We both know shit happens in this game."

"Thank you for your forgiveness, and I'll pray for your speedy recovery."

The image of the three hundred-pound defensive end bent in prayer amused Ryan. "I appreciate that."

"The league was a little less forgiving than you've been," Rodney winced.

"Hit you with a hefty fine, huh?"

"Sure did."

"Well, I know you didn't do it on purpose, so don't sweat it. Enjoy the off-season."

"Oh, I plan to, but I would've enjoyed it a whole lot more if we'd beaten you guys."

Ryan laughed. "Maybe next year."

"Take care, Ryan."

"You, too."

He returned the phone to its cradle and rested his head back on the sofa, infuriated to realize he was already tired again. But rather than fight it, he gave into it and slept for a couple of hours. The doorbell awakened him. Stiff after his nap, Ryan shuffled through the house like an eighty-year-old man and swung open the door to find a bunch of his teammates on the front porch holding grocery bags and cases of beer. Grateful Susie wasn't home at the moment, Ryan greeted them with a smile. "What are you guys doing here?"

"You missed all the fun," Bernie said. "So we figured we'd bring the fun to you."

"You gonna let us in, Sandy?" Darling hollered from the steps.

"Sure, yeah, come on in." Susie was going to kill him for this. He winced when Toad, his backup quarterback and one of the youngest players on the team, slapped him on the shoulder on the way by.

"For Christ's sake, Toad, he's hurt." Bernie smacked Toad on the side of his head. "Don't touch him again."

"Sorry, Sandy," Toad said.

"No worries. I won't break."

"I sure am sorry I let it happen." Darling shook his head with dismay at the colorful bruises on Ryan's face. "That motherfucker Johnson is *huge*."

"Tell me about it." Ryan followed them into the kitchen. A beer was pressed into his hand, and he took it only because he hadn't had any pain medicine. "He called to check on me."

Everything in the kitchen came to a halt. "Get the fuck out of here," Bernie finally said.

Ryan smiled. "I know. It was a first for me, too."

"Saved himself a trip to the confessional," Toad said, and the others howled with laughter.

As Darling dug out pots and pans, a few of the guys got comfortable on the granite counter that made up the center island, and each of the massive men had a cold beer in his hand. *Uh oh,* Ryan thought. *They're settling in. Susie is definitely going to kill me.*

"What are you making, Darling?" Ryan asked.

Darling's big white smile lit up his black face. "My world-famous chili, of course." He flipped a huge tray of ground beef into a frying pan.

The doorbell rang again, and Ryan went to answer it. "Hey, Doc. Come on in and join the party."

Doc's white eyebrows knitted with disapproval. "What's going on here, Sandy? You're supposed to be taking it easy."

Ryan glanced over his shoulder toward the voices and music that pulsated from the kitchen. "The guys just wanted to say hi."

"Do I need to remind you that you should be in the hospital?"

Ryan rested a hand on the little man's shoulder. "I know. Did you bring me something for the allergies?"

With a dour glance at the kitchen, Doc nodded.

Ryan led the doctor into the den and gently lowered himself to the sofa.

Doc had given him the allergy shot and was re-taping Ryan's ribs when Bernie came into the den.

"Hey, Doc," Bernie said. "How's the patient?"

"He should be in a hospital, not partying with you fools."

"I'm offended on behalf of all the fools in the kitchen," Bernie said indignantly.

Ryan chuckled, but his smile faded when Doc tightened the tape. The pain shot through him like wildfire, causing him to break into a cold sweat.

"*Damn,* man," Bernie said. "Are you all right?"

"He is *not* all right," Doc said. "He needs to be resting."

Ryan would have defended himself if he could've spoken. He wished he had taken the pain pills.

"Almost done," Doc said.

By the time Doc left, Ryan was stretched out on the sofa trying to breathe his way through the pain.

"Jesus," Bernie uttered. "You're freaking me out, Sandy."

"Sorry," Ryan rasped. "Hurts like a sonofabitch."

"Don't you have drugs or something?"

"Yeah, but I'm trying not to take them."

"Why the hell not?"

"They fuck me up." Ryan rested a hand on his pounding head. "Just give me a minute. It'll pass."

Bernie sat down across from Ryan.

Darling came into the room. "Ready for some chili?"

"Sandy's down for the count, man," Bernie said. "We should probably go."

"I'll be all right," Ryan said. Under normal circumstances, he would have razzed his friends for being so concerned. Right now, he just didn't have it in him. "You don't have to go."

Someone turned up the rap music in the kitchen, and it pounded through the house.

A few minutes later, Susie came in through the front door and made a beeline for the den. With her hands on her hips and her eyes shooting daggers at Ryan, she said, "What the hell is going on here?"

Chapter 4

BERNIE GOT UP TO HUG SUSANNAH. "SO GOOD TO SEE YOU, Susie." He kissed her cheek. "Mary Jane and I have missed you."

"I've missed you, too," Susannah said with a smile.

Ryan was relieved to see her soften as their old friend embraced her.

"I was so happy to hear you and Ryan are back together," Bernie said.

Ryan winced. *Oops.*

Susannah's eyes narrowed. "We are *not* back together." She tossed a pointed look at Ryan. "I don't know where you got that idea."

From his place on the sofa, Ryan shrugged with innocence.

"Oh," Bernie sputtered. "I thought, I mean, Coach said . . ."

"Don't sweat it, Bern," Ryan said.

Darling broke the tension in the room when he planted a loud kiss on Susannah's cheek. "You look gorgeous, as always."

Despite her annoyance at Ryan, she smiled and patted his cheek. "Still a charmer, aren't you, Marcus?"

"Yes, ma'am, so they tell me."

She cast a glance at the kitchen where voices competed with loud music. "Is the whole team here or does it just sound that way?"

"Oh, no," Darling said. "Only about fifteen of us."

"Well, that's a relief," Susannah said dryly. "What are you cooking?"

"Oh, shit!" Darling bolted from the room. "The chili! Stay there. I'll bring you some."

"Great," Susannah muttered as she removed her black leather coat and draped it over the chair in front of her antique roll-top desk. "Fifteen football players and a bowl of chili."

"Sorry about all this, darlin'," Ryan said with a sheepish grin. "The guys just wanted to see for themselves that I'm still alive." He could tell she was working hard at not being a poor sport in front of his friends. "How was your meeting?"

"Fine," she said. "The Black and White Ball is next weekend."

"And you're the chair again?" he asked, ashamed he didn't know for sure and embarrassed that Bernie was witnessing just how out of touch he was with his wife.

She nodded.

"Does that make five years in a row?"

"Seven," she said quietly. Her sad blue eyes were a reminder of one of the many issues that had come between them—his inattentiveness to the things that mattered to her.

Ryan cursed himself for being so stupid. Children's Hospital was one of the Mavericks' favorite charities, and Susannah had been leading the team's involvement in the hospital's largest annual fundraiser for almost as long as Ryan had been leading the team itself. Their pending divorce apparently hadn't stopped her work on behalf of the hospital.

"Well, I'll leave you to visit with your friends. Good to see you, Bernie."

"You, too, Susie. Give Mary Jane a call. She'd love to hear from you."

"Don't go." Ryan pulled his feet back to make room for her on the sofa. "Stay and have something to eat. You'll hurt Darling's feelings if you don't."

"I'm not hungry, and I have some phone calls I need to make."

Ryan lifted an eyebrow and hoped it was enough to remind her of their deal. He held his breath while he waited for her to get the message. After an endless moment during which he had no idea what she was thinking, Susannah sat down on the sofa but took pains to stay as far from him as she could get. He smiled at her, and she looked away.

They made small talk with Bernie until the rest of the guys began filtering into the den, carrying beers and bowls of chili. Darling handed one to Ryan and offered another to Susannah.

"Thanks," she said. "What's in it?"

"That's a Darlington family secret."

"No peanut butter, right?" she asked.

Darling scoffed. "You offend me. That'd be cheating."

The rest of the guys chuckled at the face Darling made as he left the room. He returned with a six-pack of beer and a bowl of chili for himself. "How is it?" he asked.

"Hotter than hell," Toad said in a choked voice.

"No shit," Ryan agreed, reaching for the beer Darling opened for him. That's when he noticed Susannah holding her throat and gasping for air. He moved so fast he never felt the pain that must have radiated from his ribs as he dumped his bowl of chili on the coffee table and sprinted from the room.

"Sandy?" one of the guys called after him. "What's wrong?"

"Call 911!" Ryan yelled as he ran for the kitchen cabinet where she had always kept it, praying she hadn't moved it in the year since he had lived there. He was filled with relief when he found what he was looking for and returned to the den, pulling the cap off the EpiPen as he ran. When he reached her, his heart almost stopped when he saw her struggling to breathe as red welts exploded on her face. He plunged the needle through her pants into her thigh and held it tight against her leg until he felt her begin to relax.

Tears streamed down her face as he brought her into his arms. "It's okay, baby," he whispered. "You're okay. I've got you."

"The 911 lady wants to know what happened," Bernie said, his face white with shock.

The other guys stared at Ryan and Susannah.

"Anaphylaxis," Ryan said. "She's allergic to peanuts."

"*Sweet Jesus,*" Darling gasped. "I thought she was kidding!"

"She wasn't." Ryan held Susannah close to him. "Keep breathing, baby. I can hear the ambulance." He brushed his lips over her damp forehead.

"What can we do?" Bernie asked.

"Nothing," Ryan said as he struggled to swallow the hot ball of panic lodged in his throat. The whole thing lasted less than thirty seconds, but to him it had felt like a year. "She's okay now.

The siren grew closer, and Bernie went to get the door. He returned with two paramedics, who peppered Ryan with questions about Susannah's medical history and what she had eaten.

"Her blood pressure is elevated," one of them said. "We're going to take her in." His eyes widened when he suddenly recognized Ryan and the other players.

"I'm her husband. I'm going with her."

"Of course, Mr. Sanderson. No problem." They loaded Susannah onto a stretcher and covered her with blankets.

Ryan grabbed his coat from the rack in the foyer and tugged on the boots he had left there the night before. His ribs screamed in protest at the sharp movements, but he ignored the pain in his haste.

"I'm so sorry, Sandy," Darling said, his eyes bright with tears.

"It's okay." Ryan squeezed Darling's shoulder. "She's going to be fine." He wasn't sure who he was trying to convince—himself or his distraught friend.

"We'll clean everything up," Bernie called after Ryan, who waved as he rushed out the door behind the paramedics.

Ryan groaned when Henry pulled into the driveway and leaped from his car.

"What's going on?" Henry asked. "Is it Susannah?"

"*What* are you doing here?" Ryan asked.

"I wanted to check on Susannah. What's wrong?"

"She had an allergic reaction to something she ate." Ryan struggled to be patient when all he wanted was to get to Susie. "They're taking her in as a precaution. She's fine."

"I want to see her," Henry said, rushing toward the ambulance.

"Not now." Ryan pushed past him and winced as he climbed into the ambulance. His head and ribs pounded, but he ignored his own discomfort as he sat on the bench across from Susie and reached for her hand. "How are you doing, baby?"

"Better," she said.

"Susannah!" Henry called from outside. "Honey, I'm here."

The paramedics closed the doors, and the ambulance jolted as it pulled out of the driveway. Ryan could have fainted from the pain radiating from his ribs, but instead he gritted his teeth and forced himself to stay focused on Susie.

"Was that Henry?" she asked.

"Yeah." Ryan brought her hand to his lips. "I told him you're okay." All at once, the whole thing came crashing down on Ryan and tears filled his eyes. "You scared me." He rested his forehead on her hand as he struggled to get a hold of himself.

"You saved my life, Ry."

Ryan kissed her hand. "I was so relieved the EpiPen was where you always kept it."

"I can't believe you remembered that."

"I used to live in fear of it happening, but nothing I ever imagined could've prepared me for the reality of it." Ryan released Susie's hand so the paramedic could check her blood pressure.

"It hasn't happened since I was thirteen. I'd forgotten how terrifying it is."

The moment the paramedic removed the blood pressure cuff, Ryan reclaimed her hand. The hives on her cheeks had faded, but her eyes were still big with shock.

"Darling was freaking out. He thought you were kidding about the peanut butter."

"It's not his fault. I should've come right out and said I was allergic."

"Or I should've. I should've been more protective of you—not just today, but always," he whispered since the star-struck paramedic hung on his every word. "I'm sorry I wasn't."

Susannah's eyes filled with tears as she squeezed his hand.

They arrived at the hospital a minute later, and the paramedics whisked Susie into an exam room. A nurse stopped Ryan when he tried to follow her. "Please wait here, Mr. Sanderson. The doctor will be right with you."

Henry came dashing through the E.R. doors. "How is she? I want to see her."

"You can't," Ryan said, annoyed by the pesky man who had somehow convinced Susie to marry him. "Why don't you go home, Henry? There's nothing you can do here. I'll make sure someone calls you later with an update."

"I'm not leaving until I see my fiancée," Henry said, his face set into a stubborn expression.

A nurse with a clipboard approached them. "I need some paperwork," she said, holding out the board.

Henry reached for it. "I'll do it."

The nurse raised her eyebrow. "And you are?"

"Her fiancé."

Ryan took the board from her. "I'll take care of it."

The nurse looked from Henry to Ryan and shook her head as she left them to fight it out.

"Do you even know her date of birth?" Henry asked, his hands on his hips and his chin raised with indignation.

Today his bow tie was a yellow paisley, and his gold-rimmed glasses had slid down his nose, giving him the appearance of a nutty professor. *What the hell does Susie see in this guy?*

"It's official," Ryan said. "You're annoying me." He sat in the waiting room and did the best he could to complete the forms. Like an irksome gnat, Henry buzzed around him while Ryan did some quick math to determine the year Susie was born before Henry could figure out that he didn't know it by heart. But *yes,* he *did* know her birthday.

What kind of asshole did Henry take him for? *The inattentive, forgetful kind,* Ryan admitted to himself. *The kind that forgot her birthday, forgot our anniversary, and just about everything else that mattered to her.* Ryan glanced at Henry, who paced the length of the waiting room. *Oh my God. I don't deserve her. I don't deserve her, and he does.* The thought terrified him, almost as much as seeing her on the verge of anaphylactic shock.

A doctor came into the waiting room. "Mr. Sanderson?"

Ryan stood up as quickly as his ribs would allow and shook hands with the doctor.

"It's an honor to meet you," the doctor said. "I'm a big fan."

"Thank you."

Henry groaned and rolled his eyes. "How's *Susannah?*"

"She's doing well. Her blood pressure is better, and all her other vitals are within normal ranges. You got the epinephrine into her before any damage was done, Mr. Sanderson."

"*Great,*" Henry muttered. "That's just *great.*"

"Do you think you could just shut up?" Ryan said to Henry. "Can I see her?" Ryan asked the doctor.

He nodded. "She's asking for you."

"She is *not,*" Henry snorted.

"Who are you?"

"Her fiancé."

The doctor looked to Ryan for confirmation.

Ryan shrugged.

"I'm sorry, but my patient is asking for Mr. Sanderson," the doctor told Henry.

"If I give you five minutes with her, will you leave?" Ryan asked Henry.

Henry met Ryan's fierce gaze with one of his own. "For now," he finally said.

"Fine. Go."

After Henry had scurried away with the doctor, Ryan lowered himself to a hard chair. His legs were weak from his own injuries and the shock of Susie's sudden attack. As he realized just how close he had come to losing her forever, he became even more determined to get her back. This was the most important game of his life, and he had every intention of winning.

Chapter 5

SUSANNAH REACHED UP TO SMOOTH THE HAIR OFF HENRY'S forehead. "I'm fine, really," she assured him. "I was lucky Ryan knew exactly what to do."

Henry's jaw tightened with tension. "Always the hero, isn't he?"

"He saved my life, Henry. Do you resent him for that?"

"Of course not. But I suppose I'd be pointing out the obvious by saying if he hadn't forced his way back into your life you wouldn't be in a hospital bed right now."

Susannah sighed. "That's not fair."

"You know what's not fair? Your superstar ex-husband pushing me to the sidelines just weeks before our wedding. Is *that* fair?"

"No, it's not. It's terribly unfair." She squeezed his hand. "I love you, Henry. You have to have faith in that and in me."

"I do." He traced a finger over one of the faded welts on her cheek. "I have all the faith in the world in you, Susannah. It's him I don't trust. He hurt you so badly. I can't just sit back and watch that happen again."

"Shh, don't. I'm going to be fine, and in a few short weeks I'll be your wife. I'll be where I always should've been—with you. I can't wait until we have the rest of our lives to spend together."

He bent over the bedrail to hug her. Trailing kisses along her jaw, he said, "I can't wait to finally get you back in my bed again. Eleven years is a long time to wait for that, too."

She smiled. "We'll be glad we waited. Our wedding night will be extra memorable."

His ears flamed with color.

Susannah adored him. He was the one person she could always count on. His devotion to her had never wavered, even after she made the biggest mistake of her life by leaving him for Ryan when they were in college. She had paid a mighty price for that mistake, and so had Henry.

"Time's up," Ryan said from the doorway.

Henry lifted his head off her chest and leaned in to kiss her.

Susannah combed her fingers through his hair and brought him back for a better kiss.

"I'll call you later," he said, breathless from her passionate kiss.

She nodded.

He left without looking at Ryan.

"Does it make you feel like a big man to make him feel small?" she asked.

Ryan stepped into the room. "He is small."

"Compared to you, he's a giant."

"So then why aren't you sleeping with him?"

She gasped. "You were *listening* to us?"

"I overheard by accident."

"You disgust me."

"Does that mean you've already forgotten about me saving your life? I thought my heroics would buy me at least one day of sweetness. I feel cheated."

She glared at him.

He pushed his hands into the pockets of his jeans. His strapping presence made the small room feel crowded. "So why *aren't* you sleeping with him?"

"That's none of your business."

"I'll bet I know why," he said with a cocky grin.

"I can't wait to hear this."

"You're afraid you'll be disappointed after me, and it'll be better if you're married when that happens."

Susannah fought to keep the indignation off her face. She wouldn't give him the satisfaction. "I'm afraid you're way off, but I wouldn't even try to explain my relationship with him to you. We both know you're incapable of real intimacy. All we ever had was sex, not intimacy."

His eyes flashed with anger. "That's not true," he said, stepping closer to her bed. "It was more than that, and you know it." When his ribs bumped into the bedrail, his face went chalky and sweat beaded on his upper lip. He reached out for something to hold on to and stumbled when he came up empty.

"Ryan! What's wrong?" When he didn't answer her, she called for a nurse. "Something's wrong with him!"

The nurse eased Ryan into a chair and checked his pulse. "How did he get hurt?"

Susannah realized she was dealing with one of the three people currently alive in Denver who had no idea who Ryan Sanderson was. "Playing football. Three broken ribs and a concussion four days ago."

The nurse, who was old enough to be his mother, clucked her tongue with disapproval as she shone a flashlight in his eyes. "He needs to lay down." She put her arm around Ryan. "Come on, big fella."

He didn't resist when she helped him up and led him to the other bed in the room.

"Do you know if he's taken anything for the pain today?"

"No, I don't." Susannah was more worried about him than she cared to admit. "I wasn't with him earlier. Is he all right?"

"He will be. He probably just overdid it. Concussions can make you feel really sick if you're not careful."

"He saved my life earlier," Susannah said softly, her eyes fixed on Ryan in the next bed.

"I'd say that probably qualifies as overdoing it," the nurse said with a smile. "I'll send the doctor in to check on both of you in a few minutes." She glanced at Ryan who appeared to be asleep. "He sure is a handsome devil. You're a lucky lady."

"Yes," Susannah whispered after the nurse had left the room. "Lucky me."

"You're both going to have to take it easy for a few days," the doctor was saying.

Susannah was still focused on Ryan's face, which had yet to regain any of its usual robust color.

"You've had a bad knock to the head, and broken ribs are nothing to mess around with. If you don't want me to admit you, you'll have to promise me you'll do nothing more strenuous than take a leak for the next five or six days. You got me?"

"Uh-huh," Ryan said.

"You're not convincing me. I don't care who you are, I've got a bed with your name on it upstairs if I don't think you're taking me seriously."

"I got you, Doc. I'll lay low."

Somewhat mollified, the doctor turned to Susannah. "You should feel much better by tomorrow, but you've had a shock to your system. You need to take it easy, too."

"I'll make sure she does," Ryan said.

The doctor raised an eyebrow. "And how do you plan to do that when you're going to be flat on your back or in the hospital?"

"We're going to our place in Breckenridge tomorrow morning," Ryan said.

"No, we're *not*," Susannah said.

"Yes, we *are*. It's just what we need: no phones, no visitors, no distractions."

"That sounds perfect," the doctor said, seeming pleased his message had gotten through to Ryan. "How will you get there?"

"I'll get a couple of my buddies to drive us."

"Have a blast." Susannah folded her arms across her chest. "I'm not going."

Ryan dug his cell phone out of his pocket. "We'll see about that."

The doctor watched them with amusement, which added to Susannah's irritation.

"Go ahead and call your damned lawyer. I don't care."

"If that's what you want." Ryan pressed the number on his speed dial. "This is Ryan Sanderson. May I speak to Terry, please?"

Susannah fixated on a water stain in one of the ceiling tiles as her heart pounded. *He won't do it.*

"Hey, Terry," Ryan said. "A little better. Yeah, it was quite a hit, but we won, so it was worth it."

Susannah rolled her eyes. *Worth a concussion and three broken ribs? Yes, to Ryan it would be. All he cared about was football.*

"Listen, the reason I'm calling is I've decided to put the brakes on the divorce."

Appearing uncomfortable to be overhearing their personal business, the doctor signed Susannah's discharge paperwork, handed it to her, and left the room.

"I know we're due back in court in nine days, but I've changed my mind." Ryan listened for a moment and then glanced over at Susannah. "She's coming around."

Susannah got out of bed and grabbed the phone from Ryan. "I'm *not* coming around, Terry," she said, slapping the phone closed.

"Thought I was bluffing, didn't you, darlin'?" he asked with the lazy smile that made her want to smack him. Or kiss him. No, definitely smack.

"You *are* bluffing. You're not going to stop the divorce."

"The judge knew what he was doing when he made us wait six more months before making it final. He could see we weren't finished with each other, yet."

"I *am* finished! What do I have to do to convince you of that?"

"Spend the next few days with me in Breckenridge. You heard the doctor. I need to take it easy, and so do you. We won't get a minute's peace if we stay in town. The phone will be ringing nonstop, people coming by—"

"And poisoning me . . . "

"Susie! That's not nice. You know it was an accident."

She sighed as she got up from the bed and slipped on her shoes. "I can't leave town right now. I've got the ball next weekend and a wedding to plan. I'm not going."

"I'll have you back in plenty of time for the ball, and you *are* going. Unless you want me to call Terry back . . . "

"What am I supposed to tell Henry?"

"I'm sure you'll think of something." Ryan attempted to push himself into a sitting position.

Without thinking, Susannah reached out to help him up.

He played the advantage by putting his arms around her. Tipping his head, he kissed her softly and then caressed her cheek. "You've got your color back."

Amazed by his audacity and her reaction to the gentle kiss, Susannah could only stare at him. *Why does he have such an effect on me, and why do my knees still go weak when he looks at me that way? I hate that!* Tugging herself free of him, she left the room.

Bernie and Darling were pacing in the waiting room.

"Susie!" Darling rushed over to her. "Are you all right?"

"I'm fine." Touched by the genuine concern on his face, she hugged him. "It was an accident. I don't want you to give it another thought."

"I'm so sorry. I had no idea you were allergic."

"You couldn't have known." The hulking football players had captured the attention of everyone in the waiting room. "Let's forget about it, okay?"

"Um, yeah, sure," Darling said. "Give me a year or two."

Susannah laughed and tipped her cheek to receive a kiss from Bernie.

"You look a lot better," Bernie said as Ryan joined them, sending a buzz through the waiting room. "But he looks like hell—even worse than before. What happened?"

"I guess I 'overdid it' today." Ryan shrugged. "I need a favor, you guys."

"Anything," Darling said with an earnestness that amused the others.

"Can you give us a lift to Breckenridge in the morning? One of you can drive my car and the other can follow us so you can get back."

"No problem," Bernie said, draping his coat over Susannah's shoulders. "Come on. Let's get you two home."

When Ryan tried to put his arm around her, Susannah scurried out of his reach. She was going to have to think fast because there was no way she could go to that cabin with him. He wasn't only trying to escape the city by making a plan to go to Breckenridge. No, he knew the cabin would remind her of a time when she had been happy with him, and he hoped it would lower her defenses. She could *not* let that happen.

As they rode home in the backseat of Bernie's Mercedes SUV, Susannah puzzled over the situation from every angle. The call Ryan had made to his attorney had rattled her. Suddenly, she was afraid to push him. He had nothing to lose by stopping their divorce, but she did. She had everything to lose—Henry, her sanity, and the peaceful, uncomplicated life she had built for herself over the last year. Her stomach twisted with anxiety when she looked up to find Ryan watching her with amusement dancing in his eyes. In that moment, she hated him for what he was putting her through and for the feelings he was resurrecting in her—feelings she had long ago put away and tried her best to forget.

When their eyes met, her heart fluttered with the startling realization that he and the judge were right about one thing: they weren't finished with each other.

The next morning, Susannah fumed in the passenger seat of Ryan's Escalade as Bernie drove them west to the cabin in Breckenridge. Darling followed in his four-wheel-drive truck. Snow had begun to fall as they left their upscale Denver neighborhood of Cherry Hills, and the bleary day was a good match for her mood.

Ryan, who was stretched out in the back seat, talked to Bernie while Susannah relived the huge fight she'd had with Henry over the trip to the cabin. She ignored Ryan's repeated efforts to draw her into the conversation, preferring to stew about the mess he was making of her new, well-ordered existence.

He has no right to make me go somewhere I don't want to go! She'd had to turn over the final plans for the Black and White Ball to her committee, telling them she had been called out of town unexpectedly. That was putting it mildly! But she couldn't very well tell them she'd been blackmailed and virtually kidnapped by her famous ex-husband. A tidbit like that would stir up years of gossip within her social circle. It was bad enough her trip to the hospital had been mentioned in that morning's *Denver Post*—and in the sports section, no less. What an insult! She was only news because she was linked to *him*.

Her day had begun with an irate call from Henry who hadn't appreciated seeing his fiancée referred to in the paper as the wife of Denver Mavericks' Quarterback Ryan Sanderson. "What am I supposed to tell my parents and friends when they see that?" Henry had asked.

Susannah had been unable to give him a satisfactory answer to that question because there wasn't one.

Henry had gone from furious to ballistic when she told him Ryan was insisting on going to the cabin for the next few days.

"I won't stand for this, Susannah."

"*What am I supposed to do?* If I don't go, he'll stop the divorce, and there goes our wedding. What choice do I have?"

"I'm beginning to think you're enjoying this."

"Enjoying *what?*"

"Having two men fighting over you."

She had hung up on him, and when he'd called back ten minutes later, she had ignored the call. At the moment, she had nothing to say to either of them. She was sick to death of all men and their boundless egos.

"I want to ski," Ryan moaned as Bernie drove through the busy town of Breckenridge. "I wait all year for the off season so I can ski my ass off. But not this year."

"I know," Bernie agreed. "What a bummer. Hopefully, you'll be back on the slopes in a couple of weeks. In the meantime, don't forget you're supposed to be taking it easy."

"Yes, Dad," Ryan said with a chuckle.

When they arrived at the sprawling log cabin set into the foothills of the mountain, Bernie and Darling wouldn't let Ryan or Susannah carry a thing.

"Put my stuff in the guest room, please," Susannah said to Darling.

With a nervous glance at Ryan, Darling reached for her bags.

Susannah took a deep breath before she walked into the house they had bought right after Ryan had signed with the Mavs. She crossed the threshold and was hit with a hundred memories and feelings and scents that, all combined, stirred her to tears. *Oh, he knew what he was doing by bringing me here.* Since Ryan had been living between the cabin and an apartment in the city since their separation, she was surprised to find none of the usual chaos she associated with him. In fact, the place was immaculate. The sound of heavy footsteps on the front porch had her wiping away the tears.

Darling and Bernie came in carrying her suitcases and Ryan's ratty Mavericks duffel bag. They put the bags in the bedrooms and rejoined Susannah and Ryan in the rustic living room.

Bernie went out to the porch and returned with an armload of wood that he carried to the stone fireplace. A few minutes later, he had a roaring fire going. "We're going to hit the grocery store to get you stocked up," Bernie said. "Any special requests?"

Susannah shook her head.

"She'll want at least a case of Diet Coke," Ryan said. "Plus Total Raisin Bran, bananas, French vanilla ice cream, anything that might go in a salad." He scratched at the stubble on his chin as he studied Susannah. "Oh yeah, tuna, Triscuits, and cottage cheese, too."

She didn't want to be impressed by his memory or moved by his attentiveness, but she was both.

"You got that, Bern?" Darling asked.

"I think so."

After they left, Susannah went into the guestroom to unpack, still fuming that she was even there.

"Are you ever going to talk to me again?" Ryan asked.

She turned to find him leaning against the doorframe. "What do you want me to say? You seem to have all the answers."

"If I had all the answers, we never would've landed in divorce court in the first place."

"I want to make one thing perfectly clear, Ryan. I'm only here because you bullied me into coming."

"Bullied is kind of a strong word. Not as bad as blackmailed, but—"

She held up her hand to stop him. "I don't want to be here. I don't want to be with you. I want to be with Henry. So I'll do my time until either you decide you've had enough of this silly charade or until our day in court, whichever comes first. Is there any part of that you don't understand?"

"No, I think I got it. Even a dumb jock can understand plain English."

Susannah hated that the hurt radiating from him bothered her.

"Since I have no plans to give up on us any time soon, do you think we could be civil to each other?"

She shrugged. "I'm not feeling very civil at the moment."

"I love you, Susie."

She rolled her eyes. "Save it."

"I haven't given you much reason to believe it, but it's true. I love you. I've loved you for so long I can't imagine ever *not* loving you. When I saw you struggling to breathe yesterday, I was reminded again that a life without you is no life at all. So you don't have to be civil. You don't even have to talk to me, but I'm going to talk to you. I hope you'll listen."

After he walked away, she sat on the bed and wept.

Chapter 6

BERNIE AND DARLING RETURNED FROM THE GROCERY STORE with enough food to feed ten people. They put everything away and brought in several days' worth of firewood from the pile outside. The four of them shared a quiet lunch during which the tension between Ryan and Susannah was palpable.

To fill the awkward silences, Bernie and Darling talked about their upcoming trip to the White House where the president would welcome the Super Bowl champions.

"Doesn't that usually happen later?" Susannah asked.

"This president is a *huge* Mavs fan," Darling explained. "He cleared his schedule so he could see us before we scatter for the off-season."

As they prepared to return to Denver, Bernie asked for a moment alone with Susannah.

She tugged on her coat and went out to the porch with him.

"Are you all right?" he asked.

"I will be."

Bernie glanced at Ryan through the window. "He's my best friend, and I love him like a brother." Bernie brought his eyes back to Susannah. "But I love you, too. If you don't want to be here with him, just say the word, and I'll take you home."

"He seems quite determined to play out this last-minute rescue scenario," Susannah said with a sigh. "I'm not going back to him. He's going to need you when that finally sinks in."

"I know he can be a thick-headed idiot at times—hell, so can I. Just ask Mary Jane. But he's one of the good guys, Susie. I'd trust him with my life, with my kids' lives. And if there's anything about him I'm sure of it's that he loves you. You guys had a tough break, but that doesn't mean—"

Desperate to stop the direction the conversation was taking, she went up on tiptoes to kiss his cheek. "I appreciate what you're trying to do, Bern. I really do. Thank you for caring, but I'm going to stay and play it out. He seems to need the closure."

"What about what you need?"

Her face lifted into an ironic smile. "It's never really been about what I need, has it?"

"If you change your mind and want to go home, call me, and I'll come get you. Day or night. If I'm in Washington, I'll send someone else."

"Thank you."

The door opened, and Ryan came out with Darling.

"Ready?" Darling asked Bernie.

Bernie nodded, and both men hugged Susannah.

"Give the president my regards," Ryan said.

"We'll miss you, man," Darling said. "Are you sure you can't come?"

"I've been there before. And besides," he added with a meaningful look at Susannah, "I've got more important things to do right now."

With her stomach in a knot, Susannah waved to their friends as they drove down the long road that led back to town. She wanted to race after them but couldn't seem to make herself move as she was filled with anxiety over how completely alone she was with Ryan.

"Do you remember the first time we were here?" he asked. "We'd never even seen the Rocky Mountains, but there was just something about this place we loved from the first minute we saw it, remember? After growing up in Florida and Texas, we had nothing to compare it to, did we? The mountains and the trees and the snow. Air so fresh and cold it almost hurts to breathe. For the first time in my life I had money, but we were hesitant to make such a big impulse purchase. Wasn't that what you called it? An impulse purchase?"

Susannah kept her back to him as a defense against the long-buried memories he was resurrecting.

"We never regretted it, though, did we? What would we have done without this place to hide out in during those crazy first few years with the Mavs? I know you love the McMansion in the city, but this is our home, Susie. This is where we belong. I know you feel it, too."

She turned around and was careful not to look at him or get too close to his sore ribs as she brushed past him on her way into the house. Once inside, she went to the guest room and closed the door.

Susannah floated between sleep and wakefulness. Music. A guitar and singing. Ryan. Her eyes fluttered open, and she lay still to listen, feeling out of sorts as she awoke in the strange room. *Oh,* she sighed. *Not that song . . . That's not playing fair, Ry.* Rod Stewart's "You're in My Heart," the song they had danced to at their wedding. Ryan's voice was deep, and his guitar playing had improved dramatically since she last heard him play. About three years ago, he'd decided to take up the guitar. Like everything else he tackled, he had mastered it in no time.

Susannah was dismayed to realize his song was having the desired effect. Her heart hurt when she remembered their wedding, just two weeks after Ryan graduated from Florida and two weeks before he was due to report to the Mavs' rookie camp. She had been so excited, so in love, and so filled with hope for their future. *That was a long time ago,* she reminded herself. *And everything is different now.*

The door opened. "Hey," he whispered. "Are you awake?"

The hallway light made a silhouette of his big frame. "Yes."

"Are you hungry?"

"Sort of."

"I made some dinner."

"You *did?*"

He chuckled. "Don't get too excited. It's just steak and a salad."

"You did this all by yourself?"

"Very funny. I've been living alone for a while now. I had to conquer the kitchen."

"An interesting development."

"There've been a few of them. I'd like to tell you about them if you'll let me."

Susannah lay there for a moment longer, attempting to marshal the fortitude it took just to be in the same room with him. Finally, she sat up. "I'll be out in a minute."

"Okay." He started to walk away but turned back. "I'm glad you're here, Susie. This place wasn't the same without you."

After he was gone, she sat on the edge of the bed for a long time before she got up and went into the bathroom. When she ventured into the living room, she felt like a visitor in someone else's home even though everything was just as she had left it. As she took in the cozy country-style living room, the stone fireplace that occupied one whole wall, and the high ceiling with the wood beams, she became aware of just how much she missed being there and how much she missed Ryan, too. Unnerved by the realization, she folded the Aztec blanket that had been left in a pile on the sofa, evidence he had napped, too. The man who never napped sacked out often at the cabin—the one place where he managed to completely relax.

Wearing a red flannel shirt with old jeans, Ryan came in from the deck with a plate in his hand. "Ready to eat?"

Susannah thought, as she always did, that nothing about his appearance gave him away as the multimillionaire that he was. Despite all his success, in many ways he was still the same boy he'd been when he picked her out of the crowd in a Gainesville restaurant more than eleven years ago.

"What can I do?" she asked.

"Not a thing." He held a chair for her at the dining room table. When she was settled, he lit the candles and poured her a glass of red wine.

Her stomach twisted with nerves. "Ryan, this is all really nice and everything, but . . . "

He reached for her hand. "It's just dinner. We always had candles and wine, didn't we?"

"Yes, I guess we did."

"Then don't sweat it." He squeezed her hand and then released it so he could serve the salad.

After they had eaten in silence for several minutes, she said, "This is very good. Thank you."

"You're welcome." He refilled her wine glass. "Can I ask you something?"

"Can I stop you?"

He flashed the smile that had made him a superstar with the women of Denver—and beyond. "Why'd you TiVo the Super Bowl?"

Susannah froze. "I didn't."

"Yes, you did."

"I didn't mean to."

He laughed. "How do you accidentally record the Super Bowl?"

"It was probably set from when you lived there."

He shook his head. "No," he said softly.

Susannah got busy finishing her dinner.

"Did you record it because I was playing in the game?"

She looked up to find him watching her intently and knew there was no point in trying to evade him. He'd see right through her, just as he always had. "Yes."

His eyes lit up with pleasure and what might have been hope. "Why?"

"I had plans with Henry that night, and I thought I might want to watch it later."

"Because I've made such a football fan out of you?" he asked with a sad smile.

"Something like that."

"Did you watch it?"

"No." She took a long drink of her wine. "But I knew you had won."

"Did you know I was hurt?"

She nodded. "I didn't know it was so bad," she said, gesturing to his battered face. "I didn't know that."

"That's why you didn't watch the game, though, isn't it? Because you heard I got hurt. You still can't bear to see that, can you, baby?"

"Stop it, Ryan," she whispered, her eyes filling despite her desire to remain aloof.

He reached for her hand. "You always took it so hard when I got hurt. I hated that."

Pulling her hand free, she cried, "Is that so wrong? That I don't like seeing the man I I—" Appalled and shocked by what she'd almost said, Susannah's hand flew up to cover her mouth.

"The man you what? The man you love? Is that what you were going to say?"

Desperate to escape him, she got up from the table and went outside to the deck. In the distance she could see the twinkling lights in the town of Breckenridge and the well-lit night ski runs on the mountain. Shivering violently, she swatted at the tears that chilled her face.

Ryan stepped up behind her and wrapped a blanket and his arms around her.

"I'm done, Suze."

"With what? Trying to get me back?"

"No, with football. I'm retiring."

She snorted with laughter. "Yeah, right. Nice one, Ry. You're really pulling out all the stops here, aren't you?"

He turned her so she faced him. "I'm not kidding. As soon as the team gets back from Washington, I'm meeting with Duke and Chet," he said, referring to his coach and the team's owner.

"You won't do it."

"I'm *going* to do it. I have three Super Bowl rings, a likely spot in the Hall of Fame, a Heisman Trophy, and more money than I can spend in a lifetime. I've got nothing left to prove to myself or anyone else. I want to go out while I'm still on top and while my body still has some life left in it."

Susannah stared at him like she had never seen him before.

"I'm serious, Susie." He held her close to him, and she let him because she was freezing. "So if you were to stay with me, you wouldn't have to live in fear of the man you love being hurt anymore."

She pushed him away but was careful to avoid his broken ribs. "This doesn't change anything."

He took hold of her chin and forced her to look at him. "It changes *everything*. There's another reason I'm retiring, and it's far more important than all the others."

She tried to look away from him, but he wouldn't let her.

"I want to spend as much time as I can with my wife. I want us to have a family."

Susannah closed her eyes against the pain and shook her head. Her eyes flew open when his cold lips landed on hers. Imprisoned by his strong arms and the heavy blanket, Susannah was afraid she'd hurt him if she struggled.

His lips warmed as they moved over hers. He tipped his head to delve deeper, his tongue gentle but insistent.

When she recovered her senses, she discovered his shirt was bunched into her hands. Her mouth was open, her tongue wrapped around his, and there was no denying that she was kissing him back.

"*Jesus*," he gasped when he came up for air. His breath came out as little puffs in the cold. "Susie . . ." He captured her mouth again, but this time there was nothing gentle about it.

She pushed at his chest. "Stop. Ryan. *Stop.* I don't want this."

"You could've fooled me," he whispered as he trailed hot kisses along her jaw and then rolled her earlobe between his teeth.

"*Please*," she moaned. "I don't want to hurt you by fighting you, but if you don't let me go right now, I'm going to hurt you."

He stopped what he was doing to her ear and stepped back from her. "I'm sorry," he said as he dragged his hands through his mop of hair. "I can't help it. I want you so much, Susie. All I can think about is how it was between us when it was good—really, really good." With his hands now on her shoulders, he leaned his forehead against hers. "Before everything . . . happened. I know you remember. You can't convince me you don't. I want us to find our way back to the good stuff. Can't we do that? Can't we please try?"

She trembled. Whether it was from the cold or the yearning she heard in his voice she couldn't have said.

He put his arm around her and led her inside, urging her down in front of the fireplace. After he had tossed several more logs onto the smoldering flame, he lowered himself down next to her, grunting when he made contact with the floor.

"Are you hurting?" she asked.

"Not as bad as yesterday."

She could tell she surprised him when she reached for his hand. "I want you to know I heard everything you said out there. And before, too."

"I meant it. All of it."

"I know."

His brown eyes widened. "You do? You believe me?"

She nodded.

He looked like he could weep as he reached for her. "It's going to be different this time, Susie. I promise. You're going to come first."

She gently disentangled herself from his embrace. "I've realized something in the last few days."

"What, baby?" he asked, tucking a lock of hair behind her ear.

"I love you, Ryan. I do."

His smile lit up his face.

"I was crazy to think that would end just because we weren't together anymore." She grasped his hands. "But too much has happened for us to get back what we had."

"No," he protested. "That's not true. We love each other. What else is there?"

"I waited *years,* Ryan—too many years—to have just the kind of conversation we've had tonight. But there was always something else that was more important, something else you had to attend to, or some*one* else."

"What's that supposed to mean?" he asked hotly.

"It doesn't matter now. None of it does. It's too late. You need to accept that and let me go."

"Never."

"You promised me. You said if I gave you these ten days and still wanted the divorce you would give it to me. You promised you wouldn't interfere with Henry and me. I'm going to hold you to it."

"I've got eight days left, and now I know you still love me," he said with the cocky smile that was all Ryan. "And if you didn't want me anymore you wouldn't have kissed me the way you did. So the way I see it, I'm still in the game."

With an exasperated sigh, she got up from the floor. "You were right when you said it's time to retire, Ry. Let's go out while we're still on top. Good night."

Chapter 7

SUSANNAH TOSSED AND TURNED. SHE LISTENED TO RYAN play his guitar and was still awake when he crept into her room, brushed the hair off her face, and kissed her forehead.

"I love you, Susie," he whispered. "I love you more than anything."

Pretending to be asleep, she struggled to keep her breathing steady as her heart pounded. He left as quietly as he had come. When she heard the shower go on in the master bedroom, she wept bitterly into her pillow.

How long have I wished for him to give himself to me this way? Only now that he's planning to give up football will I come first with him. It's too little, too late. Choked by sobs, she was reminded of all the nights she had cried herself to sleep over the man who was once again occupying her every thought. *I can't put myself through this a second time. I've already been unfaithful to Henry by kissing Ryan like kissing was on its way out of style. Henry . . . you deserve so much better. I've disappointed you so many times in the past. I can't let it happen again. I just can't.*

Despair.

Was there any other word to describe what she felt just then? From the very beginning with Ryan, she had been sucked into his orbit. She left college to marry him and moved to Denver when he signed with the Mavs. Her life revolved around him for so long that when their marriage ended, she discovered she had no idea who she was without him. She had spent the last year figuring that out and had been on her way to a whole new life when he'd come swooping back in, tipping her world upside down as only Ryan could.

Her sobs dissolved into hiccups as warm, bitter tears continued to cascade down her face.

"Susie?"

She suppressed a groan. "Go to bed, Ryan."

He came in and perched carefully on the edge of the bed. "Are you crying?" Reaching out to caress her face, he said, "You are! Baby, what's wrong?"

The light coming from the hallway made it possible for her to see that he wore only boxers. His wet hair was combed back off his freshly shaven face. He was still the most beautiful man she had ever seen, and God help her, she still wanted him. "Nothing's wrong," she said. "Go to bed. Please."

"I can't leave you here upset and alone."

"Why not? You've done it before."

He winced.

She couldn't see his eyes but could imagine the flash of anger and pain. Her own eyes flooded with new tears.

"Susannah . . . You're breaking my heart."

"You broke mine," she said between sobs. "More than once."

"I'm sorry," he said in a pleading tone. "You're the last person in the world I ever meant to hurt. You have to know that." He reached for her and pulled her up and into his arms. "I've made mistakes," he said, brushing a hand over her hair. "I don't deny that, but I want to make it right. You have to help me make it right."

"I don't *have* to do anything," she retorted. "The time for making it right was when I was begging you to engage in our marriage. You're so used to getting everything you want that you have no idea how to deal with the word *no,* do you?"

"I haven't gotten everything I wanted," he reminded her.

She pulled back from him, incredulous. "Not getting to play for the Cowboys does *not* count."

"You never understood how I felt about that, so I don't expect you to get it now."

She stared at him in disbelief. "You've had a career most men would sell their souls for, and yet you're still nursing that old wound, aren't you? You've been so blessed that you can't see how stupid it is."

"I know I've been blessed, and I know now I was meant to play for the Mavs even if I grew up dreaming of a career with the Cowboys. I wouldn't have three Super Bowl rings if the Cowboys had drafted me. I get that—now."

She had never heard him say that before, and the revelation was intriguing. He *had* changed. "Ryan, I didn't mean—"

He shook his head to stop her. "They said I was the best high school football player to come out of Texas in a decade, but I didn't get to play for the team I grew up worshiping. I know you think it's dumb in light of everything I've had with the Mavs, but it hurt. I don't expect you to understand it. Why would you? After all,

I had to tell you the quarterback is the one who throws the ball."

She chuckled when she remembered his shock at discovering she knew absolutely nothing about football and wasn't among the legions of Florida's faithful who spent autumn Saturdays in The Swamp worshiping at the altar of Ryan Sanderson. "And no one throws the ball better than you do," she said softly, regretting now that she had pulled the scab off an old wound. "I'm sorry I didn't try harder to understand how much that hurt you."

He shrugged. "It's old news now, and in hindsight, I guess it *was* kind of dumb. I hardly have anything to complain about, do I? How did we get on this tired old subject, anyway?"

She smiled. "I think it started with me saying you get everything you want."

"Ah, yes," he said, returning her smile. "And something about me not understanding the word *no,* if I recall correctly."

Amusement faded into desire when their eyes met in the milky darkness.

He combed his fingers through her hair and tugged lightly, tipping her face up. "Kiss me," he whispered.

"No," she said, even though she burned for him.

A long, breathless moment passed before he removed his hand from her hair and eased her back down to her pillow. He kissed her forehead, whispering, "See? I *can* take no for an answer."

Susannah lay awake for a long time after he left wishing he had stayed and worrying about what she might have done if he hadn't taken no for an answer.

◈ ◈ ◈

Ryan delivered breakfast in bed the next morning: coffee, toast, scrambled eggs, juice, and a sprig of evergreen in a vase. "I couldn't find a rose," he said with a shy and uncertain smile.

"Roses aren't big fans of snow," she said, impressed and touched by the effort he was making. She sat up and combed her fingers through her hair, worried that she looked like a wreck.

He rested the tray on her lap and kissed her cheek. "You look beautiful in the morning. You never believed me when I told you that."

That he read her thoughts so easily was more than a little unnerving. That he was so different from the Ryan she had come to expect was terrifying. She had no idea how to protect herself from this new sensitive, attentive version of Ryan. Reaching for the mug of coffee on the tray, she took a long sip, hoping it would wake up her defenses, because right now they were missing in action.

"Do you think maybe you could take that off while we're here?" he asked.

"What?"

He nodded at her engagement ring.

"No."

Sitting down on the bed, he reached for her hand and ran his thumb over the ring. "What did you do with the rings I gave you?"

"They're in the safe at home."

"I thought you'd hock them or something."

"Why? I don't need the money. You saw to that."

He shrugged. "I figured they'd be a bad memory, like me."

"You aren't a bad memory. Well, not entirely . . . "

His laughter filled the room, but his smile faded when Susannah's cell phone rang. He got up and retrieved her purse, dropping it on the bed next to her.

"Sorry," she said with a weak smile. They had a rule about no phones at the cabin. They'd never had a phone installed there and used to make a big show of turning off their cell phones the minute they entered the town of Breckenridge. Susannah had been so annoyed at him when they arrived the day before she hadn't thought of it.

"Hello?" she said as Ryan stalked from the room.

"Susannah," her sister said. "What the hell is going on out there?"

"Hello to you, too, Missy," she said with a sigh.

"I just got off the phone with Henry. He's going out of his mind. Tell me he's not serious about you being in Breckenridge with Ryan."

"I wish I could."

"Oh, that rotten son of a bitch!" The curse sounded almost comical in Missy's lilting accent. Susannah's sister, who lived in Savannah, was the ultimate southern belle. "Did he really threaten to stop the divorce if you didn't go with him?"

"Yes."

"That's *outrageous!* Have you talked to your lawyer? He can't do this."

"He has all the power, Miss. He's not the one who's engaged to someone else."

"He's only doing this *because* you're engaged to Henry. His rampant ego can't handle the idea of you with another man."

"I don't know if it's only that." Susannah nibbled on the breakfast he had made for her as she talked to her sister. "He seems different somehow. I can't really put my finger on what it is, but he's changed."

"Oh, Susannah, *please.* Tell me you're kidding me! Ryan Sanderson will *never* change. The universe revolves around him, and it always has. You can't have forgotten what your life with him was like, especially the last few years."

"I haven't," she said with another deep sigh. "He said he's retiring from football."

Melissa laughed long and hard. "And you're *buying* that? What the hell happens to you when you're around him? It's like you've been abducted by aliens or something."

No, just my ex-husband. "He seems to mean it," Susannah said meekly, worried now that Ryan had taken her for a ride. It wouldn't be the first time.

"Listen to me, Susannah. Are you listening?"

"Yes," Susannah said in a small voice.

"That man is poison. Your life was all about *him.* You were like an accessory, not a wife. I can't watch you be sucked back into that. You've worked so hard to break free of him. How can you forget about that after just a few days with him? And what about Henry?"

"I know, I know," Susannah said.

"That poor man has waited his entire adult life for you to come to your senses and get over this obsession you have with Ryan."

"It's not an obsession, Missy. I love him. I'll always love him."

"And he'll always hurt you because he doesn't know how to love anyone but Ryan Sanderson."

"That's not true," Susannah protested. "He loves me. He does."

Melissa was silent, which was never a good thing.

"Say something."

"You're going back to him, aren't you?"

"No! I never said that."

"But you're thinking about it."

"I didn't say that, either."

"It's because of what he did for Daddy, isn't it? That's why you won't tell him to go screw himself the way any rational person would. You feel obligated to him."

"No, I don't. There were no strings attached to what he did."

Missy snorted. "That's what you think."

"He kept Daddy from going to jail and our parents from ending up homeless," Susannah reminded her sister. "You should feel obligated to him, too."

"It's very heroic to throw money at a situation, especially when you have tons of it to throw."

"He didn't have to do it," Susannah said. "He did it because he loves me and cares about my family." She wondered for a moment why she felt so compelled to defend Ryan to her sister. It just seemed like the right thing to do.

"He's got your head all twisted around again," Missy said with a sigh. "I can't bear it."

"You're leaping to all kinds of conclusions just because I'm spending a couple of days with him."

"I'm not the only one who's jumping to conclusions, Susannah. Have you spoken to your fiancé today? Remember him? He's reached a few conclusions of his own."

Susannah's stomach twisted into knots as she thought about Henry.

"Well, I've got to go," Missy said. "George and I are planning to come out with Daddy and Mama for the wedding—if there *is* a wedding."

"There *will* be," Susannah insisted.

"If that's what you want, then take a piece of advice from your big sister—end whatever this is with Ryan and go back to your fiancé. Weddings tend to go better when the bride isn't shacking up with her ex-husband."

"Gee, thanks, Missy. I don't know what I would've done without that advice."

"You could do with less sarcasm and more common sense."

"Don't go blabbing all of this to Daddy and Mama."

"I wouldn't dream of upsetting them by telling them you're back with *him*."

"I'm *not* back with him," Susannah insisted.

"Who are you trying to convince, Susannah? Me or yourself? I've got to go. George and I have a tee time. Call me in a couple of days, and be careful. I love you. I don't want to see you hurt again."

"I love you, too. I'll talk to you soon."

Susannah ended the call, turned off the phone, and tossed it into her purse. She flopped back against the pillows and exhaled a long, deep breath. Everything her sister had said was true, and Susannah knew it. But no one—not her parents, her sister, or especially Henry—had ever understood the special bond she shared with

Ryan. While other women envied her handsome, sexy, successful, famous husband, the people closest to her had questioned the match from the very beginning.

Even when Ryan hired the best lawyer in Florida to keep her father out of jail after his business partner embezzled from their clients—even *then*—her family withheld their approval of her marriage to a professional athlete. Despite his obvious devotion to Susannah, they were convinced he would eventually stray. Oh, they were always friendly and civil to him, but they never made Ryan feel like a member of their family, which was something he desperately wanted after growing up as the only child of a single mother who had worked two jobs to support them.

Susannah's head spun as she took a shower and got dressed. Carrying her breakfast tray, she went into the living room where Ryan was stretched out on the sofa with the remote control aimed at the T.V.

"Thanks again for breakfast," Susannah said.

Without looking away from the television, he said, "No problem."

She expected a mess when she went into the spotless kitchen, but once again he surprised her. The Ryan she used to live with might have made breakfast, but he would've left the mess for her to deal with.

They had argued about hiring household help. Susannah felt that because she didn't work she could take care of her own home. He hadn't wanted her to have to deal with it, saying her volunteer commitments were equivalent to a full-time job and they could well afford help. In truth, she hadn't wanted a stranger in their home.

Their lives were so public there had to be somewhere they could be completely alone.

She put her dishes in the dishwasher and wiped off the tray. The sprig of evergreen caught her eye. Susannah picked it up and breathed in the fragrant scent that brought back memories of Christmas trees and cozy holidays—some of them right here in this house. When there was nothing more to keep her in the kitchen, she took a deep breath to prepare herself to face him, wondering how she would ever stand eight more days alone with him.

He came into the kitchen and refilled his coffee cup. "What did non-lover lover boy want?"

She shot him a withering look. "It was Missy."

"*Oh,* another of my biggest fans. How *is* my sister-in-law?" he asked, leaning back against the counter.

She noticed the bruises on his face were beginning to yellow and fade a bit. "She's not happy I'm here with you."

"Why am I not surprised?"

Susannah shrugged.

"I'm sure she gave you an earful."

"And a half."

He raised an amused eyebrow. "Do you remember what we used to say when we'd get that disapproving vibe from your family?"

Susannah felt her cheeks grow hot with embarrassment. "Don't say it."

"Why not?" he asked, enjoying her discomfort. "If they could see us in bed, they'd never wonder what kept us together."

She rolled her eyes. "It takes more than good sex to keep a marriage together. We found that out, didn't we?"

Putting his mug on the counter, he crossed the room and rested his hands on her shoulders. "What we had was not *good* sex. It was *great* sex." He kissed her cheek and then her neck. "Need me to refresh your memory?"

"No, thank you." She pushed gently on his chest. "I appreciate the offer, though."

He chuckled but didn't remove his lips from her neck. "Want to get out of here for a while?"

Thrown off balance by the question and trying not to be breathless from what he was doing to her neck, she asked, "And do what?"

"We could take the snowmobile for a ride."

"Should you be doing that?"

"I feel a lot better today, and if I don't get some air, I'm going to lose it."

She pushed him away with more insistence as her sister's warning echoed through her mind. "You always were a terrible patient."

"I won't deny that."

"I'll agree to the air, but not the snowmobile. How about we start with a walk?"

He made a face of distaste.

"I know a walk won't pacify your need for speed, but one wrong move on the snowmobile and you're back in the hospital."

"Why do you always have to be such a grown up?" he asked, his lips forming a pout that reduced him to a twelve-year-old. He'd asked the question often during their life together.

"One of us has to be," she said, and the familiar retort made her ache for what used to be. From the look on his face, he felt it, too.

"Susie," he whispered, cradling her face in his hands. "Kiss me like you did last night. Just once."

This time she didn't say no. She kissed him because she wanted to. It was a simple as that. Besides, the lump in her throat made it impossible for her to do anything but hold on for the ride as he crushed his lips to hers. Her arms slipped around his neck, his hands on her hips molded her to him, and her breasts pressed against his chest. Heat, the one thing she could always count on from him, blazed through her, making her feel weak and empowered at the same time.

He had asked for just one kiss, so he made sure he got his money's worth. By the time he pulled back from her, Susannah was clinging to him.

"Let me make love to you," he whispered in her ear, sending a tremble through her. "I was awake all night thinking about what might've happened if you hadn't said no. I want you so much, Susie." He inched her back against the counter to make sure she could feel just *how* much.

"I can't." She sidestepped out of his embrace and moved as far from him as she could get without leaving the room. "I can't do this to Henry."

Ryan exploded. "*I don't want to hear another word about him!* How can you stand being with that seventy-year-old trapped in a thirty-year-old's body?"

"I love him!" Susannah cried.

"If you loved him, you wouldn't have kissed me the way you just did, the way you did last night. You love *me!* You said so!"

Susannah burst into tears.

He went to her and brought her into his arms. "You love me," he said in a softer but no less urgent tone. "You don't want him. That's why you're not sleeping with him. You want me."

"I don't *want* to want you," she said, pummeling his chest with her fists.

Before she could connect with his ribs, he tightened his hold on her.

"I just can't do this again, Ryan. I barely survived it the first time, and the only reason I did was because Henry was there for me."

"He was *always* there for you," Ryan fumed. "He's been the third person in our marriage from the very beginning. I tolerated your friendship with him, but I always knew he was in love with you. He couldn't wait for us to break up so he could swoop in and rescue you."

"That's not true."

"*The hell it isn't!* He's been poisoning your mind against me for years."

"No, he hasn't," Susannah protested, even as something about what Ryan said rang true. She couldn't remember Henry ever having anything nice to say about Ryan, but she had always thought it was because she left him for Ryan. Had Henry deliberately tried to sabotage her marriage?

"He hates me because you love me, and he knows it," Ryan said quietly. "He's willing to marry a woman who's in love with another man. Who does that, Susie?"

"He loves me!"

"Yes, he does. But you don't love *him.* He knows it, I know it, and you know it. You *know* it, Susie."

Trapped by the truth and overwhelmed by her feelings for Ryan, Susannah pulled herself free of him and left the room before she could humiliate herself by crying again.

Chapter 8

Ryan watched her go and then kicked one of the kitchen chairs in frustration. He winced when pain cut through his midsection. "*Goddamn it!*"

Nothing was going according to plan. He hadn't expected it to take this long to bring her around.

He'd had more than enough time over the last year to think about what had gone wrong between him and Susie and to take responsibility for his share of it, which was most of it if he were being honest. He was trying to show her he'd changed, but he was finding she had changed, too. She was no longer the wide-eyed girl who loved him unconditionally, who stood by him through all the highs and lows of his illustrious career, and who made him feel adored even in the most trying of times. That girl was gone, and in her place was an older, wiser woman who wouldn't be so easily led this time.

But he couldn't give up, especially now that he knew she still loved him. They needed more time. The only problem was they didn't have much time. In just over a week they were due back in court, and unless he was somehow able to convince her to give their marriage another chance, he was going to be handed a divorce he didn't want. If that happened, how was he supposed to live the rest of his life without her? Since she was no longer susceptible to what he'd often been told was his formidable charm, he was going to have to take his game up a notch. But how? He had no idea, but he had to think of something—and fast.

Desperate and panicky, Ryan went on a futile search for her in the house. In the front hall, he noticed her coat was gone. Grabbing his coat, he shrugged it on and went outside.

"Susie?" he called but was greeted by silence. The sky was thick with stormy-looking clouds, and the air heavy with moisture. *We're going to get pounded with more snow,* he thought, studying the sky for a moment before he looked down to find her footprints in the old snow. "Susie!" he called, breaking into a jog that made him painfully aware of his weakened state. He hadn't even traveled the length of a football field when he had to stop to catch his breath.

He found her perched on a ridge that overlooked the town. They had whiled away many an hour in that spot but not when the slope leading to the ridge was slick with ice like it was now. "Susie," he said, weak from exertion and relief. "Susie, come down from there. Come on."

She didn't move or even indicate she heard him.

"I can't do a goddamned thing for you if you fall off that rock!" he yelled, still clutching his side as he tried to catch his breath. "So get down. Now!"

"Leave me alone, Ryan. Will you please just leave me alone?"

He hated the tears he saw on her cold-reddened cheeks—and hated knowing he had put them there.

"If you don't come down, I'm coming up."

"I got myself up, I can get myself down. Now, go away."

He scaled the six-foot climb with his eyes, groaning inwardly at what it would cost him to climb up there in his current condition. Reaching for the first notch in the rock, he grabbed hold of it and grunted as he eased his way up the craggy slope.

"Oh, for God's sake," she said, descending with ease. She wiped her hands on her jeans and glared at him. "Happy now?"

"No," he said. "I am *not* happy right now."

She tried to push past him, but he blocked the path.

"I need you to leave me alone for a little while." Her bright blue eyes spit fire at him. "Can you do that? I can't think when you're taking up all the space."

He fought to conceal his smile. "Out here?" He gestured to the snow-capped aspens and pines. "Or in there?" he asked, resting a finger on her chest.

She swatted his hand away. "*Ugh! You're driving me crazy!*"

"Right back atcha, darlin'. You drive me crazy. You drive me wild. You drive me. That's what I've been trying to tell you."

"Well, *I've* been trying to tell *you* it's time for you to get a new driver, but you refuse to listen to anything other than what you want to hear."

"I don't want another driver. I want you."

"*You can't have me!* What part of that do you not understand?"

"Um, the 'can't' part?"

She shrieked with frustration. "You could have any woman in that town." She gestured toward Breckenridge off in the distance. "Hell, you could have three of them at once if that's what floats your boat. Why don't you go find one who wants you and *leave me alone?*"

"Maybe I *can* have any woman I want." He worked at not showing her she had hurt him by being so anxious for him to find someone else. "But the only one I want is the one who's standing right in front of me."

"Well, I'm sorry to disappoint you—"

"I know you're hoping I'll get bored with this and give up because that's what I would've done in the past. But that's not going to happen."

"Let me ask you something, Ryan."

"Anything you want."

"What happens, hypothetically speaking, if you were to 'get' me?" She made quotation marks with her fingers. "What happens then?"

He shrugged. "We spend the rest of our lives together."

"And when you're not in what you consider to be the fight of your life, are you going to be this concerned about how I feel and what I'm thinking and if I'm happy?"

"Of course I will," he stammered. "*I will.*"

She snorted. "Whatever. Once the thrill of the chase is gone, the thrill will be gone, too, and we'll be right back to business as usual—you being the great and wonderful Ryan Sanderson and me being a piece of furniture in your life. You can't convince me *anything* would be different."

"Do you know what your problem is?" He told himself to just shut up before he said something he couldn't take back. But somehow his mouth never got the message from his brain.

"Oh, please, *do* enlighten me." She folded her arms across her chest.

"You've never forgiven me."

"For?"

He kicked at the snow with the point of his boot. "You know."

Her face went pale. "Don't go there. That's completely and totally off limits." She pushed past him.

"Why?" He chased after her. "Why is it off limits? You've never talked to me about it. I know you've talked to other people about it. Why not me? Why not the only other person in the world who feels the same way you do?"

She stopped and turned to him, a look of disbelief on her face. "You do *not* feel the same way I do, and you've got a lot of nerve to say that!"

"*Why?*" he cried. "Because I wasn't the one who carried him? That doesn't mean I didn't want him! I wanted him. More than I've ever wanted anything!"

Susannah put her hands over her ears and shook her head. "Please stop."

He reached for her arm. "No, I won't stop," he said, plunging forward despite the hurt that made every nerve ending in his body feel like it was on fire. "This conversation is long overdue. It's the reason we're on the verge of a divorce."

"It's not the only reason."

"It's a big one, and nothing was ever the same after it. Talk to me, Susie," he pleaded. "I needed to share it with you, but you shut me out."

"You went back to work!" She tugged her arm free. "If you wanted to share it with me, you should've stayed home."

Following her as she started back down the path, he said, "I had a job to do. My team was counting on me."

"Your *wife* was counting on you," she shot over her shoulder.

"My *wife* treated me like the whole thing was my fault. Going back to work was a relief."

"How typical. Of course it was all about you." Her movements were jerky as she went into the cabin and tugged off her coat.

He hung his coat next to hers and summoned the strength to pursue it, knowing if he didn't, nothing else he did would matter. "It wasn't all about me, Susie," he said in a quiet tone as he fought for control of his emotions. "But it wasn't all about you, either. I was in that room when they couldn't find his heartbeat. I was right there with you. And then I had to watch my wife give birth to a baby we knew was dead." His voice caught. "So don't try to tell me it didn't happen to me, too." He walked up behind her and rested his hands on her stooped shoulders. "It was the worst thing that's ever happened to me, Susie," he whispered. "Even worse than losing my mother."

Sobs wracked through her petite frame. "It was my fault."

"*What?*" He turned her around so he could see her face. "Why would you say that?"

"I must've done something wrong. He was moving all around. For thirty-two weeks he lived inside me, and then he was just gone. How could that have happened?"

"No one knows, baby." Tears slid down his face. "But it was *not* your fault. You did everything right. I wanted to help you. After. I wanted to be there for you, but you didn't want me. That made me crazy, Susie. I felt like I had lost you, too. That's why I went back to work. I know I shouldn't have, but I couldn't bear to spend another day in that house waiting for you to turn to me. Your mother was there and your sister, so I knew you'd be well cared for. I just needed to go back to something I could control."

"And how did that go?"

His mouth twisted into an ironic smile. "You know. The biggest blowout of my career."

"Which led to all the press coverage of our loss. It was *ours,* Ryan. It never should've been in the papers."

His jaw clenched with old anger. "I know that. I tried to find out who leaked it to the press, but I never did. I was on the warpath for weeks over it."

She shrugged. "It could've been anyone—a nurse in the hospital, a trainer on the team. Who knows? It didn't matter. Nothing did, for a long, long time."

"I've thought of him every day for two years," Ryan confessed. "I wonder what he'd be doing, what he'd be saying, what he'd be interested in. I have this picture in my mind of what he might look like—he'd have to be blond with us as his parents. I hope he'd have gotten your pretty blue eyes and maybe my dimples. Girls always went crazy over them."

Susannah looked up with surprise, her eyes bright with new tears. "I never knew you thought about him that way."

"You never let me tell you. I couldn't stand having to pretend like nothing happened when the worst thing in the world had happened. After Bernie and I cleaned out the nursery before you came home, I bawled for hours. I was a total mess, but you refused to let me even mention his name."

She shook her head. "Don't."

"Justin," Ryan whispered. "His name was Justin, and he was our son, Susie. *Ours.*" He pulled her tight against him when she broke down into sobs. "I loved him as much as I love you, and I miss him. I miss him every day." He brushed the tears from her face. "We should've tried again."

"I couldn't," she said. "I couldn't bear the idea of it happening again."

"The doctors said there was no reason to believe it would. It was a fluke thing, baby. And don't you think we owe our son more than to let his death ruin our marriage? He wouldn't have wanted that, Susie. We were so happy for so long, and then it was over. Just like that."

"It wasn't just because of what happened with . . . "

"Say it, Susie. Say his name."

"Justin," she whispered. "It wasn't just because of him."

He sat on the sofa and brought her down onto his lap, wrapping his arms around her. "It didn't help that we weren't able to share our loss, that we both turned to other people to get us through it."

"No," she conceded. "That didn't help. I'm sorry if you felt like I blamed you. I didn't. I just felt like I had failed you so profoundly."

"Failed *me?*" He was incredulous. "You didn't fail me. You could never fail me."

"I knew how much you wanted a family of your own, and I wanted to give you that. I wanted to do that for you."

"You already had. The day you agreed to marry me, I had my family. If I'd had only you, it would've been enough. Justin and any other children we might've had would've only been frosting on the cake."

Susannah stared at him, seeming amazed by his confession.

"So what do you say?" he asked. "Do you think you can forgive me?"

"For what?"

"For going back to work when you needed me. For letting you think football was more important to me than you were, which it wasn't—ever."

She raised a skeptical eyebrow. "Never?"

He shook his head. "Never."

Caressing his bruised cheek, she studied him for a long time. "I do forgive you, Ryan. I pushed you away after everything happened. You're right about that. I knew I was doing it, and I knew I'd regret it." She looked almost ashamed. "In a way, I think I was testing you."

"I guess I failed then, miserably, by rejoining the team," he said, feeling sick as he said it.

"You did what I expected you to."

"I would've stayed. If you had given me even the slightest indication you wanted me there, I would've stayed. I would've sacrificed the rest of the season if I'd thought it would matter to you."

She rested her head on his shoulder. "We've made a terrible mess of things, haven't we?"

"It's nothing we can't fix."

"I'm marrying someone else," she reminded him.

He tipped her chin up and brushed his lips over hers. "No, you're not."

"Yes, I *am*."

Chuckling, he caught her bottom lip between his teeth. "You'll marry him over my dead body."

"If that's what it takes," she said with a saucy grin. Her eyes danced with amusement, which he much preferred to the devastation of a few minutes earlier.

He tossed his head back and laughed but went silent when he felt her lips on his neck. "*Susie . . .* " he groaned. "What're you doing?"

"Remembering."

"Remembering what?" he asked as she moved on to his ear, sending a ripple of desire shooting straight through him.

"How I used to be able to get you to do anything I wanted with just a few well-placed kisses." She trailed her lips along his jaw.

"I believe what you're doing right now was how you ended up with a Chippendale dining room to show off Grandma Sally's china," he said dryly, but his heart felt like it was going to jump out of his chest. He was in pain again but not from his injuries.

She giggled at his restrained grimace as he let her have her way with him.

"So what are you after now?" he asked with a grin, sliding his hands under her sweater to find the soft skin of her back. He had forgotten just how silky smooth she was. She felt like a dream he never wanted to wake up from.

She dropped gentle kisses on the battered side of his face. "I'm not sure."

"Just so we're on the same page, now would be a very good time to ask for anything you want."

"How about a divorce?" she asked with a teasing smile.

Stung, he eased her off his lap and got up.

"Ryan . . ."

He kept his back to her. "I'm going to take a walk."

She got up and went to him. Resting her hands on his chest, she said, "I'm sorry. That wasn't fair in light of what I was doing—"

He stopped her with a finger to her lips. "I'll be back in a bit."

"Do you want me to come with you?"

"You wanted some time to yourself, and I could use a minute, too."

"Ry?"

He turned to her on his way out the door.

"I really am sorry."

With a curt nod, he closed the door behind him.

She realized after he left that he had forgotten his hat.

Chapter 9

HE WAS GONE A LONG TIME. SUSANNAH MADE SOUP AND grilled cheese sandwiches for lunch, but he didn't come back, and she couldn't eat until he did. During his absence, snow began to fall softly at first and then more steadily. As she put several logs on the fire, she worried he had fallen or reinjured his ribs or worse.

The afternoon had grown dark, and she was pacing in front of the fire by the time he finally came in, his hair white with snow and his face red from the cold. He carried a soggy newspaper.

Susannah flew across the room and leaped into his arms.

He hissed from the pain of impact but scooped her up anyway.

"I'm sorry. I was mean, and I hate myself for hurting you."

"Be quiet, darlin', and kiss me, will ya?"

His lips were cold and demanding, but the kiss was hot, so hot that Susannah melted into him, oblivious to the snow dripping all over both of them. He eased her back down without losing the kiss.

She pushed his coat off his shoulders, and it fell into a wet lump on the floor. Pulling back from him, she led him to the hearth in front of the fireplace and urged him down. "You're so cold. Why did you stay out there for so long?"

"I went into town to get the paper."

Her mouth fell open. "You walked four miles to get a paper? Are you out of your mind? You shouldn't be doing that! You have a perfectly good car sitting out there."

"I needed the exercise. All this lying around is turning me into a noodle."

She pulled off his boots and rubbed his feet through his socks. "Are your ribs okay? Do they hurt?"

"They weren't hurting until you launched yourself into them," he said, but there was amusement, not reproach, in his tone. He toyed with her hair. "I like this concerned Susie. I'll have to get you worried about me more often."

"All I ever did was worry about you."

He took her hands to stop her from rubbing his feet. "You've never told me that before."

She shrugged. "You're forever climbing something, scaling something, flying something, testing your limits. It's bad enough you let three-hundred-pound men crash into you for a living." She shuddered. "The other stuff was unbearable. I spent a lot of time waiting to hear you were paralyzed or dead."

"Why didn't you ask me to stop?"

"Because that would be like asking you to stop breathing. It's who you are. I couldn't ask you to be someone you weren't."

"You're very silly, do you know that?"

She huffed with indignation. "Why does that make me silly?"

"Because all you had to do was tell me it bothered you, and I would've stopped." He kissed her hands. "The team hates my *extracurricular* activities as much as you do. I've gotten in trouble with Chet more times than I can count," he said, referring to the team's owner. "He says 'insurance doesn't pay for stupidity.' If I've heard that once, I've heard it a thousand times."

"He's right, but of course you know that."

He shrugged. "You only live once."

She rolled her eyes. "Are you hungry? I made lunch a while ago. I could heat it up for you."

"Sure. Thanks."

She got up and went into the kitchen. When the food was ready, she carried it into the living room on a tray. Ryan had tilted his head back against the sofa and his eyes were closed. *He overdid it again,* she thought, kneeling down next to him. She combed his wet hair with her fingers.

"Ry," she whispered, tracing his jaw with her index finger. He didn't stir, so she leaned in and kissed him.

He awoke with a start and stared at her. "Do it again."

She kept her eyes open and fixed on his when she did as he asked. But before the kiss could spiral out of control, she pulled back. "You need to eat."

"What did you make?"

"Tomato soup and grilled cheese."

"Yum, cabin food." He accepted the bowl of soup from her. "I used to crave that combo when I was here alone."

"Why didn't you just make it?"

"Without you?" he asked, horrified.

She smiled. "Eat up. I made you the usual three sandwiches."

"My girl knows me." He drained the bowl of soup and polished off three sandwiches in the time it took Susannah to eat one.

"How you manage to eat the way you do and not gain a pound I'll never understand."

With a big grin, he said, "Metabolism, baby." He reached for a book on the coffee table. "*The Grapes of Wrath?* Are you reading this?"

"Yep."

"Why?"

She laughed. "It *is* a classic, you know."

"I read it in college."

"So am I."

He looked at her with surprise. "You're finishing school?"

"Uh-huh. I took this semester off because of the wedding, but I should be done by the end of the year. *The Grapes of Wrath* is on the reading list for next semester, so I figured I'd get a jump on it."

"That's great, Susie. I always felt so bad about you leaving school to marry me."

"We said I'd go back, but it didn't quite work out the way we planned, did it?"

He smiled. "Nothing did."

"The minute you signed on the dotted line with the Mavs, everything got so insane."

"It was exciting, though, wasn't it?"

"When I wasn't terrified, I guess it was exciting."

"Why were you terrified? I don't remember that."

She shrugged. "We had just gotten married. I wanted to settle in and nest, but we had nonstop obligations, events, fund-raisers, fans, security, money. So much money. It was mind-boggling. I was so afraid you'd forget you had a wife or you'd forget to come home."

"I never did, though, did I?"

"You never forgot to come home."

"I never forgot I had a wife, either," he said emphatically.

"Never?"

"Not once. Ever."

Susannah studied him. "All those women, Ryan, throwing themselves at you everywhere you went. You're going to tell me you didn't ever, you know . . . "

"I was never unfaithful to you. Never. Not once. I never thought about it. I never considered it. I never did it. I still haven't."

"You're not serious," she said, snorting with disbelief. "We broke up more than a year ago. In all that time—"

"There's been no one else."

She shook her head. "I know you. I know what you . . . need. I find that very hard to believe."

"I'm telling you the truth."

"There were rumors when we were still together," she said quietly.

His face turned as stormy as the weather. "Whatever you heard, none of it was true." He took her hand and looked into her eyes. "You can believe the gossipmongers or you can believe your own husband."

Susannah was torn. She wanted so badly to believe him, but there was a nagging doubt deep inside that left her chilled. She must have shivered because he reached for her. The moment she was close to him she was warm again.

He kissed the top of her head. "I have something for you."

"You do?" She tipped her head back so she could see him.

"Stay put. I'll be right back." He eased himself up, went down the hall to the bedroom, and returned with a small box wrapped in red foil paper.

Puzzled, she asked, "Where did you get that?"

"I've had it for a while. I saw it in a window in Houston, and I've been hoping I'd get the chance to give it to you." He handed it to her. "Open it."

She tore open the paper to find a jeweler's box. Inside was a charm: the number ten, encrusted with diamonds. "Ryan . . . "

"Our anniversary was a big one, and we *were* technically still married." He sat down next to her by the fire and put his arm around her. "I forgot a lot of important stuff when we were together, unforgivable things. But I wanted you to know I remembered our tenth anniversary, even though we weren't together for it."

Susannah rested her head on her knees and wept.

Ryan tipped his head into the groove of her shoulder and rubbed her back.

"I have no idea what to do with this new and improved Ryan."

"I could offer a couple of suggestions if that would help."

Lifting her head off her knees, she smiled and fingered the delicate charm. "I stayed home alone on our anniversary. I didn't see anyone or take any calls. I stayed in my pajamas all day."

"I came up here and went for a long hike. I wanted so badly to call you. I should have. But things had gotten so hostile between us. I wanted to tell you I was sorry and beg you for another chance, but I didn't think that was the day to do it."

"I wanted to call you, too," she confessed. "You were the only one I wanted to talk to that day. I don't know what I would've said. I just . . . I missed you."

He brought her into his arms.

She rested her head on his chest. "Thank you for this, and thank you for remembering," she said, admiring the charm again. "I'll add it to my bracelet."

"I was going to get you something bigger, something more significant . . . "

"No, this is perfect. There's nothing else I'd rather have." She returned the charm to the box and put it on the table. "It'll also remind me of ten crazy days one February."

"Ten days that were maybe the start of something new?"

Raising her head to look at him, she said, "Maybe."

He kissed her with a passion and a thoroughness that took them both by surprise. She was startled to realize the almost chemical attraction they'd always had for each other had grown and intensified during their long separation. His tongue tangled with hers, and the taste that was so uniquely his only fueled her desire for more. When she slid her hand into the back of his jeans, he moaned and tumbled down on top of her.

Without breaking the kiss, he filled his hands with her breasts and pushed his erection into the V of her legs. He tore his lips free of hers and dragged in several deep breaths. "Susie . . . God, I want you. I want you more than I ever have before."

With a coy smile, she lifted her hips to press against his pulsing erection. "I know. I can tell."

He gazed at her for a long moment before he dipped his head and reclaimed her lips. What had been frantic now became soft and sensual. The air was electric with the sounds of wet mouths, urgent moans, the crackling of the fire, and the howl of the wind. The lights flickered once, twice, and then went dark.

Ryan lifted his head. "Well," he said with the dimpled grin that made her knees weak. "Isn't this romantic?"

She laughed and brought him back down to her. "You planned this."

"You're damned right I did." He kissed her cheeks, her nose, and her chin.

By the time he made it back to her lips, Susannah was desperate for him. Forgetting about his injuries, she held him tight, and he winced. "Oh, God, I'm sorry."

"I'm fine," he whispered against her lips as he tugged at her sweater. "Take this off."

She sat up, aware she was about to cross a line. But she wasn't thinking about Henry or their engagement at that moment. No, her every thought and emotion belonged to Ryan. His eyes, hot with desire, devoured her as he waited breathlessly to see if she would do what he had asked. Filled with her own power, she let her fingers linger at hem. He ran his tongue over his lips as he waited, waited. Finally, his patience ran out, and he reached over to do it himself. The sweater sailed over her head and landed on the sofa.

Trailing her fingers over his chest, she unbuttoned his shirt and pushed it aside. The hair on his muscular chest and washboard stomach was bright gold in the firelight. "Ry," she whispered when she uncovered the horrible bruises above and below the tape on his ribs. "I'm afraid to touch you."

"I won't break."

Careful to steer clear of his midsection, she caressed his chest. Even bruised and battered, he was magnificent. His nipples stood at attention as she nuzzled through the soft hair to run her tongue over one of them.

He lay back on the floor, exhaled a long deep breath, and closed his eyes. "Once won't be enough," he said. "You know that, right?"

"Hmm?" she asked, intent on what she was doing to his nipple.

"Susie . . . " With his hands on her face, he found her eyes. "If you make love with me and then go back to him, you'll ruin me."

His words were like a blast of cold air. She sat up and ran her fingers through her hair.

He reached for her. "Come back."

She lay down next to him, resting her head on his chest.

"Are you warm enough?" he asked.

"Yeah."

"It's going to get cold in here if the power doesn't come back on. We'll have to sleep by the fire."

"We've done it before."

"I'm going to hook up the generator for the fridge." He kissed her cheek. "I'll be right back."

"Do you need help?"

"Nah, I've got it."

"Watch those ribs."

"Yes, Mother," he said with a teasing smile as he buttoned his shirt and pulled on his boots. Before he got up, he kissed her. "Don't go anywhere."

"I won't."

Susannah curled up to watch the fire. *If he hadn't stopped me, we'd be making love right now.* She didn't often think of Ryan as being vulnerable, but he had shown her more with one simple statement than he had during all the bigger, deeper subjects they had covered during the course of that extraordinary day.

The firelight reflected off her engagement ring, and she realized she hadn't thought of Henry in hours. In fact, she rarely thought of him when she wasn't with him. She loved Henry, but she wasn't *in love* with him. She couldn't be because she was still in love with Ryan. This time alone with him had shown her that. Now she had to decide if she had it in her to give him another chance.

Ryan stomped through the snow to the shed where he kept the gasoline for the generator. "Fucking idiot," he muttered under his breath. "You could be in there with her right now. Why'd you have to stop her?"

She had never fully appreciated the hold she had over him. He'd often suspected she was waiting for him to grow tired of her and move on to one of the ever-present groupies who followed the team from city to city. But he'd never grown tired of her. If anything, he had grown so dependent on her that when she left him he'd been completely lost without her.

He had told himself at the start of his ten-day campaign that he would do anything it took to get her back. But today he'd discovered he had limits, and now he wanted to shoot himself for showing her that she rendered him defenseless. Somewhere in the course of discussing the son they had lost, the anniversary they had missed, and the life they had shared, the stakes had gone up. Ryan was even more convinced that if she left him for good he wouldn't survive it.

Chapter 10

THEY COOKED HOTDOGS IN THE FIREPLACE AND OPENED a bottle of red wine. After he polished off his third hot dog, Ryan pushed the sofa closer to the fire. Just six feet from the fireplace, the cabin was freezing. Susannah snuggled under a heavy blanket and picked up her book to read by the firelight. Ryan reached for his guitar but stuck his feet under the other end of her blanket.

"Do you take requests?" she asked with a smile after she listened to him for a long time.

"Depends on who's asking."

She chuckled.

"What do you want to hear?"

"Anything by The Eagles."

He played a song she hadn't heard before, called "No More Cloudy Days," that was all about second chances and new romances.

"I like that," Susannah said softly.

"You're supposed to be reading."

"I'd rather listen to you. You've gotten really good."

"I've had lots of time to practice." He played "Peaceful Easy Feeling," which he knew was her favorite song by The Eagles. The concert continued with a slice of "American Pie," a bit of Toby Keith, and ended with a blast of Kiss that had her howling with laughter.

"Hot dogs and Kiss," she said, recovering from the laughing fit. "Just another night with my millionaire husband."

He kept his eyes fixed on her as he continued to strum the guitar, singing along to a tune of his own creation. *"She called me her husband, so I have to believe, she loves me enough not to leave. She looks at me with eyes so blue, and I love her more than I ever knew."*

He was three feet from her, but he touched her everywhere. "Maybe you'd better not quit your Sunday job after all," she said in a dry attempt to hide her true feelings.

"Are you implying my dream of a second career as a songwriter is a nonstarter?" he asked, feigning offense.

"Pretty much."

"You liked it."

She shrugged with pretend boredom. "It was all right."

Laughing, he put down the guitar and tunneled under the blanket to her end of the sofa. He popped out and rested his head on her leg. "Read to me."

"You've already read it," she reminded him.

"I can't remember. Come on. Read it to me."

"All right. If you insist."

He shifted onto his good side, and Susannah combed her fingers through his hair absently. Absorbed in the story, she didn't notice when he released the bottom two buttons of her denim shirt. Her words got stuck when he pressed his lips to the skin he had uncovered.

"Keep reading," he whispered as he opened two more buttons and kissed her breasts through her bra.

She clutched a handful of his hair. "Ry . . . What're you doing?"

"I was listening to you read, but then you stopped."

"I can't read when you're doing that."

"Doing what?"

Overwhelmed by him, she was gentle but insistent when she pushed him away. "Let me up. I want to get changed."

He sat up slowly, favoring his injured side.

Susannah dashed down the dark hallway to the guest bedroom and made quick work of changing into a flannel nightgown and heavy socks. She was shivering by the time she went into the bathroom to wash her face and brush her teeth. No more than five minutes later she returned to find that Ryan had inflated the air mattress they used on the rare weekends when they invited friends to join them at the cabin.

"Come on, blue lips," he said, lifting a blanket.

She grabbed her book as she lay down on the mattress.

He layered the blankets on top of her. "Good?"

She nodded. "Thanks," she said through chattering teeth.

"There should be enough hot water for a quick shower," he said when he finished building up the fire. "Get that bed warmed up for me."

Susannah planned to read but found she was too cold to do anything but burrow deeper under the covers. Over and over she relived what he'd said earlier: *If you make love to me and then go back to him, you'll ruin me. You'll ruin me.* Since she still didn't know if she was ready or able to reconcile with Ryan, she was fearful of getting too close to him until she decided for certain. Still puzzling it over, she dozed off. She woke up when Ryan crawled in with her wearing only a pair of sweats. Since he usually slept nude, the sweats were a major concession to the cold.

"It's really coming down out there," he whispered as he curled around her. "We might be stuck here for weeks."

"All part of your evil plan," she said with a yawn. He felt so good and so warm that she put her arm around him and discovered the tape was gone from his ribs. "You unwrapped them? Can you do that?"

"It was starting to itch."

"Does it still hurt?"

"Now it's more like a toothache than a heart attack."

"Did it really hurt that much?"

"Worse than anything ever has . . . except for losing you, of course."

"Cute."

"You think I'm kidding."

She found his eyes in the amber light and discovered he wasn't kidding. "Ry," she said with a sigh.

He brought her even closer to him and kissed her.

"We can't," she said. "What you said earlier . . . I haven't decided anything yet, and until I do . . . I don't want to hurt you."

"About four seconds after I said that I decided I'm willing to risk it."

"But what," she stammered. "What if . . . "

"What if it never stops snowing and we're stuck here forever?" He trailed soft kisses on her neck. "What if? What if? How about we talk about what *is?*"

"And what's that?"

"Well, let's see." He sprinkled kisses on her face, seeming to avoid her mouth on purpose. "There's you, and me, and this dark, cold cabin, and this nice fire. It seems silly to let all this atmosphere go to waste, don't you think?"

As she listened to him, she caressed the rippling muscles on his back. His lips hovered over hers, but she turned her face away. "Wait, Ry."

"What, baby?"

"I just don't want you to think if we, you know, do this, that it means . . . "

"All it means is we want to make love. You're still my wife, Susie."

"But I'm also—"

"Don't say it." His eyes were dark and fixed on her. "Do *not* say that."

She reached for him.

His lips came down on hers and swept away any final doubts that she was exactly where she belonged. Everything about him was familiar, yet new, too. This wasn't the same man she'd wanted to divorce. He wasn't the same man she had decided she could easier live without than try to live with. Which Ryan would she get if she agreed to stay with him? That uncertainty still nagged at her. But when he reached for the hem of her nightgown, sat her up, and swept it over her head, she ceased to think of anything but him.

"Oh, Susie, is that from the EpiPen?" he asked, smoothing his hand over the fist-sized bruise on her thigh.

She trembled from both the chill and the heat of his gaze. "Yeah."

He replaced his hand with his lips. "I hate that I did that to you."

"You saved my life. I think I can forgive you for a little bruise."

"It's a *big* bruise."

"It's nothing compared to all of yours." She ran her hands over his arms. "Are you comfortable up there?"

"No." He took his lips on a trip to her inner thigh. "I'm very uncomfortable, and you're the only one who can fix it."

Her giggle turned to a gasp. "Ry . . . "

"Hmmm?"

"Oh, *God*," she moaned when he nudged her legs apart. She had forgotten what it was like to make love with Ryan—the all-consuming passion, the endless pleasure. Or maybe she hadn't really forgotten but rather locked the memories away somewhere deep inside where they couldn't be easily found as she built a life without him.

He teased her with his tongue, dragging it on a sensuous trail over one inner thigh and then the other.

Susannah's legs quivered, so he rested them on his broad shoulders.

"What do you want?" he whispered against her thigh.

The feel of his soft lips against her skin made her crazy. "You."

"Where?"

She lifted her hips. "You know."

He kissed his way closer. So close . . . "No, I don't. You have to tell me."

She had also forgotten the way he liked to talk to her when they made love and how much he enjoyed getting her to say things she would never say any other time.

Nuzzling at her core, he said, "You can't have it until you tell me you want it."

"I want your tongue," she whispered.

"Where?"

Her face burned with embarrassment, but desire burned brighter. "In me. On me. Everywhere."

"We'll get to that." He ran his finger over her slickness. "Oh, you're so wet, Susie. So hot."

Susannah shuddered, and her gasp sounded more like a sob by the time it broke free of the lump in her throat. She cried out when he slid two fingers deep into her. "Ryan!"

"Tell me."

Feeling like she was outside of herself watching someone else, she let her legs fall open in surrender. "Move them," she whispered.

He kept his fingers torturously still. "How?"

At any other time, Susannah would have died of embarrassment. Right now, she cared only about the throbbing tension between her legs. "In and out."

His fingers twisted, ever so slightly. "Fast or slow?"

"Fast," she panted, raising her hips to beg for more. "Fast."

"When we were apart, I dreamed about this," he whispered against her thigh as his fingers moved in and out of her. "I dreamed about how wet you always got for me and how you smell." Keeping up the steady movement of his fingers, he burrowed his nose into the soft blond hair on her mound and took deep breaths. "And how you taste . . . so, so sweet." He replaced his fingers with his tongue.

She came instantly, crying out as she pushed against the gentle but insistent thrusts of his determined tongue. When she would have retreated into recovery, he wouldn't let her.

"Do it again," he whispered, his breath hot against her sensitized skin.

"I can't," she whimpered.

"Yes, you can." Clutching her bottom in the palms of his big hands, he held her in place and set out to prove her wrong.

"*Ryan!*" she cried the instant a second orgasm, this one even more powerful than the first, sent her flying into orbit. Trembling and weak, she floated as the aftershocks rippled through her.

He lowered her legs from his shoulders and entered her with a swift thrust of his hips that brought her soundly back to earth.

She gasped and struggled to accommodate his width and length.

For a long, breathless moment he was still. "Susie," he whispered in her ear. "How have I lived without you, without this, for more than a year?"

With her hands on his face and tears in her eyes, she brought him to her for a deep, soulful kiss as he began to move. When she sensed his injuries were bothering him, she carefully eased him onto his back and straddled him. Bringing the blankets up and around them, she teased him by refusing to grant him entry.

Growling, he held her hips still and surged up and into her. Once he was back where he wanted to be, he reached up to comb his fingers through her hair. "I love you, Susie. I love you so much."

"I love you, too."

"Do you? Do you really?"

She nodded, tossed her head back, and rode him with abandon, steeped in the thrilling sensation of being filled by him, consumed by him.

He cupped her breasts and ran his thumbs over her nipples, lifting her into yet another climax. "Ryan," she panted, looking down at him with eyes that she was certain were glassy with passion and what might have been shock—that it was still possible to feel this much . . . so much . . . even more than before.

"*Susie,*" he moaned. "God, don't stop. Don't ever stop."

She leaned back, took him deeper, took him all the way.

"This reminds me of the first night we ever spent together," Ryan said much later as they lay facing each other. "Do you remember?"

"Of course I do. We were in that fleabag apartment you rented off campus."

"There were no fleas," he said with indignation.

She laughed at the face he made. "I was expecting something pretty fabulous, since you were supposedly this *big star.*"

"I *was* a big star and the apartment *was* fabulous. At least it was until we moved in. I remember clearing the other guys out and scrambling to clean the place up before you got there. I'd spent months trying to get you into bed, and I didn't want anything to mess it up. Of course I didn't expect the bed to break . . . "

Susannah laughed until she cried at the memory. "As I recall, it didn't slow us down any."

"Just like the cold hasn't slowed us down tonight."

She turned her face into the pillow. "Stop."

"You'd think we were out to beat our own record."

"Ryan . . . "

He laughed at her discomfort. "Is it just me or is what was always amazing now extraordinary?"

"It's not just you," she said softly.

"Maybe it's because we appreciate each other more after being apart for so long."

"That's not it. Although that might be part of it."

He reached out to twirl a lock of her hair around his finger. "Then what is it?"

"It's what I tried to tell you was missing before. The way we talked today, about stuff that really matters . . . It's made me feel connected to you in here," she said with her hand over her heart.

"I get it now, Suze. I really do. I know what I had, what I lost, how I felt without it." He brought her hand to his lips. "Do you know I still look for you in the stadium where you always used to sit? Whenever we scored this season, I'd look for you, wanting to share it with you. It was like losing you all over again every time I looked for you and you weren't there."

Overwhelmed by him, Susannah fought the urge to cry.

"So many times over the last year I wanted to call you," he continued. "Especially when . . . "

She studied his face, which was suddenly tight with tension. "What is it?"

He sighed. "I heard from my father."

"*What?*" she gasped. "When?"

"About six months ago."

"But, what, I mean . . . What did he say?"

"That he'd followed my career, that he wanted to see me." He shrugged. "Nothing much."

"So what happened? Did you see him?"

Ryan nodded. "He came to a game, and we went out to dinner after."

"How did you even know it was him?" Susannah asked, hanging on his every word.

"I look just like him," Ryan said with an ironic chuckle. "It's unreal. He's an older version of me."

"Wow, that must've been so weird. How did you feel when he just called you out of the blue like that?"

"Stunned," he confessed. "I wanted so badly to talk to you about it. I didn't know what to do."

"I wish I'd been there with you. All those years you wondered about him . . . "

"I wish you'd been there, too, especially when I found out what he really wanted."

"I'm almost afraid to ask . . . "

"Money, of course."

"Oh, Ry," she sighed as her eyes filled. "What'd you do?"

"Gave it to him. What else was I supposed to do?"

She clutched his hand. "I'm so sorry."

He shrugged, but the hurt was written on his face. "I was stupid. I got my hopes up. Since my mother died and you and I broke up, I've been kind of short on family. But I should've known better than to pin any hopes on him."

"He's not a father," Susannah said fiercely. "He's a sperm donor."

Ryan smiled. "I guess I sort of suspected what might happen. That's why—"

The lights flickered back on, startling them.

When he began to get up to turn them off, Susannah stopped him. "What were you going to say?"

"Just that I had a hunch about how it might turn out. That's why I didn't tell anyone he had called. Not even Bernie."

"Did you find out where he's been all these years?"

"In California. He's remarried. He didn't even know my mother had died."

"Does he have other kids?"

Ryan nodded. "Three of them."

Susannah studied him as she absorbed it all. "You have siblings."

"Yeah. I'm not really sure what to do about that. I go back and forth about contacting them. They can't help who their father is any more than I can."

"Why did he ask you for money?"

"Apparently he'd gotten into some trouble with gambling."

"How much did you give him?"

"Half a million."

"*Ryan! Oh my God!*"

"Yes, I know it's outrageous," he said, chagrined. "But by the time he told me how much he needed, I just wanted to be rid of him."

Susannah held out her arms to him.

He slid into her embrace with a deep sigh of relief. "He looked like a grown up, Suze, nothing like those old pictures I have of him. But he's still the same guy who left his wife and two-year-old son and never looked back."

"It's a good thing I wasn't there." She was furious with a man she had never met. "He wouldn't have gotten a dime out of you if I had been."

"I know," Ryan said with a chuckle. "I thought the same thing at the time. After I gave him the check, I drove over to the house. I sat outside for an hour trying to work up the nerve to call you or knock on the door or something. I just wanted you so badly."

Tears slid down her cheeks. "I'm sorry," she whispered. "I'm sorry he hurt you and that I wasn't there for you. I would've punched the snot out of him."

He laughed, but his eyes were bright with emotion. "I love when my little debutante talks like a truck driver."

"I'm serious. I would've hurt him."

"I have no doubt." He wiped the tears from her face. "Thank you."

"For what?"

"For listening and for being so mad on my behalf. I was pretty numb for a while after it happened."

"And you were all alone."

He shrugged. "I feel better now that you know about it." He kissed her cheek. "You must be getting tired, baby."

She glanced at the clock on the mantle and found it was after three. "Not really. How about you?"

"I'm hungry," he said as he kissed her and got up to turn off the lamps.

"Why am I not surprised?" She watched him move around in the nude. Even with the bruises that colored his chest and face, he was so gorgeous she couldn't look away.

He caught her watching him and grinned. "See something you like, darlin'?"

"Uh-huh."

He turned off the last of the lights and returned to their makeshift bed on the floor.

Susannah squealed when he landed on top of her. "Watch your ribs!"

"They're fine." He captured her mouth in a passionate kiss.

"I thought you were hungry," she said as he turned his attention to her neck.

"I am."

She tilted her head to give him better access. "Want me to make you something?"

"You'd really leave this nice, warm bed for me?"

"If I have to."

He drew back to look at her. "You *do* love me."

"God help me," she joked.

"What're you going to do, Susie?"

"Make you a sandwich if you'll get your big self off of me."

He held her face so she couldn't look away. "That's not what I meant, and you know it."

"This has been the most amazing day and night." She reached up to touch his hair and then his face. "I just want to enjoy being here with you without any pressure to decide anything. Can we do that?"

He studied her for a long time, and it seemed to cost him to say, "Okay."

"How about that sandwich?"

"You don't have to." He pulled on his sweats. "I can do it. Want half?"

"Just a bite and some water."

"Coming right up."

He returned a few minutes later with a huge turkey sandwich and a bottle of water to share.

"Ry?"

"What, baby?"

"I was just wondering . . . "

"About?"

She rolled her lip back and forth between her teeth.

He took her hand. "There's nothing you can't ask me, Susie."

"If you love me so much, why'd you wait until the eleventh hour to do this? To come back?"

He swallowed the last bite of sandwich and took a long drink of water. "I didn't plan to wait so long. When the judge ordered us to wait six more months before he would grant the divorce, the season was just starting. I wanted to get you alone with no distractions, and you know how crazy everything is during the season."

She nodded.

"No one expected us to do anything this year. It was supposedly a 'rebuilding year,' but everything went our way. We beat teams we never should've beaten. I was starting to feel desperate because time was getting away from me, and we kept winning. We played Miami in the playoffs."

"I watched that game," she confessed.

"Then you know we shouldn't have won."

"I was jumping all around when Willy returned that fumble for a touchdown."

"It was insane. I couldn't believe we were going to the Super Bowl again. It was an incredible season, in many ways more exciting than any of the others. Then I got hurt, and they stuck me in the hospital. I was freaking out. I was down to ten days until our court date, and they were telling me I needed to spend at least three of them in the hospital. So I checked myself out against the doctor's orders."

"You shouldn't have done that."

"You were engaged." He fiddled with the blanket. "I was desperate. You should've seen me when I heard you were going to marry that guy. I just kept picturing you . . . with him, and I thought I'd go crazy. I got stinking, filthy drunk. I even missed a practice for the first time ever."

Susannah swallowed hard. "I'd planned to tell you myself."

He turned to her. "So why didn't you?"

"Henry told a couple of people, and the word got out. After it was mentioned in the paper, I knew there was no point in calling you."

"You should've called me, Susie. You owed me that much."

"You're absolutely right. I did."

He studied her intently. "Were you hoping to hurt me?" he finally asked.

"No."

"You did."

"I know. I'm sorry."

"Old Henry didn't waste any time, did he? How long did it take him to move to Denver after we split up?"

"Three or four months."

"He gave up a cushy job on Wall Street to run the First Mercantile Bank of Denver. Quite a step down, but I'm sure it was worth the sacrifice since you'd finally unloaded the dumb jock."

"It wasn't like that," she protested.

"Sure it was."

"Ryan, please . . . Don't do this." She put her arms around him and kissed his back. "Please. Don't ruin everything."

"I thought I already had. Isn't that what you said when you asked me to leave?"

She leaned her forehead against his back. "Ry," she said, her voice catching on a sob.

He turned and put his arms around her.

"I never meant to hurt you," she said. "We hurt each other so much. I don't want to do that anymore."

"Neither do I."

"Do you really think, in light of all that's happened, we have a prayer of putting our marriage back together?"

"If I didn't, we wouldn't be here." He lay down and brought her with him. "We can do it, Susie. I know we can."

"Are you really going to retire?"

"Yes."

"And do what?"

"Run my businesses, and I've been toying with the idea of maybe coaching."

"In the NFL?"

"High school."

She looked up at him. "For real?"

"I think I could have a greater impact at that level. I was a messed-up kid with no father and a mother who worked all the time. Jimmy Stevens is the number one reason why I'm where I am today," he said, referring to his high-school football coach. "He showed me what I was capable of."

"But you could write your own ticket with the league."

"Where would the fun be in that? Coaching a bunch of overpaid egomaniacs? No thanks."

"And what would *you* know about *that?*" she asked with a smile.

"I don't know what you're talking about." He returned her smile with his trademark cocky grin. "When I went into town today, I called Duke. I'm meeting with him and Chet the day after tomorrow when they get back from Washington. I'm dreading telling them. They're going to go nuts. I want you there with me when I tell them."

"I don't know, Ry. It's got nothing to do with me."

"Of course it does," he insisted.

She yawned. "How?"

"You're tired, baby." He kissed her. "We'll talk about it in the morning."

Her eyes closed. "I want to talk about it now."

"The heat's back on. Do you want to sleep in a real bed or stay here?"

"Here. With you."

He kicked off the sweats and slid in next to her. "I'm here."

She took his hand and pulled his arm tight around her.

"Susie?"

"Mmm."

"I love you." He kissed her shoulder and then her cheek. "I missed you so much."

"Mmm. Me, too."

Chapter 11

RYAN HELD HER CLOSE WHILE SHE SLEPT AND WAS HOPEFUL they had taken a big step back to each other. Having her warm and soft and naked in his arms was like a dream come true. How many nights had he fantasized about being with her like this again? They had covered a lot of ground and righted a lot of wrongs, but was it enough? When they got back to the real world, would it be enough to keep her from leaving? He didn't know what else he could do or say to convince her their marriage would be different this time.

She had given herself to him so completely earlier and rendered him, as she always had, helpless. He'd never understood how one woman could have such power over him. Susannah had been right when she said other women were forever coming on to him, but none of them appealed to him the way she had from the first time he spotted her at the Purple Porpoise in Gainesville. After that, it had taken him two days—and all his campus clout—to track her down. He could still remember the look on her face when she opened her dorm room door to find him there.

That she'd really had no idea who he was or what he meant to the university had utterly charmed him. He was beginning his senior year, and by then he had grown weary of his own buzz. She'd had a refreshing way even then of bringing him soundly back to earth by refusing to buy into all the hoopla that went with dating the biggest man on a big campus.

She grounded him. She had then, and she had in all the years that followed in the NFL. Without her around to remind him he was nothing more than an ordinary mortal with an extraordinary arm, he would've become completely insufferable rather than just somewhat insufferable. He chuckled softly to himself when he recalled arriving home after he won his first Super Bowl. They had walked into the house, and she'd said, "Ew, something stinks. Figure out what it is, will you, Ry?" No, his big win wasn't going to his head with her around to remind him he was just a guy with something stinky in his house.

He shifted to relieve the ache in his ribs and ended up with a handful of soft breast that made him want her all over again. But rather than disturb her, he pressed his lips to her back and shoulder. Closing his eyes, he finally drifted off to sleep but kept his hand right where it was.

When Susannah awakened after ten that morning, Ryan was wrapped around her and sharing her pillow. She remembered teasing him on many a morning about sleeping in a king-sized bed but having to share a pillow with him. "I get lonely over there without you," he would say with his child-like pout. Placing her hand over his on her breast, she lay still for a long time reveling in the feelings he aroused in her—feelings she now knew had only lain dormant during their long year apart. Despite what she tried to tell herself, they hadn't disappeared.

As she gently extricated herself from Ryan's embrace, the one thing she knew for sure was she couldn't think clearly when she was naked and in bed with him. Reaching for her nightgown, she slipped it over her head and pulled on her socks. The fire had died down, but the room was warm from the heat. She padded to the kitchen to make coffee before she went into the bathroom. After she had brushed her teeth and done what she could with her hair, she examined her reflection in the mirror. Her lips were swollen and almost bruised, and her cheeks were flushed with color. "You look like you've been making mad love," she whispered. With a giggle, she added, "Is there any other kind with Ryan?" He made love the same way he lived—with everything he had, which was why she was sore and achy in some interesting places today.

On her way back to the kitchen, she stopped to look at him sprawled out in their bed on the floor. The covers had slipped to his waist, giving her a panoramic view of his injured ribs. She winced when she imagined the pain he must have been in when it first happened. *I should've been there with him, but part of me is glad I wasn't.* Watching him get hurt playing football had been one of the most difficult parts of a difficult marriage.

He sure is handsome, she sighed, thinking as she often had that the word "handsome" didn't begin to describe him. She had never fully gotten over her awe at being picked out of the crowd by a man who could've had any woman he wanted. Over the years, she'd made an effort not to let him see her awe because keeping him humble was a big enough job as it was.

She poured herself a cup of coffee and took it with her to look out at the shiny, white morning. The sun was back, and all signs of the storm were gone. The town appeared to have been frosted by the snow, and the mountain was littered with tiny dots—skiers taking advantage of the fresh powder. If he had been healthy, Ryan might've been up there with them. Or maybe this new Ryan would've stayed home with her and enjoyed some precious time alone.

As she stood there daydreaming, she remembered another morning in that very spot, the morning she had felt Justin move inside her for the first time. The memory had Susannah unconsciously reaching for her belly where her baby boy had once lived. The grief and emptiness still struck at odd times, like now when she hadn't even been thinking about him. She'd been comforted yesterday to hear that Ryan thought of him often, too. Somehow, knowing that made her feel less alone with her loss.

Ryan startled her when he came up behind her and kissed her neck. "You were a million miles away. What were you thinking about?"

"Justin," she said without hesitation.

Wrapping his arms around her from behind, Ryan held her close to him. "What about him?"

"I was standing right here the first time I ever felt him move. Remember?"

"How could I forget? You were screaming and yelling for me to come. You scared the crap out of me."

Susannah smiled, and all at once the memory was a

happy one. She turned to him and wasn't surprised to find him still naked and on his way to being aroused. Turning her eyes up to his, she said, "Before yesterday I wouldn't have told you I was thinking about him. I would've said I was thinking about nothing or made up something else. I was sad just now, but sharing it with you made me feel better. That's what I should've done all along, and I'm sorry I didn't. I'm sorry if I made you feel like it wasn't your loss, too."

He caressed her face. "It's in the past now. We have only good things ahead of us." Wiggling his eyebrows, he added, "Maybe we made a new baby last night."

"After what we went through to get pregnant the first time, I doubt it." She cringed at the memory of ovulation kits, thermometers, and invasive tests that found nothing at all wrong with either of them. "Lightning might not strike twice."

"My boys were *very* well rested," he said with that grin of his.

Susannah's stomach twisted at the thought. "God, it didn't even occur to me to use protection because we had such trouble before. Wouldn't *that* be just my luck?"

His smile faded. "Wouldn't it just?"

"Don't be offended. I'm just saying, the timing would stink."

"With Mommy being engaged to another man and all that."

Looping her arms up around his neck, she brought him down for a kiss. At first he resisted, but she worked on him until he acquiesced.

"Do you like knowing you can have me any time you

want me?" he asked with a fierce look in his usually soft brown eyes.

Full of her own power, she met his intense gaze with one of her own. "Yes." Without looking away, she let her hands slide down his chest to grasp his throbbing erection. She stroked him the way she knew he liked it—hard and fast.

He hissed as he closed his eyes and let his head fall back.

She kept up the quick movements of her hands until he was rock hard and breathing heavily.

He backed her up to the kitchen table. "Right here?"

Susannah could tell she surprised him when she said, "Why not?"

He pushed her nightgown up to her waist and buried his fingers in her. The sound and feel of her wetness seemed to fire his already ferocious mood. "Now, Susie. Right now."

"Yes," she whispered.

"What about protection?" he asked at the last possible moment.

"I'll take my chances."

All her earlier aches and pains were forgotten when he entered her. The thrusts of his tongue into her mouth mirrored the almost angry thrusts of his hips. She had pushed him to some sort of breaking point, but rather than being frightened by his furious possession she was exhilarated by it. She hooked her legs over his hips to take him deeper, and he slapped against her.

A groan rumbled through him, and he pulled furiously at the front of her nightgown. Buttons popped off, giving him the access he craved. He caught her nipple between two fingers, and still he kissed her with deep, passionate strokes of his tongue that alone would have left her weak. The combination sent her into a soaring climax.

He tore his mouth free of hers and cried out a moment after her. Breathing hard, he collapsed on top of her and buried his face in the crook of her neck. "I'm sorry," he said when he could speak again.

Her fingers tunneled into his hair as she kissed away beads of sweat on his forehead. "For?"

"Acting like a mad man," he said, still breathing hard.

When he began to withdraw from her, she held him tighter with her legs. "Why? I liked it."

He lifted his head to look at her. "I've never treated you like that before."

"You could have. I'm not fragile."

"After all these years that you could still surprise me . . ."

"Right back at you."

They locked eyes for a long, breathless moment before he lowered his head and swept his lips over hers with all the gentle care his earlier kisses had lacked. He nipped and licked and worshiped every corner of her mouth, growing hard again in the process. "Susie," he whispered as he began to move his hips with a slow, aching patience. "You kill me." He lifted her and tugged the nightgown over her head so he could nuzzle her breasts. "You make me feel weak and strong at the same time."

He managed to put into words everything she felt for him. "Ry," she gasped when he drew on her nipple. She clutched his head to her chest, wanting him like it was their first time all over again. Maybe it was. Maybe what she'd once declared over was being reborn in that very moment. Just maybe. If the pounding of her heart and the tightening sensation in her belly were any indication, this relationship was very much alive.

"Come for me, Susie," he whispered. "I want to watch you."

Since she was already teetering on the edge, his words sent her toppling over. Watching her was all he needed to go with her.

Tears sparkled in his eyes when he kissed her softly. "I've never loved you more than I do right now."

"And I've never felt more loved by you. I could very easily drown in it."

"I'd save you," he said with another soft kiss.

"I'll never look at this table the same way again," she joked.

He smiled. "Why haven't we ever done this before?"

"I don't know," she said as he helped her up. "Maybe because there's something slightly depraved about doing it on the kitchen table?"

"If that was depraved, I gotta say I like it." He stopped her when she reached for her nightgown. "Let's take a shower."

She followed him to the huge master bedroom and came to a halt in the doorway when she saw he had rearranged the room.

"Do you like it?" he asked.

"It's different."

"I had to do something to shake things up around

here. I had no clue what it would be like to be here without you. There was many a day when I wished I had just given it to you or sold it."

"It looks good," she decided, moved by his words and feeling more for him with every passing moment. She conceded she would soon reach a point of no return—if she hadn't already—when any further talk of a life without him would be pointless.

He held out a hand to her and led her into the spacious, sky-lit bathroom where everything of hers was just as she'd left it. They stepped into the steaming shower. When she wrapped her arms around him from behind he flinched.

"What is it?"

"The heart attack seems to be back," he said with a grimace, running a hand over his injured side.

"No more mad sex for you. You're injured."

"Shoot me now and put me out of my misery if you're going to cut me off." The grin he sent her over his shoulder was lascivious, but she saw the pain in his eyes. "I'll just have to let you do all the work until I'm recovered."

"I think that can be arranged," she said as she soaped his back and kneaded his muscular shoulders.

He propped a hand on the wall of the shower and dropped his head to his chest. "Feels good."

"These bruises seem to be getting more evil looking rather than better."

"At least my gorgeous face looks better today."

"Yes, it does."

He turned to her. "What's this? No witty, ego-deflating comeback? You disappoint me."

"It *is* a gorgeous face." She reached up to caress it. "Easily the most gorgeous face I've ever seen."

"Now you're just scaring me, darlin'."

He looked so genuinely concerned that she burst into laughter. "Am I *that* mean?"

"Usually," he said without hesitation. "But that's okay. I can take it. I know you love me."

"When we were together, before, did I ever tell you what I really thought of you?"

"Now and then, but not with words. Sometimes it would be a look, or a touch, or a sigh at *just* the right moment. Don't worry. I knew."

"I used to look at you when you were sleeping—I did it just this morning, in fact—and wonder what it was about me that made such an amazing, sexy, devastatingly handsome man want me over *all* the others."

The cocky grin was back when he said, "Devastating, huh?"

She smacked his shoulder. "Don't let it go to your head."

"Too late." He leaned in for a kiss. "Do you really want to know what it was about you?"

She nodded.

"I'm glad you asked because I'd love to tell you." He trailed kisses over her neck. "The very first thing was your incredible blue eyes. It was like *wham,* a punch to my stomach when you first looked at me. You were sitting there, so pretty and prim, surrounded by all your girls."

"Prim?" she asked, raising a haughty eyebrow.

He nodded as he worked shampoo through her hair. "After I recovered from the punch to the gut and hunted you down, I'd have to say the next thing was you didn't have any idea who I was, and when you found out, you didn't really give a shit. I liked that, believe it or not. I was so sick of chicks sucking up to me because I played football."

"Oh, *poor* baby," she said, mimicking his drawl.

"Whew. You're back. There was this other Susie here a minute ago, and she was really nice to me. She scared the shit out of me."

She laughed. "They locked her back up in the loony bin."

"Good, because there's only one Susie for me—the one who calls me on my crap and doesn't let me get away with jack shit. That's the Susie I need. That's the Susie I've missed coming home to over the last year." He kissed her. "And that's the Susie who's going to leave a gaping hole in my heart and my life if she doesn't give me another chance."

"Ry," she sighed, smoothing her soapy hands over his chest.

He tipped her chin up so he could see her face. "What do you say, Suze? Can we try again? If you want me to beg, I will. I'll do whatever it takes to show you I've changed. I'm not the same guy I was a year ago."

"I know. I can see that."

He brightened. "Is that a yes?"

"I want so much to believe it could be better."

"It *would* be better. I promise you."

"I just need some more time. There's so much to consider."

"You mean Henry," he said with a flash of anger as he turned off the water.

"Among other things."

He stepped out of the shower, wrapped a towel around his waist, and handed another to her. "Take all the time you need, but just remember—we're due back in court in six days. So think fast." Turning on his heel, he walked out of the bathroom and into the large walk-in closet, closing the door behind him.

Saddened by the pain she was causing him, Susannah went to the guestroom and got dressed. She reached into her purse for her hairbrush and grabbed her cell phone instead. With a guilty glance over her shoulder, she turned on the phone, and it went wild beeping with messages.

Dialing into voicemail, she discovered six new messages. The first four were from Henry. "Susannah, I'm sorry about the way we left things. I know none of this is your fault. Call me when you can. I love you." She winced as she erased the message and listened to the next one. "I thought I would've heard from you by now. Call me." The third one said, "Are you trying to punish me? If you are, it's working." The last one gave her a stomachache. "Don't sleep with him, Susannah," he pleaded. "Please don't sleep with him. I think I could forgive anything but that."

The next message was from her sister. "You need to call Henry, Susannah. What you're doing is so unfair. Are you sleeping with that man? Don't be weak. Do you hear me? Remember what he's capable of. Remember how he left you after you lost the baby to go play football. Remember that, Susannah."

The last call was from Diane, her divorce attorney. "Heard an interesting rumor about you and your soon-to-be

ex-husband. I need you to call me right away. We might
have a problem. A big problem."

Susannah exited out of voicemail and called Diane.
She was put right through to her.

"Susannah, thank goodness you called. Is it true? Are
you back with him?"

"Not technically. How did you hear I was with him?"

"In the paper."

"Oh, the hospital! We were at the hospital, and it was
mentioned in the paper."

"There's been all kinds of speculation about you two
the last few days."

"Oh my God," she whimpered. *Henry. Oh, dear God.
The news was all over town that his fiancée was back
with her ex-husband.*

"Are you with him right now?"

"We're in Breckenridge for a few days. Why?"

Diane was silent.

"Diane? What is it?"

"Did you read the judge's order like I told you to?"

"The thing is like a cinderblock. I flipped through
it. Why?"

"He inserted a couple of clauses in there—at the very
end. Did you get that far?"

Susannah's stomach twisted with anxiety. "What kind
of clauses?"

"Oh, the kind that says if you spend a single night
under the same roof as your husband, the six-month
waiting period reverts to day one."

"*What?*" Susannah gasped. "*Where does it say that?
I never saw that!*"

"Right before it says if you re-consummate the marriage, the divorce is null and void."

"*It does not.*" Susannah sat down on the bed as all the oxygen left her body at once.

"You didn't want to hang around after the hearing to go over it, so I *told you* to read it," Diane insisted. "This judge is out to keep you two together for some reason. He refused to explain his ruling to either counsel, but he stuck all kinds of funky stuff in there neither of us had ever seen before." She paused before she asked, "You didn't sleep with Ryan, did you? Susannah?"

"I've got to go." Susannah flipped her phone closed and stormed into the kitchen where Ryan was eating toast and drinking coffee at the very table where they had made mad love—*twice*—just half an hour ago.

He was reading the newspaper he had bought in town and looked up when she came into the room. "I made you some toast," he said in a clipped tone that told her he was still pissed about their conversation in the shower.

She glared at him.

"What's the matter?"

"You *son of a bitch*."

Chapter 12

"WHAT'S WRONG?" HE ASKED, CONFOUNDED.

Tears tumbled down her face as she stalked across the room and pelted him with her fists. "*You rotten son of a bitch!* You knew, and you *tricked* me!"

He fended off her attack and tried to grab her hands. "*What the hell has gotten into you?* Watch the ribs! Are you trying to kill me?"

"*Yes!*" she shrieked. "Apparently that's the only way I'll ever be rid of you!"

Standing up so fast he knocked over the chair he'd been sitting in, he grabbed her flying fists before she could hit him again.

She struggled to break free of his tight hold but was no match for him. Breathing hard and still crying, she seethed, "Let go of me! Right now."

His face was taut with anger. "Not until you tell me what the hell's going on here."

"*You tricked me!*"

"I don't know what you're talking about!"

She butted her shoulder into his midsection.

He gasped and released her hands.

Leaving him bent in half, she went into the guestroom, wiping away tears as she threw clothes into a bag. "You're a fool," she muttered to herself. "You've been a fool over him from the very beginning. Everyone tried to tell you, but you didn't want to hear it. Well, now you know for sure."

"What do you think you know?" he asked from the doorway.

"That you're a slimy bastard."

"I wish you'd tell me what you think I've done."

"I want to go back to the city."

"How're you going to get there?"

She glanced at him and had to work at not caring that his face was pale and pinched with pain she had caused. "I'm taking the car."

"The hell you are. You're not going anywhere until you tell me what's gotten you so fired up."

She crossed her arms. "Fine. You want to know? Here it is: your little scheme's a bust. I know exactly what this 'reconciliation' trip is all about."

He took a deep breath and glanced up at the ceiling as if in search of guidance or maybe patience. "You still haven't told me what you think I've done."

"Once again you're getting exactly what you want— you've screwed up my life just as you set out to do. Congratulations. Now, do me a big favor and drop dead so I can marry Henry as planned. It's the least you can do."

"You don't want to marry him," Ryan said quietly.

"*Yes, I do!* Don't tell me what I want!"

"If you really wanted to marry him, you wouldn't have been doing me on the kitchen table less than an hour ago."

Susannah put her hands over her ears. "*Shut up!* Just shut up! I'm so sick of the sound of your voice I could puke!"

"What's going on, Susie?" he pleaded, taking a step into the room.

She held up her hand to stop him. "Don't call me that, and don't you dare touch me. I'm *through* with you. Do you hear me? *Through!* It's over. O-V-E-R."

He took another step toward her. "It's not over."

"Do you need another shot to the ribs to get the message?"

"No."

"Then give me the keys."

"You're not leaving until you tell me what's wrong. What did you mean when you said I'd tricked you?"

Determined not to be taken in by his concern or the gentle drawl of his voice, she kept her arms folded across her chest.

"The last time you went into a rage like this, I ended up in divorce court, and I'm still not entirely sure why." His voice was calm and patient, but his eyes were hard. "This time you won't get rid of me so easily. I can wait all day, but you're not leaving until you tell me what happened between the shower and breakfast."

"I talked to my attorney. That's what."

"And what did she say to make you think I'd tricked you?"

"She told me about the clauses in the divorce agreement—both of them."

"I'm still not following you."

"*The hell you aren't!* You know *exactly* what I'm talking about."

"Susannah, you're seriously trying my patience. What clauses in the agreement? The thing was an inch thick, you can't expect me to know it by heart."

"You know the two parts that matter."

"The only part that mattered to me was the one about you not being my wife anymore. I didn't read much past that."

"Your lawyer didn't tell you the rest?"

"I told him I didn't want to talk about it. I had to report to camp the next day, and my mind was anywhere but on my job. All I cared about was the six months the judge had given us to cool off and rethink things. I was thrilled we left court still married when I'd expected to be divorced."

"So you want me to believe you didn't know about the clause at the end that says if we spend a night under the same roof, the six months restarts at day one?"

His face went slack with shock. "No," he said hoarsely as his face registered awareness. "So you thought . . . Oh, Susie, *no.*" He reached for her.

She sidestepped his grasp. "What about the sex clause?"

He swallowed hard. "There was a sex clause?"

"Like you don't know if we have sex during the six months, the divorce is cancelled."

Shaking his head, he grasped her arms. "I didn't read the thing, Susie. I swear to God!"

"I don't believe you." She tugged her arms free. "You did this on purpose. Yesterday was all about getting me into bed so you could get out of a divorce you never wanted in the first place. You said everything you knew I needed to hear, and I fell for it like the fool I've always been where you're concerned. It was quite a performance, and it worked like a charm, didn't it?"

"Is that what you think?" he asked with disbelief. "How can you say that?"

"Because it's the truth."

"We talked about our son. The son we loved and lost. You'd really accuse me of using him to get you into bed?"

She looked at his anguished face for a long moment before she said, "No. But the rest, yes."

"Everything that happened between us yesterday was real. I swear on my life I knew nothing about either of those clauses. You have to believe me."

"No, I don't. You blackmailed me into coming here with you, so why should I believe you wouldn't play dirty to get what you want, no matter what it costs me?"

"What I *want* is you. That's all I've ever wanted."

"I meant what I said before. It's over between us. I can't live like this anymore."

"I didn't do what you're accusing me of. If you don't believe me, call Terry," he said, referring to his divorce attorney. "He'll tell you I was so happy to get a stay of execution I barely glanced at the judge's order. I left the next day for camp. I swear to God, Susie. I didn't know."

With her hands on her hips she studied him, not wanting to admit she was starting to believe him. "Let's just say, for the sake of argument, you didn't know—"

"I *didn't*," he insisted.

"If that's true then you'll tell the judge you stayed with me because you were hurt and didn't have anywhere else to go, right?"

"He won't believe that. He knows I have scores of people I could've called on."

"But no other family."

"So let me get this straight. You're suggesting I tell the judge that in my hour of need I turned to the woman who threw me out of my own home and was trying to divorce me?" He snorted. "Shit, darlin', even *I* don't believe that. Why would he?"

Susannah bit on her thumbnail as her mind raced. "Well, you got us into this mess by blackmailing me into spending time with you, so you'd better think of something he'll believe."

"Why?"

She was incredulous. "So we don't have to restart the six months, and so the divorce won't be cancelled."

"I was sort of getting the vibe there might not be a divorce."

"What gave you that feeling?"

"Oh, I don't know. Maybe it was the five times you got it on with me in the last twelve hours."

"I told you before it happened it didn't mean anything," she reminded him. "It was just sex."

"Maybe the first time. By the third time, I'd say it meant something."

"It didn't," she said, lifting her chin defiantly.

He studied her for a full minute before he said, "You know, I'm starting to wonder why I wanted you back so badly." He turned and left the room.

Susannah began to go after him but stopped herself. "The hell with him," she muttered, flopping on the bed next to her half-packed bag. "I don't want him back, either." But if that was true, why did it feel like she'd just let her best friend walk away? Why was she so remorseful about leading him to believe their lovemaking had meant nothing to her? And why was she so determined to push him away when she still loved him as much as she ever had, if not more? If she kept pushing, one day he'd go, and if she knew Ryan, he wouldn't come back a second time.

She lay there stewing over it for a long time before she got up, ran her fingers through her still-damp hair, and wiped the tears from her face. In the living room, she found he had put away their bed by the fire and moved the sofa back to where it belonged, leaving nothing to remind them of their magical night together.

Ryan sat with stooped shoulders in front of the fire he had rebuilt. He seemed so alone that Susannah felt her heart go out to him and the last of her anger fizzle away. "It meant something," she said softly.

He didn't look at her when he said, "I know it did, darlin'. I was there, remember?"

She knelt down next to him on the rug in front of the fire.

"It hurts me that you won't give me the benefit of the doubt, Susannah. I was a crappy husband to you at times. I don't deny that. But I never lied to you. So why would I start now when there's so much at stake?"

Because she had no good answer, she said nothing.

He reached for her hand. "It was rotten of me to show up the way I did and to cause you all this trouble with Henry. I know that. But I *didn't* know about those clauses. I wasn't trying to trick you."

"Okay."

Crooking his eyebrow at her, he said, "You believe me?"

"I want to."

"Well, I guess that's a start." He looped a lock of her hair around his finger. "You must be hungry."

She shook her head. Her stomach was so churned up that the thought of eating made her sick.

"Do you still want to go back to the city? I'll take you if you do."

Surprised, she glanced at him. Her heart ached at the expression on his face—longing and hope and fear and love. All in one place, and all of it wrapped up in her. "When's your meeting with Chet and Duke?"

"Five o'clock tomorrow."

"I guess tomorrow is soon enough to go home."

His expression softened to relief. "Good," he said. "That's good."

"Are you going to get sick of me and walk away before I decide what to do?"

"I probably should," he said with a bitter laugh.

"But you won't?"

He released the hair he'd been playing with and caressed her face. "No, baby, I won't."

She fought a losing battle to contain the tears that suddenly reappeared.

He brought her into his arms and held her tight against him while she cried it out.

"I'm so confused, Ry," she said several minutes later.

"Tell me."

"I want to believe things could be different, but then we have a huge, ugly fight that brings back all the memories of when things were bad between us." She brushed at the remaining tears on her face. "I died a little bit inside every time we had one of those horrible fights."

He nuzzled her neck. "Yeah, but remember making up?"

"Stop. I'm trying to be serious."

"So am I. Our relationship is passionate—in the bedroom and out of it. That's just the way we are together."

"I want some peace. That's what I have with Henry. It's peaceful. We don't fight."

"You don't have sex, either," he reminded her.

"We will. When we're married."

"You're starting to piss me off by continuing to insist you're going to marry that guy."

"I'm engaged to him."

"Stop reminding me! I get it! But he's all wrong for you."

"And you're so right for me?"

He took both her hands and held them tight. "If he wasn't in the picture, would there still be a decision to make about us?"

"Yes," she said but could tell he didn't believe her. "One has nothing to do with the other."

"I want you to promise me something."

She shot him a wary glance.

"This is important, Susannah."

Whenever he called her by her full name, it usually was. "What?"

"I want you to promise me that even if you don't stay with me you won't marry him."

She tried to tug her hands free, but he tightened his grip. "You can't ask me to promise that."

"You'd be miserable with him."

"I was miserable with you!"

"No, you weren't. Not always. We had a rough time after we lost Justin, but you weren't miserable before that, not the way you'd be with him. You'd be sacrificing so much of who you are if you marry a man you don't love just to keep from being alone."

"That's not fair. I've been alone for much of the last year, and I was fine."

"Promise me you won't marry him," he pleaded.

"I can't do that."

"You can't or you won't?"

"Both."

His sigh was deep and pained. "You may get your peace with him, but you'll pay an awful price for it." He leaned in to kiss her cheek. "I'm going to take a walk. I need to get some air."

"You're not going all the way into town again, are you?"

"No." He got up slowly and winced when his ribs protested. "I don't think I could do that today. I've had a setback in my recovery."

"I'm sorry," she said, chagrinned, as she reached a hand up to him. "I can't believe I did that to you, but it's your fault. You make me so crazy."

He smiled and squeezed her hand. "I know. Sometimes that's a good thing, and sometimes not so much."

"What are we going to do about the judge?"

"I told you if we spent these ten days together and you still want the divorce I wouldn't stop it. If it's what you really want, I'll do everything within my power to get it for you."

"Do you mean that?"

He sighed. "Yes, Susannah, I mean it. I don't want a divorce, but I won't hold you hostage in a marriage that makes you unhappy."

"Thank you," she said, saddened by his weary resignation. She followed him with her eyes as he put on his boots, coat, hat, and gloves. "Be careful," she called as he opened the door.

His grin had lost some of its cockiness. "You wouldn't want me to think you care, now would ya, darlin'?"

He was out the door before she could tell him she *did* care.

Susannah stayed by the fire and wallowed in the quiet she had craved, except there was no peace amid the turmoil in her heart and mind. Ryan had surprised her with what he said about the divorce. That he was willing to sacrifice his own happiness to give her what she wanted told her a lot, but it also added to her confusion.

With a heavy, sinking feeling she got up and went into the bedroom to get her phone so she could take advantage of Ryan's absence to call Henry.

He answered so fast she suspected he had been willing the phone to ring. "Susannah."

"Hi."

"I've been so worried. Are you all right?"

"Yes, I'm fine," she said, but she barely managed to convince herself.

"You don't *sound* fine. Is he treating you all right?"

"Yes."

"When are you coming back to the city?"

"Tomorrow."

"Oh, good," he said with a deep sigh of relief. "I'm dying here, honey, imagining you in a secluded cabin with *him*."

"I'm sorry." All she could think about was Ryan pleading with her not to marry this man. "I know it's terribly difficult for you."

"Difficult. Yes, you could say it's difficult. The woman I'm going to marry later this month is alone in the woods with the man *People* magazine recently called the sexiest athlete alive. Yes, Susannah, it's difficult."

"I'm sorry," she said again, this time in a whisper. "I don't know what to say."

"You sound funny. Are you sure everything's okay? He's not badgering you for sex, is he? I wouldn't put it past him."

She winced. "No, he's not."

"That's a relief. My imagination has been a little overactive, to say the least."

Anxious to change the subject, she said, "You should know there's going to be some news regarding Ryan and the team in the next few days."

"What kind of news?"

"I can't really say much about it right now, but I wanted you to know because there might be . . . talk . . . about me and him."

"What kind of talk?"

"It's nothing to worry about. It'll blow over in a day or two. Well, I'd better go. I'll call you when I get back to town tomorrow."

"I can't wait to see you. I've missed you, honey. I love you."

Her eyes filled and her throat closed. "Yes," she managed to say. "Me, too. Bye."

She turned off her phone and curled into a ball on the bed. "Oh, God, what am I going to do?" she whispered to the empty room.

Chapter 13

RYAN BLAZED THROUGH THE NEW POWDER ON ONE OF HIS favorite trails. The storm had left behind the kind of Colorado day he loved best—bright sunshine, cold, crisp air, and an endless stretch of bright blue sky. When the glare of the sun off the snow made his eyes water, he pulled a pair of Oakley sunglasses from his coat pocket. Only the piercing pain from his injured ribs detracted from his enjoyment of the perfect day. He'd almost passed out from Susie's well-placed hit to the gut. In hindsight, he could see why she thought he deserved it. But *damn,* it had *hurt!* Mixed in with his pain, though, was grudging respect. He liked knowing his little debutante could take care of herself if she had to.

He took as deep a breath of the sharp, cold air as his ribs would allow and gazed at the spectacular view of the Rocky Mountains. As a good old boy from Texas, he'd never imagined he would love a place outside his home state as much as he loved it here. After these last few days with Susie, however, he knew he wouldn't come here again without her. If they were unable to salvage their marriage, he would sell the cabin.

Things were changing. In just over twenty-four hours, his professional football career would be over, and a few days after that, maybe his marriage, too. Those were two awfully big things to lose within the scope of a couple of days. His decision to retire still felt like the right one, but as the time approached to pull the trigger, he was filled with so many thoughts, memories, and emotions. Tied up in those emotions, inevitably, were his worries about his marriage.

His mind wandered to the clauses in the divorce agreement. *That judge sure is a sly, old coot,* Ryan thought with a chuckle, remembering Susannah's face when the judge had ordered an additional six-month waiting period before he would grant their divorce. He'd said he didn't believe for a minute that they really wanted a divorce, which was certainly true for Ryan. Susie had sputtered with indignation, but the judge had dismissed her arguments with the wave of his hand. After they left court, she had accused Ryan of bribing the judge, but he couldn't have paid for the kind of ally he'd found in the old man.

Ryan was still hopeful there would be no more days in court, but if Susannah insisted on going forward with the divorce, he wondered how they would get around telling the judge that not only had they spent several nights together under the same roof, but they'd had some damned good sex, too. Just the thought of it made Ryan want more. He turned around to go back to the cabin and was hit with a piercing pain in his chest that took his breath away.

Propping himself against a tree, he fought his way through pain that brought tears to his eyes. He gasped for air and wondered if he was having a heart attack as his legs gave out under him and he slid down to the snow.

"Ryan!" Susannah screamed as she scrambled into a squat next to him. "Oh my God, Ryan! What's wrong?"

"I'm okay," he whispered. "Just a pain."

She cradled his face in her hands. "You're all clammy and pale. How long have you been here?"

"Maybe an hour?"

She gasped. "Do you think you can get up?"

"I don't know."

"Come on, let me help you." She hooked the arm on his good side over her shoulder. "Ready?"

He grunted.

Susannah made a futile attempt to haul him up, and he howled with pain.

"*What're we going to do?* We've got to get you out of here. You're wet and cold."

"Give me a second. It's getting better." With his eyes closed he rested his head against the tree, taking shallow breaths in and out. "Okay," he said a couple of minutes later. "Let's try again."

This time they succeeded. With his arm around her shoulders, they made their way slowly back to the cabin.

"You said you wouldn't be gone long, so I didn't know what to do when you didn't come back. I followed your path through the snow."

"Glad you did. I was getting cold."

"What happened?"

"I'm not sure. I think it was a bad cramp. Seems to be gone now, but I'm afraid to move too fast. I don't want it to come back."

She whimpered. "It's because I hit you."

"No, baby. I probably overdid it again."

"You're just being nice."

He squeezed her shoulder in reassurance.

A slow twenty minutes later, they reached the cabin. Susannah helped him inside and disposed of his wet coat.

"We should get you to a doctor."

He shook his head as he shivered uncontrollably. "I don't need a doctor."

"But Ryan—"

"Do you know what would help?"

She shook her head. "What?"

"Hot tub."

"All right, but I still say you need a doctor. I'll go open up the tub. Will you be okay?"

He nodded, and Susannah rushed toward the deck off the kitchen.

By the time she returned, he had stripped down to his boxers.

She took his hand to lead him outside.

His movements were slow and careful as he dropped his shorts and eased into the bubbling water.

"Feel good?" she asked.

"Yeah." He closed his eyes and leaned his head back. "Come in with me."

"I'm going to go deal with your wet clothes."

"I want you with me."

She hesitated before she said, "I'll be back in a few minutes."

"Hurry."

After she went inside, Ryan relaxed as the warm water and jets worked him over. His skin tingled from the sudden heat after the cold, and he wondered what he would have done if Susie hadn't come along when she did. The pain had passed by the time she arrived, but he'd been left drained by the ordeal.

The sliding door opened and Susie came out with her hair in a high ponytail, wearing a skimpy red bikini that stirred a whole other ache in him as she joined him in the tub.

He reached for her.

She took his hand and slid closer to him. "How are you feeling?"

"Much better, except for this new pain I seem to have."

"Where?" she asked, alarmed.

He guided her hand to his arousal. "Here."

"Ryan! *Stop!*"

"Why?"

She tugged her hand free. "You're hurt, and you need to take it easy."

"I *am* taking it easy. Come here." He guided her onto his lap, arranging her so she faced him. He tugged her closer, until she pressed against his erection. "Susie," he sighed. "You know I love the red bikini."

She kneaded the tension from his shoulders. "It was the only bathing suit I could find."

"You're so sexy," he whispered. "Just thinking about you gets me hard, and then you come out here in the red bikini. That's not fair."

She smiled. "Only you could go from being incapacitated to thinking about sex in half an hour's time."

"I'm resilient." He cupped her breasts and teased her nipples.

"Ry," she said as her bikini top floated away. "Your cramp might come back. Stop . . ."

He slid her up and rolled his tongue over her nipple. "Don't fight me," he whispered. "Doesn't it feel so good?" Lifting his warm hands off her breasts, he watched as her nipples hardened in the cold air. "Oh, look at that . . . "

"Ryan . . . "

He ran his thumbs in little circles around her breasts, taking his time getting to the main event. "What?"

"It *hurts*," she moaned.

"Mmmm, we can't have that." His tongue settled on one of the pebbled points, infusing it with warmth.

Completely unaware of the effect she was having on him, she gyrated against his erection. He took it out on her breast, pulling the nipple deep into the hot center of his mouth and running his tongue back and forth.

She gripped his hair as he gave her other breast the same treatment.

"Ry," she panted. "I need . . . "

He could feel her control slipping away. "What, baby? What do you need?"

"*More.*"

He tugged on the bows at her hips, and the bottom half of her suit went the way of the top. Using only the tip of one finger, he brought her to a hard, fast climax.

When she had recovered, she wrapped her arms and legs around him and rested her head on his shoulder as the bubbling water embraced them in heat and steam. "What about you?"

He held her snug against his pulsating erection. "I'm saving it until I can get you horizontal in a bed."

"We shouldn't."

"Why the hell not?" he snorted.

"You're supposed to be resting and healing. Instead you're having mad sex and taking walks in the cold."

"I'll give up the walks if you let me keep the mad sex."

She laughed, and his heart was so full of her that he was left breathless for reasons that had nothing to do with her being naked and wrapped around him.

"Let's go in," he said several quiet minutes later.

They disentangled themselves, and Susannah reached for her suit and their towels. Once they were inside, Ryan smelled something coming from the kitchen that made his mouth water. "What did you make?"

"Stew."

"I love cabin food." With his hands on her hips, he directed her to the master bedroom.

"Where are we going?"

"To snuggle." He tugged her towel free and dropped the one he had slung around his hips.

"You don't like to snuggle," she reminded him.

He slid between the flannel sheets and invited her to join him. "I do now."

"Who are you and what have you done with Ryan Sanderson?" she asked as she got into bed with him.

"Are you knocking it? Isn't this what you wanted?"

"Yes. It is."

He wrapped his arms around her. "Then why so solemn all of a sudden?"

She shrugged.

"What is it, baby? Tell me."

"Where was all this before? When I was asking for it? It's like you went away to camp and learned how to be the husband I always wanted."

"I was sent away," he reminded her. "And I discovered the only life I want is the one I had."

"I'm still having trouble believing you've made permanent changes."

"There's only one way to find out."

Tilting her head so she could see his face, she nibbled on her lip and appeared to be thinking it over. "What do you think of snuggling so far?"

He chuckled. "I've definitely been missing out."

She pressed her lips to his chest. Careful to avoid his injured side, she left a trail of soft, wet kisses down to his belly.

"Susie," he gasped. "What are you doing?"

"Snuggling," she said with a coy smile.

Ryan was slick with sweat and panting by the time she finished with him. "Jesus," he said on a long exhale. "Where did you learn *that?*"

"I read about it in *Cosmo.*"

He laughed. "You don't read *Cosmo.*"

"It was in the waiting room at the dentist."

"Must've been one hell of a trip to the dentist."

She giggled, and her cheeks turned a fetching shade of pink. "I thought you might like it."

"Can I ask you something?" he asked, running his fingers through her hair.

"Uh-huh."

"When you read about it, did you imagine trying it out on Henry or me?"

Her smile faded. "I don't remember."

"Be honest, Susie."

Her eyes, when they met his, were serious. "You," she said in a tiny voice.

He tugged her into his arms and held her tight. Tears burned in his eyes at the realization that she had thought of him during their long separation, that she wanted him, that she imagined herself performing an intimate, self-less act of love for him. No gift she could ever give him would mean more.

"Tomorrow, when we get back to town, I'm going to tell Henry it's over."

Ryan's heart stopped for the briefest of instants. Okay, that gift meant more. "Really?"

"Yes," she said with a sigh. "You were right before when you said I shouldn't marry him. If nothing else, the time we've spent here has shown me that. But just the thought of telling him makes me sick."

"I know it'll be hard for you."

"It'll be impossible. He's waited his whole life for me, and all I've ever done is disappoint him."

"Susannah, listen to me." With his hand on her chin, he forced her to look at him. "While he was waiting for you, he was also hoping for our marriage to fail. If he really loved you the way you think he does, why would he wish for you to be unhappy with the man you'd chosen to marry? That doesn't make him a very good friend, does it?"

"No, I guess not."

"You're doing the right thing, baby. You'd never be happy with him."

"This doesn't mean you and I are back together. I don't want you jumping to any conclusions."

"Why would I jump to conclusions? Just because you're naked and all over me at the moment . . . " When she pinched his rear end, he jolted and then laughed softly. "And clearly you can't keep your hands off me. But no, we're not back together or anything."

"Oh, shut up, will you?"

"Why don't you shut me up? I'm sure you can think of some way to—" He was cut off when her tongue invaded his mouth. Burying his hands in her hair, he devoured her. The kiss was endless and thorough and deep. When she would have pulled back from him he held her still, infused with hope after hearing she planned to end her relationship with Henry. She was coming back to him, one small step at a time, even if she didn't realize it quite yet. In a burst of passion, he rolled over her, ignoring the protest from his ribs.

"I'm supposed to be doing all the work," she reminded him.

"Shut up," he whispered, kissing his way to her breasts. Running his thumbs over her nipples, he watched her eyes go liquid and her mouth form his name. He replaced his hands with his lips, and her back arched into him. "I could spend a whole day right here," he said the instant before he drew her deeply into his mouth.

"*Please . . .*"

He looked up to find her eyes wild with desire. Knowing she wanted him that much aroused him more than anything ever had. But he thought nothing of his own needs, instead focusing all his care and attention on her. With his hand, he urged her legs apart. His fingers caressed her as he nibbled first on one hipbone and then the other. Finally, he settled between her legs.

"Ry," she gasped, burying her fingers in his hair. "Oh my *God,* what are you doing?"

"I've been reading *Cosmo,* too."

The statement was so ridiculous that she laughed, but her laughter quickly turned to a moan that was followed soon after by a sharp cry of ecstasy.

Chapter 14

SUSANNAH INSISTED ON DRIVING THEM BACK TO THE CITY the next day. They were quiet as they left the cabin, each wondering if they would ever again be there together and anxious about what was waiting for them outside their idyllic cocoon. She glanced over and found Ryan staring out the window as they made their way down the hill to Breckenridge. The plow hadn't been back for a second pass since the storm, so Susannah kept the Escalade to twenty miles per hour.

"I love the new car smell," she said.

"Uh-huh."

"What did you do with the other one?"

"Donated it to the Boys Club."

She was impressed by his gesture. The Boys and Girls Club of Metro Denver would probably get more than a hundred thousand dollars for the car Ryan had been given as the Super Bowl MVP two years ago. "I'm sure they appreciated it."

He shrugged. "I guess. My office handled it."

"This one has a lot more stuff than the other one did," she said, gesturing to the elaborate navigation and stereo systems.

"Uh-huh."

"What's on your mind, Ry? You're a million miles away over there.

"A lot of things."

"Care to share any of them?"

"I'm just thinking about the next few days and everything that's about to happen."

"You know, nothing says you have to do this now."

"Actually, I do. My contract expires on Sunday. I haven't signed the new one yet, so everyone's on edge. I can't drag it out any more. That wouldn't be fair. They need to start making their plans for next year now that this season is finally over."

"I meant if you're not ready to retire, there's always next year."

"No. I'm ready. I've thought a lot about it, and it feels like the right time."

"So how's it going to go? The next few days, I mean."

"When we get home, I'm going to call Aaron," he said, referring to his agent. "I owe him the courtesy of a head's up before I meet with the team. He's spent a lot of time hammering out my new contract, so he's not going to be very happy to hear my news."

"It's not his life," Susannah said hotly, reflecting her longtime dislike for "The Shark" who ran Ryan's career.

"There's also my endorsements to consider. I'm not sure what impact my retirement will have on them. I've got to call Chuck about that," he said, meaning one of his attorneys.

"What else has to happen?"

"After I meet with Chet and Duke this afternoon, I'd like to invite the team over to the house so I can tell as many of them as possible in person. Do you mind?"

"No," she said, even though she was worried about giving his friends the impression they were back together when nothing had been decided yet.

He tuned into her hesitation. "Are you sure?"

"Yes. It's fine. I'll call Carol when we get home and order some food."

Reaching for her hand, he brought it to his lips. "Thank you, baby." He dropped their joined hands to his lap as he continued. "Sometime tomorrow there'll probably be a press conference to announce it to the world. Maybe you can help me come up with the statement I'll have to make. You're so good at that kind of thing."

"Um, okay, if you think it'll help," she said, feeling an awful lot like a wife again.

He turned in his seat so he could see her. "It's going to be crazy for a day or two, but I want you to remember it's not the most important thing I'm dealing with right now." Squeezing her hand, he added, "Patching things up with you is my top priority, and the only reason I'm letting this other stuff in is because my contract is set to expire right around the same time our marriage ticket comes due."

"Ironic coincidence."

"Yes. Ironic is the word. In five days, I'm either going to have everything or nothing."

She glanced at him. "No pressure, though, right?"

His dimples were on full display when his face twisted into a lazy grin. "None at all." Sweeping his thumb over the palm of her hand, he asked, "How's my mug looking?" He stuck out his jaw in a dramatic pose.

She rolled her eyes. "Much better."

"So I'm not going to look hideous in all the pictures that'll be plastered on the front pages of every newspaper in the country?"

She snorted with laughter. "There's that legendary Sanderson ego on full display."

"What ego? It's an honest question." He flipped down the visor and opened the mirror to study his reflection. "Looking *good,* my man."

"Puleeze. Listen to yourself. *Looking good, my man.*"

"I love giving you the opportunity to burst my bubble," he said with a chuckle.

"You do it often enough."

"I need to keep you sharp."

"Keeping *you* humble was my greatest challenge as your wife."

"*Is* your greatest challenge."

"Was."

"Is."

"Was."

"Is."

"Shut up."

"Shut me up."

"I'm driving."

"So?" He slid his hand up her thigh.

When he reached his destination, she inhaled sharply and grabbed his hand.

Not to be deterred, he kissed her neck, whispering in her ear, "Is."

"Shut up."

He laughed and sat back in his seat but kept a firm hold on her hand.

❖ ❖ ❖

They weren't home twenty minutes and already Susannah yearned for the peace of the cabin. Ryan was in the den engaged in a heated telephone conversation with The Shark, who was apparently none too pleased by his client's news.

Susannah went to the doorway to listen.

Ryan held the phone away from his ear as Aaron yelled at him.

She made a face of distaste and signaled for Ryan to cut off his irate agent.

Ryan smiled at her before he barked into the phone. "That's enough, Aaron. I'm sorry you're so upset, but this is my life and my decision. Now, I've given you the courtesy of advance notice. Don't you dare breathe a word of this before the press conference tomorrow. Am I clear?" He paused to listen. "Fine. I'll talk to you then." Slamming the phone down, he looked up at Susannah. "He's thoroughly pissed."

"So I gathered. You were very firm with him, though. Authoritative."

He wiggled his eyebrows at her, the tension of the last few minutes forgotten as he got up from the desk and went over to her. "And does that turn my little debutante on?"

She reached up to fix the collar of his shirt. "Maybe."

"It *does*," he said with a delighted grin. Gathering her in his arms, he brushed a light kiss over her lips. "I'll have to remember that. She likes authoritative. Maybe I should try it on her. Hmm, let's see if it works: kiss me."

"No."

"Oh, she's feisty. I like that." The phone rang, but he didn't let her go. "I said to kiss me."

"And I say answer the phone."

"Not until you kiss me."

"Fine." She gave him a quick peck on the cheek, pulled free of his embrace, and darted from the room, squealing when he chased her.

He caught her in the kitchen and maneuvered her against the center island. "I *said* to kiss me."

The phone rang again.

"And I said *no*."

His smile was sexy and lascivious. "I can see I'll have to try a different tack." With his erection pushed snug against her, he said, "Will you please, please kiss me?"

Her arms encircled his neck. "Just for the record, one 'please' would've done the trick." She brought him down for a soulful kiss that quickly blazed out of control. Somehow she ended up flat on her back on the counter with half of him pinning her down. Her hands had slipped inside his jeans and clutched his ass.

She gasped when he squeezed her breast under her sweater. Through her lacy bra, he grazed a fingernail over her nipple as his tongue explored every corner of her mouth.

"What the *hell* is going on here?" Henry roared from the doorway.

As he continued to kiss her like nothing had happened, Susannah swore Ryan flexed his ass to keep her hands from escaping.

"Get off of her, you brute." Henry pushed Ryan. "And get your hand out of her shirt."

She tugged her hands free as her face burned with embarrassment.

Ryan finally lifted his head and locked eyes with Susannah for one long moment. "Don't you knock?" he asked Henry without breaking the intense eye contact with her.

"I don't have to. I have a key. Now get off of her. Right now."

"Henry, please," Susannah said, still breathless from passion and the shock of being caught. "Wait for me in the den. I'll be right there."

"I'm not leaving you here with him. I've had just about enough, Susannah. To come in here and find you doing . . . well, doing *that,* with *him* . . . What am I supposed to make of this?"

"Maybe you should make like a tree and leave," Ryan said, slowly lifting himself off Susannah and helping her up. "This is our home, and you have no business just walking in here."

"My fiancée invited me to come and go as I please," Henry retorted, reaching for Susannah's hand. "You're the one who doesn't belong here."

"You think so, huh?" Ryan asked with steel in his brown eyes.

Susannah ignored Henry's outstretched hand as she ran her fingers through her hair and tried to calm her racing heart. Being caught in a passionate embrace with her ex-husband—on the kitchen counter in broad daylight, no less—was *not* how she'd planned to tell Henry that their engagement was off.

With his hands on her hips and a pleading look in his eyes, Ryan helped her down from the counter. He brushed a finger over her swollen lips.

She found it hard to look away from him until Henry grabbed her hand and pulled her from the room.

"Hey!" Ryan called. "Don't you dare drag her like that. Susie, if you're not up to talking to him right now, just say the word, and I'll show him the door."

"You'll show me the door," Henry snorted. "Listen to the big man."

Ryan moved so fast Henry had no time to react before the big man was staring him down. "You're just begging me to kick your ass."

Henry swallowed hard but didn't look away from Ryan. "You're such a cliché, Sanderson."

Ryan's eyes went from steely to furious.

"That's enough," Susannah said with a hand on Ryan's chest. "Just give us a few minutes. Please?"

Ryan kept his eyes fixed firmly on Henry, but he took a step back. "Don't be rough with her, or I'll be rough with you. You got me?"

Susannah hustled Henry from the room before he could throw more gas on Ryan's fire.

The moment they were alone in the den, Henry enveloped her in a tight embrace. "Are you all right, honey? Did he hurt you?"

She pushed him away. "Hurt me? What the heck are you talking about?"

"He was attacking you. Right there in the kitchen. I saw it with my own eyes. That's the only possible explanation for what I just witnessed."

"Oh, for God's sakes, Henry. Maybe you didn't notice I was wrapped around him. I was hardly being attacked. I was being ravished."

Henry blanched. "Are you telling me you were *letting* him molest you?"

"He was *not* molesting me! If anything, I was molesting *him!*"

"You disappoint me, Susannah."

She ran a weary hand through her mussed hair. "Yes, I know. I would think you'd be used to it by now."

"What's that supposed to mean?"

"We need to talk, Henry," she said with a deep sigh.

He shook his head. "Not while you're cohabitating with him. I won't 'talk' to you when he's waiting in the next room, probably listening to every word we're saying."

"But—"

"On Sunday, we've got the ball. On Monday, we're going to court to get you a divorce, and in twenty-five days, we're getting married."

"Um, about the divorce—"

"Five days. Then you'll *finally* be divorced."

"There were clauses, in the agreement—"

"I don't care about clauses. I don't care about anything but you and our wedding. Unless you want to talk about that, I don't have anything else to say to you until he's gone."

"I was kissing him back."

"You're weak where he's concerned. Do you think I don't know that after all these years of watching you put up with his crap?"

Stung, Susannah took a step back from him. "I want you to leave." He was too proud to let her call off their engagement when Ryan was in the next room. She got that. But she also now knew for sure that whatever feelings she'd thought she had for this man were gone. Love had just turned to contempt.

"Honey, don't be offended," he said in a softer tone as he ran his hands up and down her arms. "You know you have a blind spot a mile wide for him. How else could you have stayed with him for as long as you did?"

"Yes, Henry, you're right." She tugged her arms free. "I'm weak and spineless. It's a good thing I had you to remind me of that every chance you got when I was married to him."

He kissed her cheek and was unfazed when she turned her face away. "I never said you were weak or spineless. I never said that, Susannah. Everything will be fine after Monday. You'll see. Once you get rid of him you'll get your perspective back. I'll pick you up at seven on Sunday for the ball." With a quick kiss to her forehead, he was gone.

Susannah trembled and wrapped her arms around herself as protection against a sudden chill.

Ryan came into the room, led her to the sofa, and brought her down to his lap. He held her until the trembling had passed.

Chapter 15

"I'M NOT WEAK," SUSANNAH SAID.

"Of course you aren't. You're the strongest person I know."

She rested her head on Ryan's shoulder. "He thinks I'm spineless when it comes to you."

He chuckled softly and touched his lips to her forehead. "We know better, don't we?"

"Yes, we do. Why was it so hard for him and everyone else in my life to believe we genuinely love each other?"

"I don't know, but they did their best to fill you with enough doubts to sink the *Titanic*."

"I *was* weak because I let them. I should've put you and our relationship off limits with them."

"You live and learn, baby. The next time around we'll put up a wall around us so none of that crap can get in."

She raised an amused eyebrow. "You're awfully certain there'll be a next time."

He kissed her cheek. "I think there already is."

"I didn't get a chance to tell Henry the engagement is off. He wouldn't let me."

"So I gathered."

"You *were* listening."

"Hell, yes, I was listening. I don't trust that guy as far as I can spit him. I wouldn't put it past him to get physical with you when you tell him it's over."

She scoffed. "Henry would never lay a hand on me."

"I wouldn't be so sure, Susie. He's obsessed with you. He always has been, only now he sees everything he's waited years for about to slip through his fingers. He's getting desperate. He'll do whatever it takes to keep you."

"You're overreacting, Ry. He's harmless."

"No, he isn't. He's manipulative and vindictive."

"And you're very sexy when you're jealous," she said with a teasing smile.

He cupped her cheek. "I'm serious, Susannah. I want you to be careful."

"I will be." She wrapped her fingers around his wrist. "You don't have to worry."

"I *am* worried." He turned her face and kissed her so softly, so gently, that the effect was devastating. "I'm worried about so many things, and all of them involve you."

She reached for him, wanting more of those kisses he was handing out. But there was nothing soft or gentle about the possessive burst of passion he responded with. She met his ardor with an equal dose of her own, and when he finally pulled back from her he looked stunned.

"That's one way to change the subject."

"Did it work?"

He shook his head. "Promise me you'll be careful, Susie. If anything ever happened to you . . . "

The phone rang again, but neither of them moved.

"Hey," she said, shaken by his concern. "Nothing's going to happen to me. I can take care of myself, remember?"

"How could I forget? I can still feel your shoulder in my ribs." Twirling a lock of her hair around his finger, he added, "You haven't promised me."

"I promise. I'll be careful, but you don't need to worry."

"I don't want you to be alone with him again." When she began to protest, he silenced her with another gentle kiss. "This isn't me being jealous, Susie. I swear it isn't. I just have this feeling there's going to be trouble when he finds out you're not going to marry him."

Taken in by the sincere concern reflected in his brown eyes, she leaned her forehead against his. "I won't be alone with him. Does that make you feel better?"

"Yes," he said with a deep sigh of relief. He hugged her tightly. "Yes, it does."

The phone rang again, and this time Susannah got up from his lap to answer it. "Hi, Bernie. Yes, he's here. Hang on a minute." She handed the phone to Ryan and left him to take the call.

She went into the kitchen and listened to the messages on her answering machine. Several were from members of her committee about last-minute issues with the Black and White Ball, as well as two from Henry's mother inquiring about wedding invitations and seating plans. Susannah leaned against the counter and hung her head as she listened to Henrietta's excited messages. She'd been so sure she was doing the right thing by marrying Henry. That she could have been so wrong left her shaken. Erasing the messages, she reached for her cell phone to return the calls from her committee and to order the food for later.

Ryan came into the kitchen holding the portable phone to his chest. "Wives and kids?" he whispered, raising a questioning eyebrow.

"Of course." She recalculated her numbers for the caterer. "Why not?"

He smiled and turned back toward the den, talking to Bernie with animated gestures.

Susannah was relieved to see his spirits were high on the day he planned to end a career that had taken them both—but him in particular—on an extraordinary journey.

He spent most of the day on the phone tracking down his teammates while she attended to the party preparations and fielded calls from her ball committee colleagues, who were relieved to hear she was back in town and back in charge.

Just after four, Susannah went upstairs to change.

Ryan joined her a few minutes later.

"How are you doing?" she asked. "Feeling okay?"

"Yeah, you know, a little sad, but I guess that's normal."

"I'd be worried if you weren't sad."

"I feel better knowing you'll be there with me." He reached for her hand and laced his fingers through hers. "I appreciate you coming along."

"Sure. It's no problem."

He kissed her hand and released it so they could get dressed.

She put on a dark suit with heels and the two-carat diamond earrings he had given her on their wedding day.

He emerged from his walk-in closet wearing navy dress pants, a starched white shirt and a tweed sports jacket. "I'm glad I still had some clothes here. Saved me a trip into town."

"Since you never came to get them, I'd been thinking about donating them to the Salvation Army."

He smiled. "Not so fast, darlin'." Crossing the room, he hugged her from behind. "You look beautiful, as always."

"Thank you." She turned to him as she secured the back of the second earring. "So do you—as always."

He toyed with one of the earrings. "I'm glad you still wear them."

"I love them. You know I do."

"And I love *you*. I don't think I've mentioned that yet today."

She sent him a teasing grin. "No, you haven't. Are you already taking me for granted again?"

His eyes were serious. "Never again."

"I was kidding, Ry."

"I know."

"Listen, before we go and before everything gets crazy, there's something I want to tell you."

"What, baby?" he asked, concerned.

"It's nothing bad," she said as she smoothed her hands over his crisp shirt. "I want you to know that even though I didn't say it very often because of the situation with your ego and all of that . . . "

"Oh, *God*, where's this going?" he groaned.

She chuckled at the pained expression on his face. "I was just going to say I was always proud of you and everything you accomplished in your career. I'm proud of the way you handled yourself with class in every situation—even the ones that didn't deserve it. You always took the high road." She reached up to brush the hair off his forehead. "And I'm proud that despite everything that's happened to you—all the acclaim and attention—the most important parts of you are exactly the same as they were the day I met you. I just wanted you to know that."

"Susannah," he whispered, his voice full of emotion as he took her into his arms. "Thank you. It pleases me more than you could ever know to hear you say that. I may have done all those things you said, but I screwed up the only thing that really matters. Don't think I don't realize that."

"I know you do."

He leaned in to kiss her. "Come on, let's go do this, so we can get home and do *this*," he said, pressing his hips into hers.

"Stop!" she squealed. "You've had enough of that for a while."

"Oh, no, I haven't. You owe me a year's worth. But I'm willing to let you work it off on the installment plan."

She rolled her eyes. "You're just *too* good to me."

"I couldn't agree more."

Ryan didn't say much on the short ride to Mavericks' Stadium on the city's south side, and Susannah decided to leave him alone with his thoughts. He used his pass to gain access to the players' parking lot. "We've got about twenty minutes," he said. "Let's take a walk."

Wearing a long brown leather coat with his Stetson, he came around the car to help her out. Not a soul was in sight as they walked hand-in-hand through the hallways under the stadium that led to the sprawling locker room, which was sparkling clean and almost surgically neat. The purple floor and yellow walls were adorned with the Mavericks' logo. Purple helmets lined the top shelf over the long row of lockers.

An older bald man came in through one of the many doorways that fed into the locker room.

"Sandy! Hey, you look great. How're you feeling?"

"Hi, Tony. I'm doing much better. You remember my wife, Susannah, right?"

Tony glanced at Ryan before he extended his hand to Susannah. "Of course. Nice to see you again, Mrs. Sanderson. It's been a while."

"Hello, Tony." She was unsure how she felt about being referred to as Ryan's wife—as if the whole world didn't know they were minutes from a divorce. "Nice to see you, too."

"What're you doing here?" Tony asked Ryan. "I thought you were home recuperating."

"I've got a meeting with Chet and Duke. I wanted to get a few things out of my locker, if that's okay with you." To Susannah, Ryan added, "We know better than to touch anything in here without checking with the chief first."

Tony chuckled. "You think it's easy being the head counselor at Camp Runamok?" He swept his hand toward Ryan's locker in the center of the long row. "Feel free."

Ryan shook his hand. "Thanks, Tony. For everything."

"Sure, Sandy," Tony said with a puzzled expression. "You take care now."

"You, too."

Tony nodded to Susannah and left them alone.

Ryan walked over to the door bearing the large number eighteen and ran a hand over the helmet on the shelf above his locker. "This must be a new one. I heard the E.R. doctors used a saw to cut off the one I wore in the Super Bowl."

"You don't remember?"

He shook his head. "Not a thing after Rodney Johnson hit me, until about eight hours later."

Susannah winced.

"Sorry, baby." He kissed her forehead. "I know you don't like to talk about that stuff." Opening the yellow locker door, he rifled around in the chaos.

Susannah stepped closer to get a better look at the photos he had hung on the door: her engagement picture, their wedding, Ryan and his mother at his Florida graduation, and some group shots of current and former teammates. Mixed into the collage was an ultrasound photo. "Oh," she said with a small gasp as she fingered the yellowing edges of the black and white image. "You kept this?"

"It's the only photo of him we had."

They gazed at the grainy image of tiny fingers and toes, a sloping spinal column, the little heart.

"I was so proud of that picture," Ryan said in a hushed voice. "I showed it to everyone."

"I remember." She looked up at him. "I'm glad you kept it."

"Do you want it? You can have it."

"I still have mine, too."

They shared a small, sad smile.

"On second thought," he said, taking a deep breath, "I'll get the stuff I need from here another time." Slamming the door closed, he took her hand. "Let's go outside." On the way out of the locker room, he grabbed a football from a huge wire basket full of them.

They walked through the dark tunnel that led to the field, emerging at the Mavericks' forty-yard line. Like a rookie getting his first glimpse at the big time, Ryan stepped onto the field and made a slow circle as he took in the towering rows of purple and yellow seats, the championship banners, and skyboxes.

Susannah stayed on the sidelines and watched him.

He tossed the ball back and forth between his hands with an unconscious grace. "Do you know what I loved best about this game?"

"I can think of so many things."

"There was one in particular." He fixed his eyes on the goalpost at the far end of the field. "I know what I'm doing here. It's as clear to me as the next breath." He flipped the ball up and caught it without taking his eyes off the goalpost. "Outside these walls most things are a mystery. But here . . . Here, I get it, you know?" He looked over at her. "That sounds dumb, doesn't it?"

"No." She joined him on the field. "It doesn't."

"They talk about my skills and abilities and throw around big adjectives that—*at times*—have gone to my head. I won't deny that."

Susannah snickered.

"But so much of my good fortune on this field has been due to God-given talent and pure old-fashioned good luck—the right team, the right coaches calling the right plays, the right receiver in just the right place at the right time. It's luck as much as it is hard work and discipline. At the end of the day, I've just been lucky."

"You should say that. At your press conference, you should say everything you just said to me."

"You think so?"

"I do."

Cocking his lucky arm into shotgun formation, he said, "Want to go long for me, darlin'?"

She raised an amused eyebrow. "In high heels?"

"Yeah, I guess not."

"I never was a very good receiver anyway."

"Are we still talking about football?" he asked with a smirk.

"*Ryan!*"

He laughed, and bracing his ribs with his free hand, he let the ball rip as best he could. Even with a handicap, the ball soared more than fifty yards.

"Not bad for an old retiree," Susannah said.

"Not bad at all, if I do say so myself."

"I figured you would."

He grinned and looped his arm around her shoulders. "Let's go do this thing."

She stopped him when he would've begun to head inside. "Are you going to be able to live without the one thing that makes sense to you?"

He took a long last look around. "I'm hoping you'll help me over the bumps, but yeah, I'll be okay. Maybe someday I'll find something else that makes as much sense."

"You'd be selling yourself short if you think this is the only thing you can excel at. As I recall, that piece of paper you got from Florida said something about magna cum laude. Now, I'm no college graduate—not *yet* anyway—but I don't think they give that to dummies."

"So you're not going to let me wallow around in my skivvies and get fat in my retirement?"

She turned up her nose. "Don't even think about it."

"You're going to have to keep a very close eye on me to make sure that doesn't happen." He led her inside. "It might be a forty- or fifty-year job that requires a daily commitment."

"I'll think about that and get back to you."

"See that you do, darlin'." He punched the button for the elevator that would take them up to the executive offices. "In the meantime, I'll be waiting in my skivvies."

She laughed and followed him into the purple elevator.

Chapter 16

CHET'S ASSISTANT TOOK THEIR COATS AND USHERED THEM into his huge office overlooking the field far below. The bright yellow office walls were plastered with framed photos of the Mavericks' colorful owner with everyone from presidents to actors to athletes from all corners of the sporting world.

"There he is!" Chet roared as he got up from behind his massive desk.

Ryan was relieved to receive only an enthusiastic handshake rather than Chet's usual bone-crushing hug.

"You look great, Sandy," he said, turning his attention to Susannah. "And it's so nice to see you, Susie. Martha and I were just tickled pink to hear you two are back together."

"We're working on it," Ryan said quickly, before Susannah could protest.

"How are you feeling, Sandy?" Duke asked as he kissed Susannah's cheek and held a chair for her at Chet's conference table where the Lombardi trophy was the centerpiece.

"Much better, but the ribs are still giving me some grief."

"Takes time," Duke said. "Ribs are tough."

"Tell me about it."

"The president sends his regards." Chet chomped on an unlit cigar as he uncorked a bottle of champagne and poured four glasses. "He was sorry you couldn't make the trip, and he wants you to give him a call if you get to D.C."

Ryan grinned. "Yeah, sure. We'll go out for a few beers."

"I bet he'd love that," Duke said.

Chet reached into his pocket for a slip of paper he handed to Ryan. "He said to have you call this number if you'd like to see him. He's a huge fan of yours, but of course you know that."

Ryan exchanged amazed glances with Susannah and had to fight the urge to giggle. Even after a decade as a professional athlete, the attention and adulation could still come as a surprise.

Chet raised his glass in tribute to Ryan. "Here's to another successful year and to the best quarterback this game has ever seen."

"I'll drink to that," Duke echoed.

Humbled, Ryan said, "Thank you," as he took a sip of the foaming bubbly and eased himself into the chair next to Susannah.

"It sure is good to see you looking so much better, Sandy." Chet reclined back in his chair as he studied Ryan with wise, old eyes. "You gave us a helluva scare down there in N'awlins."

"Sure did," Duke added with a shudder. "Took five years off my life when you didn't move for what felt like an *eternity*."

Ryan reached for Susannah's hand under the table, knowing she had gone to great lengths to avoid watching or reading about the play that had caused his injuries. "Well, I'm fine now."

"And ready to sign the fat new contract The Shark hammered out for you, I hope," Chet said.

Ryan glanced at Susannah, and she squeezed his hand.

"Um, about that," he said, hesitating as he prepared to step off the precipice into the unknown.

"Is there a problem?" Chet asked. "I was pretty sure we had a deal after the last meeting."

"You've been extremely generous," Ryan said. "You know how I hate all the haggling over money and stuff."

"You're worth every dime—and then some." Chet's craggy face lifted into a big smile around the cigar. He had given up smoking them three years earlier after a health scare. "But don't tell Aaron I said that."

Ryan chuckled, took a deep breath, and said, "I'm going to retire."

The two men stared at him like he was speaking a foreign language.

Chet shook his head as if he hadn't heard Ryan correctly. "You want to run that by me one more time?"

"I'm retiring. Effective immediately."

"You can't be serious, Sandy," Duke said. "You took a hard hit down there in New Orleans, but to quit . . . "

"I made this decision weeks before the Super Bowl."

"I just don't understand . . . " Chet stammered.

Ryan leaned forward on the table. "I'm sorry this is coming as such a shock to you, Chet. I really am. You've been so much more than a boss. You've been a good friend to me and to Susie for the last ten years. We couldn't have asked for anything more than what we've had with the Mavs organization. But I want to go out while I'm still on top, rather than outstaying my welcome."

"It's not *possible* for you to outstay your welcome, with this team or any other, for that matter." Chet slapped the table. "You're Ryan *freaking* Sanderson, for Christ's sake." To Susannah, he added, "Pardon my French, honey."

Susannah held up a hand to let him know no offense had been taken.

"We've had a great run." Ryan struggled to keep his emotions in check. "I've had the time of my life here in Denver, but I'm ready for a change."

Chet studied Ryan for a long moment as if to gauge whether the younger man was open to negotiation. "What do you have to say to this, Duke?" he asked his head coach.

"I'm not entirely surprised," Duke said.

The other three looked at him with interest.

"I've noticed you working with Toad a lot more in the last few months—almost like you were grooming him for something."

Ryan shrugged. "He's worked really hard, and he's earned the opportunity to show you what he's got."

Duke folded his hands on the table. "I'm going to say something to you, and I want you to listen to me, okay?"

With a glance at Susannah, Ryan nodded.

"Chet was dead on before when he said you're the best quarterback this game has ever seen. After this last Super Bowl, there'll be no more debating that. I've never known a player with more natural ability than you have. You've got *years* left in you, Sandy. *Years.*" Duke punctuated his point by stabbing the table with his index finger. "You have the opportunity to break every QB record on the books, but you need a few more seasons to do it. I'd like nothing more than to see you get there. So if there's anything either of us can do to change your mind, I know I speak for Chet when I say all you have to do is name it."

Chet nodded in agreement.

Ryan's jaw clenched with tension and emotion. "I can't tell you how much I appreciate that, Coach. It's been such an honor to play for you, to work with you, to call you my friend. I hope you don't have a single doubt about what you mean to me personally. But I'm done with football." With his eyes on Susannah, he added, "I've learned there are other things in life more important than having my name next to every record in the books."

Her smile was full of love, and it filled him with confidence.

"You've worked awfully hard, and you're *so* close," Duke added with a pleading edge to his voice.

"I've played my last game," Ryan said firmly. "I would've liked to have gone out a little more gracefully than I did, but hey, what can you do?"

"What've you got to say about this, honey?" Chet asked Susannah.

She looked at Ryan when she said, "I think Ryan feels he's accomplished everything he set out to do in this game, and he wants to see what else is out there before he's too beat up to be able to do much of anything."

Ryan nodded in agreement as Duke and Chet exchanged resigned glances. After a long pause, Chet got up, walked over to his desk, and pressed a button on the phone. "Jenny, will you ask Bob to come up to the office, please?"

Bob was the team's public affairs officer and would guide Ryan through the press conference and media blitz that would follow his announcement.

"Thank you," Ryan said when Chet returned to the table.

"You'll have a place in this organization for as long as I have a breath left in me," Chet said gruffly. "You got that?"

Ryan's eyes filled. "Yes, sir."

"That goes for me, too," Duke added. "Whatever you want."

The lump in his throat made it impossible for Ryan to do anything more than nod.

The press conference was set for noon the next day. Bob had done his best to prepare Ryan and Susannah for the media circus he predicted would follow Ryan's announcement.

"Are you okay?" Susannah asked on the ride home.

"Yeah. I feel better now that they know, but I hated upsetting them. They've both been so good to me."

"And you've been good to them," Susannah reminded him. "You've made Chet a ton of money and helped to elevate Duke to coaching royalty. Don't forget that."

He kissed her hand. "I'll try to keep that in mind."

"Does it feel weird? To be making it official?"

"Kind of," he conceded. "I think it'll really set in when the guys are leaving for camp and I'm not going."

"You'll be so busy doing other things by then you'll barely notice."

His dimpled grin was skeptical. "It's going to be crazy tomorrow. Are you ready for that?"

"I'll be fine."

"I hate that I have to do this right now. But the media is waiting for the announcement that I've signed the new contract, so I can't put off the press conference until after we resolve things between us."

"Speaking of resolving things between us, I want to talk to you about that when we get home."

He took his eyes off the road to look over at her. "What about it?"

"You'll have to wait until we get home."

Pushing the accelerator to the floor, he said, "Well, then let's get on home!"

"Ryan! *Slow down!*"

He darted between two cars on Interstate 25. "Not unless you're ready to start talking."

"Stop driving like a maniac, or I won't say a word when we get home."

"You ruin all my fun," he pouted as he eased off the accelerator—but only slightly.

"That's my job."

After a speedy ride, they pulled into the driveway, and he spirited her inside. "Okay, start talking."

"Can I at least take off my coat?"

He peeled the coat from her shoulders and tossed it over the banister. A moment later, his landed on top of hers. "Talk."

"In a minute," she said as she started up the stairs.

Ryan followed in hot pursuit and forced himself to be quiet while she took her time hanging up her suit jacket. "You're going to torture me, aren't you?"

She flashed him a coy smile. "It's kind of fun, actually. You're like a five-year-old waiting for your ice cream treat."

"I'll give you a treat," he said with a low growl as he crossed the room to her. He put his arms around her and backed her up to the bed, coming down on top of her. "Start talking. Right now."

Her hands found his back under his sports jacket. "You might be a big bully, but you can't make me talk."

"You don't think so?" He ran his fingers over her ribs, and she shrieked with laughter. "Do I make my point?"

She pushed her pelvis into his erection. "Yes, you do," she said with a giggle.

"*Susannah . . . Come on.* I'm *suffering.*"

"I know. I'm enjoying it."

With a deep sigh of frustration, he rested his head on her shoulder.

Running her fingers through his hair, she kissed his cheek. "I love you."

Ryan all but stopped breathing as he lifted his head to look at her. "I love you, too."

"You did well today with Chet and Duke."

"I'm glad you thought so. I was a nervous wreck."

"It didn't show."

"Thank you for being there."

"Of course I was there. I'm your wife, right?"

"Yes, you are," he whispered, his heart fluttering with hope. "What are you saying, Susie?"

"I want to try again."

Ryan could only stare at her for the longest time.

"Say something."

He dipped his head and found her lips in a deep, sizzling kiss that told her everything he was feeling at the moment.

"I take it you're happy to hear this news?" she asked, breathless from his passionate kiss.

He nodded and went back for more. Unbuttoning her blouse, he dragged his tongue over each new bit of skin as he unveiled it.

"Ry," she gasped. "We have guests coming."

Glancing at the bedside clock, he said, "Not for ninety minutes."

"But Carol . . ."

"Will let herself in. She has before."

"But . . ."

"Shh." He unhooked the front clasp of her bra and nudged it aside. "I want to make love to my wife. Right now."

"I've never made love with a retiree," she joked.

"Mmmm," he said as his lips coasted over her breast. "Then I'd better make it memorable."

Susannah floated on a cloud of pleasure and contentment. In all their years together, Ryan had never made such tender love to her, as if she were the most fragile, delicate, breakable object in the world. She'd been in the throes of a third orgasm when the door had chimed downstairs, and Carol called out to see if anyone was home. They'd dissolved into helpless laughter that had only led to more passion.

Ryan slept next to her, worn out from their love-making and the emotional meeting with Chet and Duke. Knowing he had another difficult round ahead of him with his teammates, Susannah wanted him to sleep for as long as he could. She eased herself out of his embrace, sat up, and gazed at him. She wasn't exactly sure when she decided to give him another chance, but hearing him say the football field was the only place that made sense to him filled her with such overwhelming sadness. Imagining him foundering alone in the world without her and without his beloved game was more than she could bear. She believed him when he said he had changed and was prepared to give her what she needed. In return, she was going to help him through this huge transition in his life. Sweeping the dirty blond hair off his forehead, she kissed his cheek and got up to take a shower.

She was brushing her wet hair in front of the mirror when a reflection off her engagement ring reminded her that she still had a very big problem. Putting the brush down on the granite countertop, she spun the ring around on her finger and tugged it off. Tomorrow, she would give it back to Henry. Her stomach knotted when she imagined what he'd have to say to the news that she was going back to Ryan. And then she'd have to tell her parents and sister . . .

"I don't care what they say," she whispered to her reflection. "I have to put up that wall so they can't get to us like they did before. Everything has to be different this time. Ryan has changed, and I have to change, too, or this'll never work." The thought gave her a moment's pause, as she realized what a huge leap of faith she was taking.

After she dried her hair, she went into her bedroom, put the ring away in her jewelry box, and got dressed. In a show of support for what he was about to do, she put on Ryan's team jersey. *Why the hell not?* She closed the drapes in the bedroom and pulled the covers up over Ryan's shoulders, hoping he would sleep for another half hour.

Downstairs, she discovered Carol's staff had transformed the living room, den, and dining room into party central. Bars were set up in the living room and den, and empty chafing dishes stood ready on the dining room table.

"Carol, you're a miracle worker!" Susannah exclaimed when she strolled into the kitchen.

"Anything for you, darling," Carol said, lifting her cheek to receive Susannah's kiss. Carol was a tiny Hispanic dynamo in her mid-fifties.

"Thank you so much. Sorry for the short notice."

"It was no problem. I'm always ready for an emergency party."

Susannah laughed, knowing it was true.

"Dare I ask where you were when I got here?"

Susannah's shrug was full of innocence. "In the shower."

"Uh-huh. *Sure.* I noticed a sparkling new Caddy in the driveway with Mavericks plates and the telltale number eighteen, which I see you're wearing proudly tonight. Care to tell me what's going on?"

"Not yet," Susannah said, knowing she couldn't breathe a word of her reconciliation with Ryan until she'd had the chance to talk to Henry. "But soon, I hope."

Carol took her hand. "*I* hope you and that gorgeous husband of yours are back together where you belong. I never understood what could've gone so wrong between two people who are clearly mad for each other."

"Thank you," Susannah said, touched by her friend's support. "I appreciate that more than you could ever know."

"I never believed what people were saying about him and Betsy James. I know you had your suspicions . . . "

"Just the sound of that woman's name *still* makes me want to punch something," Susannah said with a shudder. "But he swears he was never unfaithful. I couldn't bring myself to come right out and ask him about her because the whole thing just makes me sick."

"You should believe him. She's got nothing on you, and Ryan certainly knows that. If he was going to cheat, Susannah, it wouldn't have been with that bitch."

Susannah laughed. "Tell me how you really feel."

"She's not worth it. So where *is* the gorgeous husband?" Carol asked with a devilish grin.

"Sleeping," Susannah said, feeling the blush creep to the roots of her hair.

Carol laughed. "Wore him out, did you?"

"He wore *himself* out, if you get my drift."

"Oh . . . I need a drink *and* a cigarette. Stat."

Susannah giggled but then became serious. "Don't mention this to anyone, okay? I need to talk to Henry."

"I understand, sweetie." Carol rested a hand on Susannah's arm. "I promise I won't breathe a word of it. But I guess this means the last Saturday in February is suddenly open on my schedule?"

"Yes." Susannah's stomach knotted again at the thought of canceling her wedding and hurting Henry. "Sorry."

"Don't be sorry. I'm actually kind of relieved."

"Relieved? Why?"

"I work with a lot of brides, and I've never seen one less enthusiastic than you've been planning that wedding. He's all wrong for you, Susannah."

"Why am I the last one to realize that?"

"That's usually the way it goes. All that matters is you *have* realized it—in time to stop it. You know where I am if you need a friend, right?"

"Always. Thank you."

While Carol darted around the kitchen, they went over a few final details for the Black and White Ball, which Carol was also catering. Before Susannah went upstairs to wake up Ryan, she asked Carol for one last favor.

"Listen, when the team gets here, do you think you could clear out your people? Ryan has something he wants to talk to his teammates about, and it's kind of private."

"Absolutely. We'll put everything out and scram."

"You don't have to go. I didn't mean you."

"I need to get back to the office anyway. No worries."

"Thanks again, Carol."

"My pleasure. Go wake up the hunk. I need some eye candy before I go."

Susannah snorted with laughter and went upstairs.

Chapter 17

SUSANNAH LAY DOWN NEXT TO RYAN, WHO WAS STILL sound asleep. She hated to wake him, but his friends would be arriving soon.

"Ry," she whispered, kissing his cheek and then his lips. "Wake up."

"Mmmm." With his eyes still closed, he pulled her closer to him. "I was having the most amazing dream."

"Oh, yeah? What about?"

"My wife told me she's giving me another chance. So whoever you are, it's over between us."

Susannah laughed as she smacked his shoulder. "Very funny. Get your butt out of bed. Your guests will be here soon." When she tried to get up, he pulled her back down and rolled on top of her.

"Ry! Come on!" She pushed at his chest with a nervous giggle. "What are you doing?"

"Kissing your neck. What do you think I'm doing?"

"Starting something you can't finish."

"I can finish it." His hand dipped under her shirt and cupped her breast. "Oh . . . you're wearing my jersey. You know how that turns me on."

"The passing breeze turns you on. Now, *get up!*"

"Under one condition."

"What?"

"You'll wear the jersey and nothing else later."

"Fine, now get up."

He kissed her long and hard. "You promise about the shirt? I need something to look forward to."

"Yes! *Get off* of me!"

Laughing, he rolled over and stretched before he got up and made a beeline for the shower. "Stop checking out my ass," he called over his shoulder.

Embarrassed to be caught doing just that, Susannah buried her face in the pillow that still held the woodsy scent she would recognize anywhere as his.

Ten minutes later, he emerged from his closet wearing faded jeans and a black polo shirt. Sitting on the edge of the bed, he tied the laces on his Nikes. "Thanks again for doing this tonight. I'll make sure they don't tear up the house too badly."

"Just keep them away from Grandma Sally's china, and I'll be happy."

"You've got it." Bringing her hand to his lips, he stopped short. "Oh, baby . . . You took it off."

She nodded.

He brought her into his arms.

Susannah held him just as tightly as he was holding her.

"I *so* wish we weren't having company tonight," he whispered.

"They won't be here forever."

"They'd better not be."

"Will you do me a favor?"

"You can have anything you want. You've made me the happiest guy in the world."

Caressing his cheek, she said, "Will you not tell anyone we're getting back together until I've had a chance to talk to Henry?"

He studied her as he mulled it over. "I guess I could do that, but make it snappy. I won't be able to keep this a secret for long."

"I'm going to go see him at his office tomorrow morning before the press conference."

"I'll drive you."

"That's not necessary."

"You promised me you wouldn't be alone with him."

"I'll be in a public place," she protested.

"I'll drive you." His face was set into a stubborn expression that told her there was no point in arguing further.

"Ry?"

"What, baby?"

"I don't want your teammates to think you're retiring because of me. They're going to get that we're sort of back together, so—"

"I don't care what they think. You and I know why I'm doing this. That's all that matters to me."

When the bell chimed downstairs, he helped her up. At the doorway to their room, he stopped her for one last kiss and ran his hands over the silky jersey. "Don't forget your other promise. I'm not going to be able to think about anything else but you and this jersey all night."

She gave him a push. "Get moving. Carol's waiting for you."

"She wants me *bad*," he said with a teasing grin.

"Right about now, she can have you."

He laughed. "Now, baby, I *know* you don't mean that."

His arm was around her shoulders when they started down the stairs to the foyer where Carol greeted Bernie and his family. Ryan had asked him to come earlier than the others, so he could share the news with his best friend first.

When Bernie's wife Mary Jane looked up and saw them together, her eyes widened with delight. She reached for Susannah and hugged her. "I'm so happy to see you," she whispered.

"Me, too." Susannah was surprised when her eyes filled with tears. Until that very moment, she hadn't realized how much she had missed Mary Jane, Bernie, and their two sons, who had grown a foot since Susannah had last seen them. "That can't be Cole."

The twelve-year-old's face turned bright red.

Ryan wrapped the boy in a headlock.

"Don't fight back," Bernie warned his son. "Uncle Ryan's injured and shouldn't be starting something he can't finish."

"Funny," Susannah said. "We just had a similar conversation."

"Something tells me you weren't talking about the same thing," Carol said with a dry chuckle.

Ryan stuck his tongue out at her, and she rewarded him with a come hither look that made everyone laugh.

"Don't tempt me, big boy," she called over her shoulder as she went back to the kitchen.

"Come on in you guys." Ryan released Cole and reached out to hug his younger brother, Hayden.

"Can we go downstairs and play with the games?" Hayden asked.

"Sure thing, buddy," Ryan said. "In fact, I was hoping you guys would be in charge of all the kids. You remember my rule about the pool table, right?"

"Yep," Cole said.

Bernie cuffed the boy's shoulder.

"I mean, yes, sir, Uncle Ryan. We won't go near it."

"Are the video games still in the same place?" Hayden asked.

Ryan looked to Susannah for confirmation.

"They sure are, honey," she said. "Play with whatever you want."

"Just don't let the other kids get wild," Bernie told the boys.

"Carol put some snacks and drinks down there for you guys," Susannah added.

"Cool," the boys called as they took off for the stairs.

"I cannot *believe* how big they are," Susannah said, linking her arm through Mary Jane's as they followed their husbands into the den.

"They shot up this year," Mary Jane agreed.

Ryan played bartender, opening beers for himself and Bernie, and a bottle of wine for the women, who settled on one of the sofas.

"I was surprised to hear you guys were having a party," Bernie whispered to Ryan. "The last time I saw you two you were barely speaking."

"We've made some progress since then."

Bernie glanced over to the sofa where Susannah was engaged in animated conversation with his wife. "I can see that."

"You sound surprised."

"A little," Bernie admitted.

Ryan grinned. "Were you betting against me?"

"I wouldn't say that. Exactly. Let's just say I wasn't as optimistic as you were."

"We're getting back together," Ryan whispered.

Bernie's blue eyes widened with surprise. "What about the fiancé?"

"He doesn't know yet. That's why I'm whispering. I can't tell anyone until she tells him."

"Well, I'll be damned." Bernie rubbed at the red stubble on his chin. "I'm happy for you, man. Truly. I just hope, you know . . . "

"That I don't fuck it up again?"

"I wasn't going to say that. Exactly."

They shared a laugh as they carried glasses of wine to their wives.

"So listen," Ryan said. "I wanted you to come early because there's a reason we're having the party tonight."

"What's going on?" Bernie asked.

Susannah reached for Ryan's hand.

"I met with Chet and Duke today."

"Did you sign the new contract?" Bernie asked.

"No."

"Why the hell not? I heard it was *outrageous!*"

"Because I've decided to retire."

Bernie burst into laughter. "That's funny. But really, why didn't you sign?"

"I'm serious, Bern."

Bernie looked at Susannah, and she nodded.

"But, why? I don't get it."

Ryan explained his reasons to Bernie.

"I just . . . I don't know what to say. I can't imagine the Mavs without you."

"Oh, you guys will be just fine. You probably won't win any more Super Bowls, but you'll be okay."

Susannah rolled her eyes at Mary Jane.

"This is why you've been spending so much time with Toad, isn't it?" Bernie asked. "You knew you were leaving."

"It was also because Toad's a damned good quarterback. He's got a big future ahead of him."

"But he's not you."

"Bern . . . "

Bernie got up and went over to the fireplace where he squatted down to add a log to the flame.

Ryan followed him.

"Why didn't you tell me?" Bernie asked.

"I wanted to wait until the season was over."

Bernie looked up at his friend. "What the hell are you going to do without this game?"

"I'm thinking about coaching."

"Pro?"

"High school."

Bernie was startled, but before Ryan could explain, Carol poked her head into the den. "We're taking off. Everything's either out or in the oven. Enjoy your evening."

Ryan and Susannah went over to hug her.

"Thanks a million, Carol," Susannah said.

"Ditto," Ryan said, making Carol's day when he kissed her cheek.

The doorbell rang, and minutes later the house was full of people.

❖ ❖ ❖

With the help of Mary Jane and Darling's wife Cindy, Susannah kept the food and drinks flowing. Toad's girl-friend Nancy balanced their one-year-old daughter Kara on her hip and did what she could to help the other women.

"I can't believe how fast Ryan bounced back from his injuries," Cindy said with a shudder. "I was so freaked out when he didn't move for what felt like forever."

With a glance at Susannah, Mary Jane said, "We all were."

"It's a good thing you weren't there, Susie," Nancy said, holding a cracker for Kara. "It was awful."

"So I've heard." Susannah reached out to the baby, desperate to change the subject. "Is she walking yet?"

"Any day now," Nancy said.

Susannah's heart hurt when the little girl's chubby fingers closed around hers in a tight squeeze.

"Are you and Ryan back together?" Nancy whispered, and all eyes landed on Susannah.

"We're working on it."

"That's good," Cindy said. "You two belong together. It wasn't the same without you with us this season, Susie."

The reminder that she had missed Ryan's final season in the NFL saddened Susannah.

With a loud whistle, Ryan summoned everyone to the den.

"He beckons," Susannah said. A knot settled in her stomach as she anticipated the reaction Ryan's team-mates would have to his announcement.

The large room quickly became small as the players, their wives, and girlfriends crowded in together. Ryan held out a hand to Susannah. He had a football tucked under his other arm.

She worked her way through the group until she reached his side.

With his arm around her, Ryan said, "Susie and I want to thank you all for coming over on such short notice. But before I tell you why I asked you to come tonight, I want you to know I'm so proud of this team and what we accomplished this year. They said we were rebuilding and the expectations were low, but we showed them, didn't we?"

The question led to hollering, whistling, and high-fiving.

"This season was the most amazing ride, and I'll never forget a minute of it." Ryan cleared his throat and glanced at Susannah.

She nodded with encouragement.

"That leads me to the reason for this shindig tonight. This afternoon, I met with Duke and Chet."

"And signed that new fifty-million-dollar contract?" Darling asked, starting another burst of whistling.

"He's holding out for more!" Toad called from the back of the room.

"No, no." Ryan held up his hand. "They said if I signed there wouldn't be enough left to pay you, Toad."

The young man's face fell, and the others roared with laughter.

"Seriously," Ryan said after they'd had their laughs. "I didn't sign the contract because I've decided to retire."

The room fell silent.

"I can't imagine a better time to go out than after the incredible season we've just had." He raised his arm and tossed the ball he'd been holding to Toad. "It's your turn now. You're ready, you've worked hard, and I'm asking everyone to get behind you and to support you the way they've supported me."

Like a deer in headlights, Toad caught the ball as his girlfriend Nancy began to weep softly.

Ryan's teammates had a hundred questions—and arguments against his decision. During the next half hour, he handled each one with unwavering patience. When there was nothing left to ask or answer, Darling stood up and raised his beer bottle to Ryan. "There's no man whose hands I'd rather have on my ass than yours," the team's center said with an expression so serious and so solemn that the others were crippled with laughter.

"Thank you, Darling," Ryan said with a big grin. "I'm touched."

"You'll be missed," Darling said. To the others, he added, "During these times that try a man's soul, the best thing to do is drink—heavily."

His proclamation was met with loud cheers.

Beers were passed around followed by shots of Jack Daniels.

In the midst of the chaos, Ryan hugged Susannah. "That went okay, huh?"

"It was great," she said. "Perfect."

He was soon swept away to do a shot with his teammates.

Susannah took advantage of the opportunity to escape into the kitchen where she found Nancy still in tears.

"What's wrong, honey?" Susannah asked the younger woman.

"I just don't know if I'm ready for all this," Nancy

said in her lilting Georgia accent. "Todd was content to play behind Ryan. He thought he had years to go before he'd be in this position. There's going to be so much pressure and attention . . . "

Susannah put her hands on Nancy's shoulders. "All you have to do is provide a warm, soft place for him to land in the middle of all the insanity. That's your job."

"Is that what you did?" Nancy asked, wiping the tears from her cheeks.

Susannah thought about it. "Not always—not as often as I should have," she said, startled to discover it was true. "You just do the best you can. That's all any of us can do. And while you're at it, enjoy the perks and use the clout you'll gain as his girlfriend—or maybe even his wife someday—to give something back to the community."

"He wants to get married."

"You don't?"

Nancy shrugged. "I don't know if this life is for me, Susie. I'm not like you. You're so calm and cool all the time. I wish I could be more like you."

Susannah snorted with laughter. "I'm a mess inside, just like everyone else. I'll let you in on a secret. When I first met Ryan, I had no idea what a quarterback was."

"That's not true!" Nancy said, scandalized. "How could you not know that?"

"I grew up surrounded by women with a father whose primary interest in sports involved horse racing. I was in no way prepared for the life I've led. You'll figure it out, Nancy, just like I did. Remember—it's not about whether this life is for you. It's about whether that *man* is for you."

The man in question picked that moment to come into the kitchen, holding Kara on his shoulders. "There you are, honey." Toad put his arm around Nancy. "Are you okay?"

With a grateful glance at Susannah, she said, "I will be."

Chapter 18

JUST AFTER MIDNIGHT, SUSANNAH TOOK A FINAL TRIP through the first floor collecting discarded bottles and cans.

Ryan came in after walking Darling and Cindy to their car. "What a great party." His eyes were bright from excitement and alcohol. "Thanks again for pulling it together so fast, baby."

"You'll have to think of some way to thank Carol. She's the one who pulled it off."

"Hmm." He scratched his chin. "I'm sure I can think of *some* way to thank her."

"She'll take whatever you're doling out," Susannah said, tying the garbage bag and leaving it by the back door to take out in the morning.

Ryan snaked his arms around her from behind. "What about you? Will you take whatever I'm doling out?" When she didn't reply, he turned her around. "Hey, what's the matter?"

Susannah looped her arms around his waist and leaned her forehead against his chest.

"Susie? What is it? You haven't changed your mind in the last four hours, have you? I can't believe I filled the house with football players ten minutes after you agreed to give me another chance. Good move, Sanderson."

"It was fine. They were very well behaved."

"Then what's wrong?"

"I realized something tonight when I was talking to Nancy about what to expect as the starting QB's significant other."

"What's that?"

"I've let you take most of the blame for what happened between us—"

"Most of it was mine to take."

"But not all of it. I wasn't as supportive of you and your career as I should've been."

His face twisted with confusion. "What are you talking about? You came to every one of my games, you've led the team's work with Children's Hospital—and continued that even after we broke up. How can you say you weren't supportive?"

"I wasn't supportive of *you*. I learned about football, mostly by being around it, but I never cared about it as much as I could have. I wanted you to do well and not get hurt, but I could've been more interested in the details."

"I wouldn't have wanted that, Suze. By the time I got home to you, the last thing I wanted to think or talk about was football. I told you the other day, I liked that you weren't a football groupie. You gave my life balance. Without that—and without you—I can't imagine what these last ten years would've been like. I probably would've become one of those overpaid athletes you read about in the police reports."

"No *way*. You were too smart and too focused to take that path."

"I don't know." With his arm around her, he flipped off the lights and steered her toward the stairs. "I might've been tempted to become one of football's famous bad boys—lots of boozing, a different woman every night, you know the type."

"Highly doubtful."

"We'll never know, though, will we? Because I had my beautiful wife to keep me on the straight and narrow." He rained soft kisses down her neck, making her tremble. "And you, my love, have miles to go and promises to keep before you sleep."

"Whatever do you mean, Mr. Frost?" she asked with a coy smile.

"You know." He sat on the bed and kicked off his shoes. "I'm waiting."

"You'll just have to wait a little longer," she said, heading for the bathroom.

He fell back on the bed with a deep sigh. "Hurry up!"

Susannah rushed through her nightly skincare routine. When she had applied her moisturizer and brushed her teeth, she took off everything except the requested jersey, which fell to mid-thigh. The silky material against her bare skin made her feel both sexy and like a nervous bride on her wedding night. In some ways it *was* like a wedding night. Everything was new again, and she was determined to make it work this time.

Filled with excitement and anticipation of all that was ahead for them—tonight and in the future—she emerged from the bathroom to find Ryan in bed with his back to her. Turning off his lamp, she went around to her side. She smiled when she saw his eyes were closed and his breathing steady. So much for his big plans.

She left her light on when she got into bed and turned on her side to face him. *How I ever thought I could live*

*the rest of my life without him, I'll never know. Well, you
do know, but there's no use thinking about that stuff
anymore. It's all in the past now.* Susannah scooted
closer to him and reached out to caress his chest.

He pounced.

She shrieked.

"You thought I was sleeping, didn't you?" he asked
with a delighted grin.

With her hand on her heart, she said, "You scared the
crap out of me."

"Do you *honestly* think I would go to sleep knowing
you were about to come out here wearing *only* my
jersey?" He lifted the hem of the shirt to make sure she
had followed his instructions. His eyes went dark with
lust when he saw she had done exactly what he'd asked
her to. "Are you *crazy?*"

"You were faking!"

"Yep."

"And here I was thinking you're all talk and no action."

"Those are fighting words," he said with a
menacing scowl.

She had forgotten how much fun he was to be with.
Nothing was ever simple or boring or routine. Not with
Ryan Sanderson. "I missed you, Ry," she confessed. "I
missed you every night. I hated going to bed alone after
sleeping with you for so many years."

He pulled her closer to him. "I missed you so much it
made me sick, especially when I imagined you sleeping
with Henry. *Ugh.* Unbearable."

She pressed her lips to his chest and ran her hand up
and down his back.

"Why didn't you ever sleep with him, Susie? Really?"

"I don't know. It wasn't for a lack of trying on his part, believe me."

"Spare me the details. Please."

"I just couldn't bring myself to actually do it."

"Why did you agree to marry him? I don't get it."

"He was very attentive and romantic. He said and did all the things I thought I needed and was just there for me. Then we went to Chicago for a weekend, and he proposed. I was completely shocked."

"You had no idea he was going to?"

"None at all."

"Why did you say yes?"

"I was so numb and lost and afraid. He represented safety and peace to me. It's hard to explain the place I was in at that time. I had lost Justin, I'd lost you . . . Nothing mattered."

"He knew you were vulnerable and took advantage of that."

"I don't think there was anything sinister about his intentions, Ry. It wasn't like that."

"He took advantage of the situation to get what he wanted. You'll never convince me otherwise."

"Then I won't try."

"By the way, you never lost me. We got a little side-tracked, but you never lost me."

"We almost got divorced," she reminded him. "With any other judge we'd be divorced by now. I'd probably be married to someone else and still missing you every minute of every day."

"Then thank God we got the right judge." He kissed

her and caressed her breasts through the silky fabric. "Mmm, so hot . . . "

Susannah nudged him onto his back and carefully rested on top of him. "Does that hurt?"

"Not my ribs, if that's what you mean."

"Yes," she said with a giggle. "That's what I meant."

"Thank you," he said, reaching under the jersey to cup her bottom.

"For?"

"Giving me another chance. I'm going to make sure you never regret it."

"I won't."

"You sound pretty confident."

"I have faith in you." She kissed him and sighed when his arms tightened around her. "Ry?"

"Yeah?"

"I want us to try again to have a baby."

"Really?"

She nodded. "I'm so tired of being afraid all the time. The doctors said it was a fluke, and I have to believe them. It's not going to happen again."

"That's right. I'm ready to do my part."

She chuckled. "Yes, I can tell."

Turning them over so he was on top, he rolled his tongue over her nipple through the silky fabric as he entered her slowly.

She moaned and clutched his shoulders.

"We'll fill this house with kids, if that's what you want," he whispered.

"Right now, all I want is you."

❖ ❖ ❖

Susannah wasn't surprised to find Ryan sharing her pillow when she woke up the next morning. As she listened to her stomach growl, she lay there for a long time wondering if she might already be pregnant. The last two mornings she had woken up starving, and her breasts were ultra-sensitive like they had been from the very beginning with Justin. Of course that could also be from all the attention they'd been getting from Ryan lately. Being ravenous in the morning, though, was unusual, and it had been an early sign of pregnancy before.

After trying so hard to get pregnant the first time, she'd been totally in tune with her body and knew almost instantly that she was pregnant. She'd just had a feeling about it. She had no such feeling now, just some signs that were hard to ignore. *Wouldn't that be something? With all we went through the last time that it could be so easy this time. Don't get ahead of yourself. Don't even think about it so you won't be disappointed if it isn't true. Yeah, sure, don't think about it . . .* She decided to make an appointment with her doctor to find out for sure.

Susannah got up to shower and get dressed. She debated over what to wear to Ryan's press conference and decided on a simple black dress that would also be appropriate to wear to see Henry. She zipped Henry's ring into a compartment in her purse and went to wake Ryan.

While he was in the shower, she went downstairs to make breakfast and an appointment for the following afternoon with her doctor since it was probably too soon for a home pregnancy test.

Ryan came downstairs wearing a navy pin-stripe suit and a Mavericks tie. "Does this look okay?"

"You look wonderful." She adjusted his tie and smoothed her hands over the lapels of the suit they had bought on London's Seville Row several years ago. "Like a man who's going out on top."

He put his arms around her. "I went out on top last night—a few times as I recall."

She groaned. "You always have to talk about it, don't you?"

"What fun is it if I can't talk about it?"

"Let's eat so we can get going."

On the way into the city, they listened to sports talk radio, which was abuzz over Ryan's press conference. Most of the chatter was about the fifty-million-dollar contract the Mavericks had offered for three more years and speculation that the press conference was to announce Ryan and the team had reached a deal.

"If you're Chet Logler, don't you give Ryan Sanderson anything he wants?" one of the hosts asked.

"I would think so," the other replied. "I know I would."

Susannah glanced over at Ryan in the driver's seat. Clearly he wasn't hearing a word of what was being said about him. "What are you thinking about?"

"I want this thing with Henry done."

"Soon enough."

"I want to go in with you."

"No, Ry. I can't do that to him. I just need a few minutes with him. You don't need to worry." She reached out to caress his cheek where a muscle pulsed with tension. "Everything's going to be fine. You need to be thinking about your press conference."

"I can't think about anything but you and that guy alone in a room together when you tell him it's over."

With a deep sigh, she rested her head on his shoulder.

A short time later, they pulled up to the First Mercantile Bank of Denver on California Street.

Ryan stopped her when she reached for the door. "If you're in there for more than fifteen minutes, I'm coming after you."

"It won't take that long." She leaned over to kiss him and got out of the car. Inside the bank, she took the elevator to Henry's second-floor office. His assistant greeted her with a smile.

"Hello, Ms. Sanderson. Mr. Merrill's in a meeting. Did he know you were coming by?"

"No, he didn't," Susannah said, wishing now she had made an appointment.

"I'll let him know you're here. I'm sure he'll want to see you."

"Thank you." Normally, Susannah would balk at calling him out of a meeting but not today.

Henry's assistant gestured for her to have a seat while she waited.

Susannah used the time to retrieve the ring from her purse. She curled it into her palm, which was suddenly damp from anxiety.

Five of her fifteen allotted minutes had passed when Henry came out of his office with a group of coworkers. His face lit up when he saw her.

"Susannah." He ushered her into his office as the others moved to the elevator. Today he wore a burgundy bow tie with a charcoal suit. "This is a nice surprise." He kissed her cheek and sat next to her on the sofa that overlooked the street. If she stretched just the tiniest bit, she would have been able to see Ryan waiting for her in the car.

"I'm sorry to interrupt your meeting."

"It's fine. We were done. What brings you into town so early?"

With a deep breath she said, "We need to talk."

His smile faded. "That doesn't sound good."

Susannah reached for his hand. "I'm sorry, Henry, but I've decided to give my marriage another chance."

He smiled but there was no warmth in it. "You didn't decide that. You had it decided for you."

"That's not true." Susannah took back her hand and told herself to stay calm. "I make my own decisions, and this is what I want."

"You must be out of your mind if you think you'll ever be happy with him."

"I *am* happy with him. I *was* happy with him for a long time."

He stood up. "Were you happy with him when he left you to go play football after you lost the baby? Were you happy when the whole town was talking about him having an affair with Betsy James? Were you happy then, Susannah?"

"No," Susannah said quietly. "I wasn't happy during any of those painful periods you love to remind me about every chance you get." She stood to face him. "Not that it's any of your business, but Ryan left me to play football after we lost Justin because I pushed him away by refusing to share my grief with him, and he did *not* have an affair with Betsy James or anyone else."

"He's really got you snowed, doesn't he?"

"I'm sorry if my decision causes you or your parents embarrassment. I'll pay for any costs incurred by canceling the wedding."

"You mean *he'll* pay, don't you?"

"Does it really matter?"

"I can't believe you would do this to me, Susannah! After I gave up my job in New York and moved out here to be with you . . . "

"I never asked you to do that!"

"You needed me, and I was here for you! I was right here for you, *always.*"

"Yes, you were. You were right there telling me what a good-for-nothing my husband was while pretending to be my friend."

"*Is that what he's been telling you?* And you're *buying* that? We've been friends since we were fifteen years old! Are you not allowed to have friends who are men?"

"Of course I am. I have many of them. But none of them has spent the last decade trying to get me to leave my husband so he could have me for himself. That's not love, Henry." She put the ring on the coffee table. "That's something else entirely."

"*Susannah!*" he cried as she moved to the door. "Wait." He put his hand on the door to stop her from leaving. "Please, honey, don't do this. I love you so much. There's nothing I wouldn't do for you."

"I'm sorry, but my mind's made up. I'd like to leave now, please."

"Tell me we can still be friends," he pleaded, grabbing her arm and pulling her to him.

Pain shot through her left arm when he twisted her wrist to keep her from escaping his tight embrace. "Henry! You're hurting me! Let go!"

"I can't lose you, Susannah. Please. Tell me we're still friends."

"We're not friends." The pain radiating from her arm brought tears to her eyes. "My friends want what's best for me. You want what's best for you. Now let go of me, and open that door before I start screaming."

"You know what?" he said as he abruptly let go and turned the doorknob. His genial hazel eyes had turned to ice. "The two of you deserve each other. He did me a big favor by coming back when he did. Be sure to thank him for me."

"I'll do that." Her stride as she left his office was quick and confident, but once she was inside the elevator her legs turned to mush and her hands began to shake.

As the elevator doors closed, Henry turned to find his assistant staring at him with her mouth hanging open. "Mind your own business," he snapped, slamming his office door closed.

He went over to the window and looked down to the street where Ryan Sanderson leaned against the black Escalade. Wearing a long leather coat and that goddamned Stetson he never left home without, Sanderson glanced up.

The two men locked eyes.

Sanderson didn't look away until Susannah emerged from the bank and threw herself into his arms. He held her for a long time while Henry watched them from above. After Sanderson helped her into the car, he looked up again, but this time his face was twisted into what could only be called a smirk.

He's gloating! That motherfucker is gloating! They drove away, but Henry stood there staring out at the busy street for a long time before he went over to his desk and picked up the phone.

"Betsy? Hey, it's Henry Merrill. I was wondering if you might be free for lunch today."

Chapter 19

AFTER A DAY FILLED WITH EMOTION AND NONSTOP INTER-
views with local and national media, Ryan and
Susannah returned home to Cherry Hills just after
nine. A light snow fell as they walked into the dark
house. Ryan hung up their coats in the front hall closet
and turned to her.

"How about a fire?"

"I'd love it," she said, wincing when he rubbed his
hands over hers to warm them.

"What's wrong?"

"Nothing."

He tilted his head to study her. "Something."

"I hurt my arm earlier. It's no big deal."

"How did you hurt your arm?" He nudged her into the
kitchen so he could look at it under the light. "And why
didn't you tell me?"

"I banged it, and I never had the chance."

He sat her down on a stool at the counter and rolled up
her sleeve to find her wrist bruised and swollen.
"Susannah! Baby, why didn't you tell me you were hurt?"

She shrugged. "You were busy with the press. I didn't
want to bother you."

"Bother me? You must've been in pain all day! We
need to get you to a doctor."

"I have an appointment tomorrow for a routine
checkup. I'll have Pam take a look at it then."

He gently turned her arm so he could see the other side of her wrist where there were four smaller bruises. "Those are fingerprints!" His eyes narrowed with fury. "Henry did this, didn't he?"

"He didn't mean to. Honest, he didn't. He was upset I was leaving, and he tried to stop me. He wasn't trying to hurt me."

Ryan released a deep breath in an effort to contain his rage. "I'm going to kill him."

"No, you're not." She rested her good hand on his chest. "How about getting me some ice to put on it?"

With his mouth tight with anger, he stared at the bruises for a long moment before he went to get an ice pack.

She took it from him with a calming smile. "Now, you said something about a fire. Why don't you get changed first?"

"Are you sure you're okay?"

"I'm fine. The ice feels good. Go ahead, Ry."

He kissed her cheek and went upstairs, but what he really wanted to do was find Henry Merrill and kick the shit out of him. *Just the thought of that guy putting his hands on Susie . . .* Tomorrow he would pay that little worm a visit to give him an idea of what would happen if he ever touched her again. Ryan hung up his suit and changed into jeans and a long-sleeved T-shirt. With his hands on the countertop in the bathroom, he hung his head and took a minute to get himself together.

Susannah came into the bathroom and sighed when she saw him struggling with his emotions. She put her arms around him and rested her head on his back. "Don't be upset, Ry. I'm okay."

"I *knew* I shouldn't have let you go in there alone." He slapped the countertop in frustration. "I *knew* it! This is exactly what I was trying to warn you about yesterday."

She turned him around so she could see his face. "Baby, I'm fine. It's no big deal. Please don't let it ruin what's been such an important day for you."

He put his arms around her and hugged her tightly.

"I want to sit by the fire and listen to you play your guitar. Will you do that for me?"

He kissed her forehead. "Anything you want. But I still want to kill him. I swear to God if he ever comes near you again I won't be responsible for my actions."

"Don't talk like that. He's not going to bother us. I told you, I made it very clear to him that it's over between us—completely."

"I'll believe it when I see it."

"Go get the fire going while I get changed."

"Do you need help?"

"No, I can do it. Thanks."

"All right. Don't be long."

"I won't."

The moment she was alone, Susannah reached for the bottle of Advil in her medicine cabinet. Her wrist hurt a lot more than she had let on to Ryan, and she suspected it might be sprained or worse. She shuddered when she imagined his reaction if it was in fact broken. She'd only defended Henry because she was afraid Ryan might actually kill him if he knew Henry *had* been trying to hurt her when he twisted her arm so violently. For a brief moment she had been frightened by the intensity of Henry's reaction. She'd known him for half her life and had never seen him lose control the way he had today.

With a shudder, she pushed those unpleasant thoughts aside and changed into a pale pink silk nightgown and matching robe. The simple tasks took much longer than usual because of her sore wrist. By the time she joined Ryan in the den, he had built up a big fire and was sitting in front of it lost in thought.

"Hey," he said when she sat on the sofa behind him. "I thought you forgot about me."

"Never. What were you thinking about?"

Rising to his knees he turned to face her. "You."

"What about me?" she asked with a smile.

He ran a hand over the silk that covered her thighs. "Actually I was thinking about the conversation I had with your father before I asked you to marry me."

Her eyes widened with surprise. "You talked to Daddy first?"

"Of course I did. The weekend before I proposed, I drove out to your folks' place. Your dad was fishing in the lake. He offered me one of the beers he had in his cooler and baited a pole for me. And then for the longest time he didn't say a word."

Susannah chuckled at the scene he described.

"I was starting to sweat when he finally said, 'You've come to tell me you're taking my Susannah away from me, haven't you?'" He mimicked her father's deep Southern drawl to perfection.

"Why haven't you ever told me this before?" she asked, her eyes filling.

He shrugged. "It was kind of between me and him, you know?"

She nodded. "So what did you say?"

"I said, 'I've come to ask for her hand, sir. I love her, and I'll take care of her always.' He said, 'You're a good boy, Ryan, but I'm worried about the life you've chosen and how my little girl is going to fit into it.' He said he had always pictured you married to a nice Southern gentleman—a doctor or a lawyer, perhaps. Someone more like Henry. He even used him as an example."

Susannah wiped away the tears that rolled down her cheeks, and her heart swelled with love as she imagined Ryan courageously approaching her father, a man who would appreciate such old-fashioned courtesy. Ryan had done it despite the fact that her father had been quite vocal in his disapproval of the career Ryan planned to pursue after graduation.

"We talked for a long time. I tried to convince him that while football wasn't as noble a profession as medicine or law, I'd be able to provide a comfortable life for you, and you'd never have to work unless you wanted to. As you can imagine, he wasn't much swayed by my description of the perks that would come with marriage to a professional athlete. He finally gave in when I told him quite simply that you'd be safe with me. He couldn't very well argue with that, I suppose."

"I can't believe neither of you ever said a word about this."

"I haven't thought about it in years, to be honest, until today when there was a very brief time when you weren't safe." He touched his lips to the bruise on her wrist. "Now all I can think about is I promised your daddy I'd take care of you, and I didn't do that today. I didn't trust the nagging feeling I had in my gut that Henry might hurt you."

Susannah put her arms around him and cushioned his head against her chest. "I love you so much."

His sigh was both contented and conflicted.

"You know that Southern gentleman Daddy hoped I'd find?"

He nodded.

"I married him. I married the best guy I've ever known, and if I had it to do over again, even after all that's happened, I'd do it in a heartbeat."

Looking up at her, he asked, "Will you?" In the palm of his hand were the engagement and wedding rings he had given her more than a decade ago. "Will you marry me all over again?"

"Yes," she said, her hands on his face. "Yes, I will."

He reached for her left hand and slipped the rings onto her finger. "I want us to renew our vows so we can put the brief period of insanity behind us and make a fresh start."

"I'd like that." She gazed at the familiar rings and was overcome with relief to see them back where they belonged. "I guess this means you haven't forgotten the combo to the safe."

"I was glad you hadn't changed it, but these are just placeholders until I can get you new ones."

"I don't want new ones. These are the ones I love. I cried all day when I finally worked up the nerve to take them off after you moved out."

He brushed at the dampness on her cheeks. "No more tears. Those days are over. We have the best of everything ahead of us."

She kissed him and urged him onto the sofa with her.

He took her in his arms and stretched out next to her. "I thought you wanted me to play for you."

"I'd rather have you hold me."

"Happy to oblige, darlin'."

"Aren't you at all curious as to what's being said about you on T.V. tonight?"

"Not in the least. I'm sure it'll be front-page news in tomorrow's sport section. We'll find out what they have to say soon enough. How does your wrist feel?"

"Okay. I took some Advil."

Ryan took a deep, rattling breath. "I sure wish you'd let me kill him. It would give me such pleasure . . . "

"What good would you be to me in jail?" she asked with a teasing smile.

"That's true," he conceded. "We took care of some major business today, didn't we?"

"We sure did. It feels good to have nothing standing in our way. We're free to do whatever we want."

He turned onto his good side so he could see her. "I just wish we could think of something to do with this newfound freedom of ours."

She pretended to give that some significant thought. "We could play a game."

"Or watch a movie," he said, his hand coasting over her silk robe.

"Uh-huh." She choked on a gasp when his roving hand found her breast. "I hope we aren't going to be bored as retirees. We might have to take up bridge or shuffleboard to fill our time."

He snorted with laughter. "From football to shuffleboard. Can you picture the headlines?"

She giggled but it quickly became a moan when he dragged his tongue over her bottom lip. "Ry," she sighed, burying her fingers in his hair to pull him closer.

But rather than give in to her need for urgency, he gave her top lip the same slow treatment.

Her heart fluttered when she looked up to find him watching her with brown eyes gone soft with tenderness. "I want you," she whispered.

"You have me. I'm all yours."

With her hands on his face, she brought his mouth back to hers.

The kiss was undemanding. He rimmed her mouth with his tongue and then delved deeper in quick fleeting strokes that made her desperate for more.

Susannah had to remind herself to breathe as he focused all his attention on the kiss. His hands never moved as he kissed her like a man who had all the time in the world to give her, all the time in the world to love her.

"Let me up so I can go get the paper," she said the next morning as sunlight streamed into the bedroom. In their haste the night before, they had forgotten to close the blinds. "I'm dying to know what they're saying about my man."

"In a minute," he murmured, his lips trailing over her neck.

When he caressed her belly, Susannah squirmed and then jolted as his hand dipped between her legs. "Ry!"

He pressed his erection against her back. "Hmm?"

"We can't."

"Why not?"

"This is nuts," she said, breathless from what he was doing to her. *How is it possible that I want him again?*

He eased her onto her belly and raised her arms up over her head.

She turned so she could see him. "Ry? What're you doing?"

"Kissing your back."

She wiggled under him. "That's not kissing! That's *biting!*"

"Details, baby." With a combination of lips, teeth, and tongue, he worked his way down her spine. Filling his hands with soft buttocks, he said, "I love your ass. Have I ever told you that?"

"Um, no." He was making her nervous. "Not in so many words."

"Too bad," he said, nibbling one cheek and then the other. "I should've told you, because I've thought it so many times." He slipped a finger in between to discover his efforts were having the desired result.

Susannah almost levitated off the bed.

"Easy, baby. Take it easy."

"How am I supposed to take it easy when you're doing that?"

He slid his finger into her wetness and tempted her with small, teasing movements. "Doing what?"

"*That!*" She thrust her hips back to try to capture his teasing finger. "Oh my *God!* Ryan . . . "

"Spread your legs a little."

"No! Stop. Come *on.*"

With his knees, he urged her legs apart and raised her hips. He entered her from behind and gave her a minute to adjust before he withdrew almost completely.

"Ryan!"

"Do you want more?"

"*Yes,*" she moaned. "*Please.*"

He kissed the back of her neck and whispered in her ear, "I love it when my little debutante is polite in bed."

"*Damn it! Do it!*"

"Oh, Christ, I like that even more," he said with a groan as he filled her again.

Careful to protect her sore wrist, he kept her on her elbows and knees as his teasing strokes drove her mad. When he reached for her breasts, her legs gave out, and she landed face down on the bed with him on top of her.

"Am I crushing you?"

"No," she panted, pushing back to urge him on. "Don't stop."

As he ground himself into her, his sweat mingled with hers. He covered her, surrounded her, possessed her. And when he whispered in her ear that he loved her, she replied with a scream of release that took him right over with her.

"Oh, God," she moaned from under him.

Ryan kissed her back, her shoulder, her neck, and finally, her cheek. "Good morning."

"This is nuts," she repeated.

"What is?"

"This," she whispered, so drained it was hard to believe she had just woken up.

He squeezed her breasts to remind her that his hands were still there. "Why?"

"We can't keep doing this all the time."

"Why not?"

She laughed. "Stop answering me with questions!"

"I'm waiting for you to give me a good reason."

"I'm trying to think of one."

He laughed, and it echoed through her.

When she closed her eyes and clenched her internal muscles, he groaned. "*Susie* . . . "

"We *have* to think of some other way to fill our time."

"Why?"

She reached up to pinch his shoulder. "*Now* can I go get the paper?"

"If you must." He withdrew from her and rolled onto his side. "How's your wrist?"

"Stiff but not as sore as yesterday." She felt his eyes on her as she reached for her robe.

"You can't go outside with just that on. You'll cause a stir in the neighborhood."

"Why? I'm covered."

"That thing clings to every delicious curve, darlin'. Take my word for it. You'll cause a stir."

"Honestly!" she said with exasperation.

Emerging from the bathroom several minutes later in a black sweat suit, her stomach growled noisily as she zipped up the sweatshirt over her unrestrained breasts. "Better?"

"Yes, but I never imagined I'd be so jealous of a zipper."

She rolled her eyes. "I'll be back in a minute."

"I'll be here."

She went downstairs, made coffee, and put a piece of bread in the toaster, hoping to calm her stomach. While the toaster did its thing, she pulled on boots and went outside to find the paper wrapped in a blue plastic bag that was in sharp contrast to the snow on the lawn. She carried the bundle inside, took the paper out of the bag, and flipped it open.

"Oh, wow," she whispered.

Chapter 20

RYAN LAY ON HIS BELLY AND WAITED FOR SUSIE TO come back. He'd expected to feel strange this morning after announcing his retirement to the world, but nothing felt different. He supposed he'd be despondent if he hadn't had Susie to give him something else to think about. Well, if he were being truthful, there was only one thing he was thinking about lately, and she had finally called him on it. He chuckled softly to himself. They'd always had an intense sexual relationship, but the last few days had been extreme even for them.

The dull throb in his ribs indicated that he had been overdoing the physical activity, but she was worth every ache and pain. She was back, she was his, and nothing was ever going to come between them again. He thought about the conversation he planned to have later with Henry, and once again his blood boiled at what that guy had done to Susie's arm. Maybe he'd do the same thing to Henry—it was the least of what that bastard deserved.

Susannah returned carrying two mugs of coffee and the newspaper tucked under her arm. "Wake up, sleepyhead."

He rolled over and sat up to receive the cup of coffee she handed to him. "How'd we do? Front of sports?"

"Not exactly." She held up the front page of the *Denver Post,* bearing the banner headline "Sanderson

Calls It Quits" over a huge photo of him dabbing at a tear during the press conference.

"*Holy shit*," he said on a long exhale. Most of the front page was devoted to him. "Must've been a slow news day."

"More like it's the story of the year in this city."

He put his coffee on the bedside table and reached for a pillow to put over his face. "Read it to me. I can't bear to look."

She chuckled as she stretched out next to him. "Are you ready?"

He grunted.

"One of the NFL's most storied careers ended yesterday with the surprise announcement that the Denver Mavericks' star Quarterback Ryan Sanderson is retiring," she read.

"Still bearing the bruises from his recent Super Bowl injuries, Sanderson, thirty-two, held a midday press conference at Mavericks Stadium, at which he charac-terized his Hall of Fame career as a combination of 'good luck and good genes.' With his wife Susannah, Mavericks' Coach Duke Simmons, and team owner Chet Logler by his side, an often-tearful Sanderson paid tribute to the many teammates, coaches, and competitors who made his ten years in the NFL a 'joyful journey.'" Susannah glanced over at him. "I liked that, by the way."

"I sound like a total geek," he said, his voice muffled by the pillow.

She laughed. "You do not! Shut up and listen. 'I also want to thank the people of Denver and the tremendous Mavericks' fans,' Sanderson said. 'You welcomed my wife and me with open arms when we first arrived in this town, and you've made playing here the most rewarding experience I ever could've hoped for. I've been guided by an outstanding coaching staff—led by my good friend, Duke Simmons—and was blessed to work for the greatest owner in the league.'

"Sanderson's current contract is set to expire on Sunday, and recent reports put the Mavericks' offer at $50 million for three more years.

"The one-time AFC Offensive Rookie of the Year led the Mavericks to three Super Bowl victories in the last five years—the only Super Bowl wins in the franchise's 36-year history—and was twice named Super Bowl MVP, including this year. He's a five-time Pro Bowler and was recently elected again but couldn't play due to the concussion and three broken ribs he sustained in the final minutes of the Mavericks' 35 to 7 Super Bowl rout of the San Francisco 49ers.

"A Heisman Trophy winner who led the University of Florida Gators to a national championship his senior year, Sanderson was named the AFC's most valuable player in six of his ten years in the league and passed for 39,620 yards during his career. A physical quarterback who wasn't afraid to tangle with opponents' defensive lines, he rushed for more than 3,500 yards and scored 23 touchdowns.

"Calling this the right time and the right place to end his career, Sanderson said he made the decision to retire before he was injured in the Super Bowl. 'I want to go on record as saying my friend Rodney Johnson's spectacular sack had nothing to do with my decision to retire,' Sanderson said to laughter from the gathered press and his teammates, who lined the room wearing Sanderson's number 18. Also wearing his jersey was his wife, who filed for divorce 14 months ago. At the press conference, Sanderson announced that the couple, who lost a son at birth more than two years ago, recently reconciled."

Ryan took the pillow off his face and winced. "They *had* to put that in there, didn't they?"

"I'm never prepared to see it in print."

"I'm sorry, baby."

She leaned over to kiss him. "It's not your fault. Listen to the rest: 'In addition to everyone in the Mavericks organization—past and present—there are three people I particularly wish to thank today,' Sanderson said. 'The first is my late mother, Theresa Sanderson, who never missed one of my games despite working two jobs. She was my greatest cheerleader, and I miss her. The second is my high school football coach, Jimmy Stevens, who was the first to suggest I might have what it takes to play in the NFL. He encouraged me to aim high and to think big. I'm here today because of him. Finally, I'd like to thank my wife, who put up with me and stood by me—while doing her best to keep me humble—during this crazy ride. I love you, Susie.'"

"That was very sweet," she said.

"It's true."

"Your mother would've been so proud of you yesterday."

"I hope so."

Susannah continued. "Sanderson, an honors graduate of the University of Florida with a degree in business, was circumspect about his future plans. He said he was looking forward to spending more time with his wife and to having the time to focus some attention on his vast business holdings that, combined with lucrative endorsement deals, have helped to elevate his net worth to an estimated $45 million."

"It's forty-six, actually," he commented dryly. He had no idea what the actual number was.

Susannah chuckled. "His endeavors include several restaurants, a car dealership, a television station, and numerous real estate holdings. He and his wife are also well known in the city for their philanthropic work, especially on behalf of the Boys and Girls Clubs of Metro Denver and Children's Hospital."

"That's it?" he asked.

"That's the main story. There're a couple of columns, too. I liked Paul Dimbroski's."

"He was always good to me."

"Listen to this: 'Sanderson ended his career the same way he played the game—with class and emotion. While shocking in its timing, coming so close on the heels of a third Super Bowl win, Sanderson's decision to go out on top says more than I ever could about his character. While many players milk the ride for all it's worth and force their teams to make tough decisions about once-dominant players, Sanderson showed us once again yesterday that the game itself was always his top priority.'

"I like that," Ryan said.

"I figured you would."

"So where's the bad news?"

"There wasn't any."

"Come on. There's got to be *something* negative."

She flipped the pages. "Well, Bobby Temple has a stick up his butt, but what else is new?"

Ryan howled with laughter. "I love that dirty talk from my little debutante. What did my friend Bobby have to say?"

"It's not worth repeating," she huffed.

"Humor me."

"All right, you asked for it: 'Must be nice to be Ryan Sanderson who can easily afford to thumb his nose at $50 million.' That's basically the gist of it."

"Bobby will never believe we're not all in it for the money."

"He irritates me."

"I know. Me, too."

She reached for her coffee. "Of course that's why he does what he does."

"Enough about him. What time's your appointment?"

"Two."

"I'll drive you."

"No, you won't," she protested. "I can drive myself."

"You have a sore wrist."

"It's my left hand, and I'm not helpless. I'll call you the minute my appointment is over."

"I want to go."

She turned on her side to study him. "What's really going on? This isn't just about my wrist."

He fixed his eyes on the cleavage visible over the top of her zipper. "Two things—one, I'm worried about Henry hassling you."

"He has no idea where I'll be today, so what's number two?"

His jaw shifted with tension. "Is Pam going to think I did that to your wrist?"

"Oh, baby, *no!* I'll tell her it had nothing to do with you."

"Yeah, right," he said with a bitter snort of disbelief. "Like she's going to buy that."

"I'll tell her the truth."

"Will she believe you?"

"I'll make sure she does."

The phone rang, and Ryan reached for it. "Yes, she is," he said. "Just a sec." He handed the phone to Susannah, kissed her cheek, and got out of bed. "I'm going to take a shower."

"Okay." She watched him go before she took the call. "Hello?"

"Hi, Susannah, it's Diane," her divorce attorney said.

"Oh, hi, Diane. I guess you saw the press conference."

"I did. I'm calling to tell you the judge saw it, too, and he'd still like to see you both on Monday at eleven as planned."

"Can't we just withdraw the petition?" Susannah asked.

"Nothing is that simple with this judge. You should know that by now."

"All right. We'll be there."

"So will I. Just in case I'm needed. Are you happy, Susannah? Is this what you really want? You were so determined to go forward with the divorce."

"I'm beyond happy. We've worked everything out. Thank you for all your help and support. You were a rock."

"I'm glad for you and for me, too. I don't get to see many happy endings."

"This is definitely going to be a happy ending. I'll see you on Monday."

"Actually, I'll see you at the ball."

"Great. I'll look forward to it. Thanks again for all you did for me, Diane."

"No problem."

Susannah arrived for her two o'clock appointment with five minutes to spare. She had managed to convince Ryan she could take care of herself for a couple of hours and had driven herself into the city. As she waited for the doctor, her heart beat with excitement and anxiety and—despite all her tough talk from yesterday—fear. How would she ever stand to wait thirty-nine weeks to find out if she could carry a baby to term, and what would she do if the same thing happened again?

Before she had time to work herself into a total state of hysteria, she was called into the exam room and handed a gown. She changed quickly and sat on the table, chilled to the bone all of a sudden. It was hard to say what she was more afraid to hear—that she was pregnant or that she wasn't. Maybe it was too soon to find out anyway. Gnawing on her thumbnail, Susannah willed the door to open so she could get this over with.

Pam Dennis swept into the room ten minutes later, full of apologies for keeping Susannah waiting. She greeted her patient with a warm hug. Besides their doctor-patient relationship, they'd worked together on several committees and had become friends over the years. "It's so good to see you, Susannah, and I was *thrilled* to hear you're back with Ryan."

"Yes, it's been quite a week."

Pam sat down and crossed her legs. "How did Henry take the news?"

"Not so great. In fact, this happened when I broke off our engagement." Susannah held up her bruised wrist. "I don't think he meant to hurt me . . . "

Pam got up, put on her glasses, and switched on a bright light to take a closer look. "Are those fingerprints?"

"I'm afraid so." Susannah winced when the doctor pressed her fingers against the bone. "It isn't broken, though, is it?"

"I can't tell without an X-ray."

"But you don't think it is, do you?"

"I really don't know. It looks like it must've hurt."

"It did."

"I can't picture Henry doing something like this."

"Neither could I—before yesterday, that is."

"You know," Pam said, appearing to weigh her words carefully, "this technically qualifies as assault. If you wanted to file charges—"

"No." Susannah shook her head. "I just want to move forward with Ryan, and I want to forget about what happened yesterday. In fact, the main reason I'm here is I'm wondering if I might be pregnant."

Pam's warm brown eyes widened with delight. "Really? What're you feeling?"

"Hungry—all the time. And kind of full and tingly," she said, with a hand over her chest. "Here. Just like before, with Justin." She dropped her hand to her lap.

Pam put her hand over Susannah's. "And you're already preparing yourself to lose a baby you don't even know for sure you're having. Am I right?"

"Something like that."

"Why don't we take this one step at a time? A quick urine test will tell us what we want to know. While we're waiting for the results, we'll do an exam. I'll also take a film of your wrist to rule out a fracture. Sound good?"

Susannah nodded. "If I *am* pregnant, it's not by much, only a week or so. It might be too soon . . ."

Pam squeezed her hand. "Then we'll do a blood test, too, just to be sure. Everything's going to be fine, Susannah."

"I'm going to do my very best to believe you."

Chapter 21

RYAN PARKED IN ALMOST THE SAME SPOT IN FRONT OF THE bank he'd scored the day before. He sat there for several minutes reminding himself that Susie had forbidden him to kill Henry. When he decided he was ready to face the other man without harming him, he got out of the car and went inside. He was so focused on his mission that he missed the stares he received from several bank patrons.

Holding his Stetson, he stepped off the elevator on the second floor and walked into Henry's outer office.

His assistant's mouth fell open when she recognized Ryan. "Um, good morning, Mr. Sanderson. May I help you with something?"

"I'd like to see Mr. Merrill, please."

"Ah, let me check to see if he's available. Would you like to have a seat?"

"I'll stand. Thank you."

She got up and scurried into Henry's office. Several minutes passed before she returned. "Mr. Merrill will see you now."

"Thank you."

Ryan walked into the spacious office and closed the door behind him.

"What do you want?" Henry asked.

"Before I say anything else you need to know the only reason I'm not here to kill you is because Susannah asked me not to."

"That's a huge relief. Thanks for clearing that up."

In a flash, Ryan tossed his hat onto a table, crossed the room, and hauled the smaller man out of his leather chair. With his face half an inch from Henry's, Ryan said, "I'm only going to say this one time, so you'd better listen up. If you *ever* lay a hand on her again, I *will* kill you, and I'll make sure it's a slow, painful death. You got me?"

Henry's face was red from rage and the chokehold Ryan had him in. "What are you talking about? I never touched her!"

"*The hell you didn't!* She's at the doctor right now finding out if her wrist is broken from what you did to her yesterday!"

"I didn't mean to hurt her," Henry said, but the coldness in his hazel eyes told a different story.

"I don't believe you, and neither does she. So I'm going to make this really simple. Stay the fuck away from her, or you'll be dealing with me, and the next time I won't be *half* as friendly as I'm being now. Am I clear?" When the other man didn't answer right away, Ryan tightened his grip.

"Yes," Henry croaked.

Ryan released him, and Henry sagged into his chair, tugging at the collar of his shirt. "You've really got the macho man act perfected, don't you?"

"I'd rather be macho than passive aggressive, which is your preferred method. At least my way is honest."

Henry's eyes narrowed. "What's that supposed to mean?"

"Give me a break. You know exactly what I mean. Your goal in life has been to fill her with doubts about me and to undermine our marriage. Ironic, isn't it, that the one she should've been watching out for was you."

"I've never been anything but a good friend to her."

"That's the biggest bunch of bullshit I've ever heard."

"You may've won this round, but this is not over, Sanderson."

"Oh, yes it is. It ends right now. You're out of her life—out of both of our lives—for good."

"You're fooling yourself if you think she won't come to her senses and realize what a big mistake she's making."

"She *has* come to her senses. The mistake she made was thinking she could trust you."

"You're playing way out of your league with her, and you have been from the very beginning. But of course you know that."

The comment was a direct hit to one of Ryan's deepest insecurities—that despite all his success, he had married up. "Sure I do," he said with bravado he didn't really feel. "But she doesn't seem to be complaining. What did this morning's paper say I was worth? Was it forty million?" He scratched his chin. "Or forty-five? I can't remember."

Henry's smirk faded. "Too bad all that money can't buy breeding, and it sure as hell can't buy class, two things you're sorely lacking. She'll wise up to you. She did before, and she will again. And when she does, good old Henry will be there to pick up the pieces, just like always."

It took everything Ryan had not to pummel the guy. "Stay the fuck away from her. I mean it. You do *not* want to screw with me."

"You've made your point. I think you know the way out."

Ryan picked up his hat, but before he left he turned back to Henry. "Why don't you just go back to New York or wherever you were before? There's nothing here for you anymore."

"Oh, I disagree. I'm giving it a month, two at the most. You'll screw it up. You always do. And when you do, I'll be waiting right here to clean up your mess. It's what I do best."

Ryan glared at him. "Leave us alone, or you'll be very sorry."

"You're the one who's going to be sorry."

Ryan decided to give him the last word. He'd said everything he had come there to say, and he was proud of himself for letting the little worm live. He decided to get out of there before he forgot he'd promised Susie he wouldn't kill the bastard. But damn, he *wanted* to!

His heart beating hard and his breathing heavy, Ryan rode the elevator to the first floor. The little worm had gotten off a few well-aimed shots, but Ryan believed he had won the battle and the war. He checked his watch and discovered it was two thirty. *Why hasn't Susie called me yet?* In the car, he tried to reach her, and when she didn't answer, he was filled with irrational fear. Some of Henry's barbs had hit too close to home, and Ryan was desperate for some reassurance that everything was all right. Hearing her on the voicemail message made him feel better. He hung up without leaving a message, certain she'd call him the minute she left the doctor's office.

"Does he think I don't know I married up?" Ryan said out loud as he pulled into traffic. He had a meeting at three with his attorneys to figure out how his retirement would affect his endorsement deals. "He's in for a rude awakening if he thinks he's going to get another shot with her," Ryan muttered. "The only way that's going to happen is if I'm dead."

Susannah finally called as he pulled into the parking lot at his lawyers' office. "Hey, baby, what did she say? Is it broken?"

"No, just a bad sprain."

"Oh, good," he said with a deep sigh of relief.

"She wants me to wear a brace for a week or two until it feels better."

"I know just what you need. I'll pick one up for you."

"That'd be great. Thanks."

"Is everything else okay?"

"Everything's fine. Where are you?"

"Heading in to see the lawyers, but I can do it another time if you need me."

"No, go ahead. I have a few errands to do. When you're done there, will you meet me at The Brown Palace?" she asked, referring to one of the city's most luxurious hotels.

"What's at The Brown?" he asked, confused.

"You'll see."

"You're being very mysterious."

"Will you meet me?"

"Wild horses couldn't keep me away."

She chuckled. "Ask at the desk. They'll tell you where I am."

"I'll do that. Susie?"

"Yeah?"

"I love you. You know that, don't you?"

"Of course I do. Why would you ask me that?"

"Just making sure."

"I love you, too, and I'll see you soon."

"Yes, you certainly will."

A liveried doorman dressed in hunter green greeted Ryan when he arrived at The Brown Palace just after five thirty.

"Good evening, Mr. Sanderson." The effort to maintain his professional demeanor was clearly a challenge for the star-struck young man. "It's an honor to welcome you to The Brown Palace. May I take care of your car for you?"

With a glance at the young man's nametag, Ryan said, "Thank you, Tom." He grabbed a plastic bag off the passenger seat and handed Tom his keys and a twenty-dollar bill. "Take good care of it for me. It's new."

"Yes, sir!" He whistled for a valet and issued strict instructions to give the car VIP treatment.

Ryan chuckled when he heard Tom excitedly whisper, *"That's Ryan Sanderson!"*

"What brings you to The Brown tonight, Mr. Sanderson?"

"I'm meeting my wife. Can you help me track her down?"

"Right this way."

Ryan followed him inside where high tea was being served in the lobby.

"Give me one minute," Tom said, gesturing Ryan toward a chair.

While he waited, Ryan acknowledged the stares—and gawks—from staff and patrons alike with a friendly nod that discouraged anyone from approaching him. It was a routine he had perfected over the years, and it allowed him to venture into public without being mobbed everywhere he went. Susannah loved to poke fun at the fact that he only needed "the nod" in Denver, where he was a local celebrity. During their separation, however, he had needed security to get through LaGuardia Airport. He'd have to tell her about that one of these days.

Tom returned with a key card for Ryan. "Your wife is waiting for you in one of the Top of the Brown suites on the ninth floor."

Perplexed, Ryan said, "She is?" He had expected to meet her at the bar or in one of the restaurants.

Tom rattled off the room number as he pointed to a bank of elevators next to the front door.

"Interesting." Ryan shook Tom's hand. "Thanks for your help."

"My pleasure. Enjoy your evening."

"I believe I will," Ryan said with a grin and a wave. Holding his coat and hat, he rode the elevator with growing curiosity. *What is she up to?*

Using his key in the door, Ryan walked in to find the elegant sitting room bathed in candlelight. Soft music filled the air and a bottle of champagne chilled next to a table set for two. He had just noticed a pair of beautifully wrapped gifts when Susannah appeared at the doorway to the bedroom.

"I thought you'd never get here."

Still absorbing the rest, he finally glanced over at her and almost swallowed his tongue. She was in black from head to toe: a lace teddy that left nothing to the imagination, garters, thigh-high fishnet hose, spiked heels, and a flowing silk robe she'd left open to ensure maximum effect, which was instantaneous and painful.

He was speechless.

Chapter 22

SHE SAUNTERED OVER TO HIM AND TOOK HIS HAT AND COAT. Laying them over a chair, she looped her arms around his neck. "Cat got your tongue, baby?" she asked with the amused lift of an eyebrow.

"You could say that." He molded her to him and leaned down to capture her mouth for a deep, sensual kiss. He found it hard to breathe as her tongue met his in an explosive burst of passion, like she hadn't seen him in days rather than hours. With his hands encircling her waist, he lifted her against his instant erection. Her lips were moist and slick as they slid enthusiastically over his.

When he finally came up for air, he managed to ask, "To what do I owe this most amazing surprise?"

"We're celebrating."

He wanted to feel her everywhere, and then taste her, and then, well . . . Forcing himself to bring his eyes back to hers, he asked, "Celebrating what?"

"Your retirement, of course. What else would it be?"

"I thought we were just meeting for a drink or something."

"We are." She took him by the hand and led him over to where champagne awaited them. "Care to do the honors?"

"Sure." He handed her the plastic bag. "I brought you this, but I can see I should've put more thought into my gift."

She chuckled when she opened the bag to find the wrist brace he had promised her. "Thank you. I'll treasure it always, but you'll understand if I don't put it on right away. It'll clash with my outfit."

He untwisted the wire covering the cork. "Just so I'm certain they gave me the right key, are you the same girl who was telling me only this morning that we needed to find something else to do besides have sex all the time?"

With a look of pure innocence, she asked, "Who said anything about sex?"

He threw his head back and laughed. A moment later he sent the cork flying across the room.

Susannah was ready with two crystal glasses. She handed one of them to him. "Here's to my husband, the retiree, who not only went out on top but did it with tremendous grace and a great deal of class. I'm very proud of you, and I can't wait to see what happens next."

As he touched his glass to hers, Ryan wanted to say, "Take *that*, Henry." Instead, what he said was, "Thank you, baby. I'm just overwhelmed. I can't believe you did all this."

"I had a little time to kill this afternoon."

"I'd hate to see what you could come up with if you had a *lot* of time to kill."

"Since we have nothing but time these days, maybe I'll show you."

Amused and amazed, he could only stare at her. "You're so incredibly beautiful. I seriously almost swallowed my tongue when I saw you in that get up."

"Don't do that! I might have a use for it later."

"Susie . . . " He reached for her, but she took a step back.

"Not so fast. We have an agenda."

"Oh, really?"

She held a chair for him at the table. "Have a seat."

"Do I have to?"

Her stern expression answered for her.

"All right. If you insist."

She served him caviar, pate, and crackers.

"Where did you get all this?" he asked.

"I had to run into Nordstrom to pick up my gown for the ball, so I hit the gourmet shop—and the lingerie department—while I was there."

Reminding himself to chew and swallow, he took a long drink of his champagne. He was hard as a rock, and she expected him to sit here and eat crackers and make small talk? "What's next on the agenda?" he asked, shifting in his seat in an effort to find some relief.

"Don't be so impatient." She spooned some of the black caviar onto a delicate cracker and handed it to him. "Remember the first time you tried caviar?"

"In Paris, after my first season with the Mavs," he recalled. "You tricked me into eating it before you told me what it really was."

She grinned at the memory. "I wish I had a picture of the face you made when I broke the news to you. It was priceless."

"I've learned to like it as long as I don't think too much about what it is I'm actually eating."

"You've learned to like a lot of things you'd never tried before. Escargot, pate, paella . . ."

He fiddled with the stem of his wine glass.

"What are you thinking about?" she asked, taking a sip of her champagne.

"Do you ever feel like you, you know, married down?"

Her eyes narrowed with confusion. "What do you mean by that?"

"You had money growing up. You were even a debutante. I was just a hard-knock kid from Dallas who could throw a ball farther than anyone else. I didn't even know what a debutante *was* until I was your date to your coming-out thingy." He laughed. "Hell, I don't even know what you call it."

She stared at him with disbelief. "Are you *serious?* You have more money than anyone I know."

"It's not the same as growing up with it."

"Where's all this coming from?"

"I was just wondering." He had decided not to upset her by telling her about his visit with Henry. "Forget about it. I didn't mean to ruin the mood."

She got up and came around the table to straddle his lap. "I don't know where you're getting these foolish ideas, but let me set you straight."

He took advantage of the opportunity to reach inside her robe and fill his hands with soft buttocks.

"Now, you have to promise me this won't go straight to your fat head . . . "

His chuckle died in his throat when she ran her tongue up his neck.

"I'm the envy of every woman I know. Not only did I land a rich, successful football player for a husband, but he also happens to be *People* magazine's most recent pick for sexiest athlete alive."

He winced. "You saw that, did you?"

"Oh, yes, I saw it. I was sorry I wasn't with you to bring you back down to earth—"

"As only you can."

"As only I can." She turned her attention to his ear. "So I don't want to hear any more talk about marrying down or any other such craziness."

"How about no more talk at all?" he asked with a hopeful smile.

She moved provocatively on his lap, drawing an agonized groan from him. "While I can see—and feel—the merits of that suggestion, next on our agenda is gifts."

He brightened. "Can I pick which gift I want?"

"Unfortunately, no." She got up and went over to where she had left one very large and one very small gift. "Let's see, which one first?" She picked up the larger of the two and brought it to him. "This one."

"That would *not* have been my first choice. I'd like that to be reflected in the minutes."

Her throaty, sexy laugh only added to his discomfort. "So noted."

The package, wrapped in shiny gold paper, was three feet tall and two feet wide. He couldn't begin to guess what he'd find inside. Since she was all but bursting with anticipation, he decided to give her a taste of her own medicine. He shook the present lightly.

"Just *open* it, will you?"

"I *am*. It's my present. I should be able to open it any way I want to."

She sighed with frustration. "You won't get any others unless you hurry up."

He tore off the paper and found the front page of the day's newspaper framed and matted in Mavericks' yellow and purple. "Susie! This is *great!* How did you get it done so fast?"

"I have a few connections of my own in this city."

"I can see that."

"I figured you'd want it for your collection."

He nodded. "I love it. Thank you."

"Where is all your football stuff? I thought you would've taken it to the cabin."

"It's at my place across town."

"I never did anything with that room after you moved out, so you can bring it all home now," she said with a shy smile. "If you want to, that is."

"I want to." He reached out a hand to her. "I want to very much. Thank you for my present. There's nothing you could give me that I'd love more."

"Oh, we'll see about that," she said with a coy smile.

He turned her hand over and pressed his lips to the palm. "Not only is she beautiful and incredibly sexy, but my wife is also very mysterious this evening. She's got me so turned on I couldn't tell you my own name right now, and still she torments me."

She glanced down at his lap, which only served to make his situation worse. "That looks kind of uncomfortable."

"Do you *think?*" he asked in a strangled tone.

"I'm reluctant to deviate from the agenda, but I want you to relax and enjoy your celebration." She urged him to his feet. "Why don't we take care of your little problem so we can get back on schedule."

He raised an eyebrow. "*Little* problem?"

"I meant *big* problem," she giggled. "*Huge.*"

"Better."

She reached up and began unbuttoning the light blue shirt he'd worn with khakis for his meeting with the attorneys. "You're overdressed for this party anyway." Pushing the shirt off his shoulders, she nuzzled his chest hair and dropped hot kisses along his collarbone.

He groaned. "Is that supposed to be helping? Because it's not working. My problem seems to be getting bigger by the second."

When she tugged on the button to his pants, he had to grit his teeth to keep from exploding on the spot. He grasped her hand. "Give me a second, baby," he said with a deep breath.

She gazed up at him with eyes so blue he could drown in them. "You look like you're in pain. I wanted you to enjoy this."

"Oh, trust me, I am." He held her tight against him. "I don't ever recall enjoying a celebration more."

"And we're just getting started."

"Am I going to be able to walk out of here under my own steam when you're through with me?"

She cracked up. "I guess we'll find out. How's it going down there?"

"The crisis has passed. Feel free to proceed."

She quickly divested him of his pants and backed him up to an easy chair.

"Let's go to bed," he pleaded.

"Not yet," she whispered, kneeling down in front of him.

He almost launched out of the chair when she dragged her tongue over his inner thigh. "*Susie . . .*" he gasped. "What're you doing?"

"While I was waiting for Pam today, I read the new issue of *Cosmo.*"

"Oh, sweet *Jesus,*" he groaned. "What did you learn this time?"

She stroked him through his boxers.

He closed his eyes, rested his head against the back of the chair, and exhaled another long deep breath.

"Did you know," she asked, as she freed his straining erection, "that men are most sensitive right here?" She used her tongue to make her point.

"*Susannah,*" he hissed.

"I had no idea. I would've guessed it to be more sensitive here."

Ryan broke out in a sweat as his heart hammered in his chest. "Susie, please . . . "

"Is this what you want?" While continuing to stroke him with her hand, she took him into her mouth.

He clutched handfuls of her soft hair in a futile attempt to regain some control over an out-of-control situation. Hanging by a thread, he almost lost it completely when she added her tongue to the mix.

He bit down hard on his lip in an effort to detract some attention away from the fire building in his lap. "Susie, that's enough . . . *Susie!*" The orgasm hit him hard as one tidal wave after another pounded through him until he was so spent it was all he could do to breathe.

She kissed her way up his belly to his chest. "Feel better?"

"Yeah," he panted, his eyes still closed and his fingers still buried in her hair. "I need to retire more often. You've never done that before . . . the whole thing like that . . . "

Her cheeks turned to a fetching shade of pink that was in sharp contrast to her sex goddess outfit. "Did you like it?"

"No, I hated it. Couldn't you tell?"

Laughing softly, she asked, "Can we get back to my agenda now?"

"You've wiped me out. I might need a nap first."

"Really?"

She sounded so crestfallen that he forced himself to rally. "Nah. Just stay here with me for another minute. Since I have no idea how long it'll take to get my hands on you again with this damned agenda of yours, I'm afraid to let you go."

"We have just a few items left before we get to new business."

"Is that when I get to take a closer look at what you've got on under that robe?"

"If you're good."

"You missed your calling as a dominatrix."

Her face lit up with what might've been pleasure. "Do you think so?"

"I'm terrified to answer that question."

She chuckled as she got up to get the other present. When she returned, she snuggled onto his lap.

"What've you got there?"

"Just something I found today at the Sixteenth Street Mall."

"You got around this afternoon, didn't you?"

She became serious. "Open it, Ry."

He tore off the paper and found what had to be the tiniest Ryan Sanderson jersey in all of Colorado. "Very cute, but I don't think it'll fit."

"It's not for you."

"Then who . . . " He stopped and stared at her. "Susie?" She nodded.

"Really?" he asked, his eyes filling with tears. "Already?"

"It probably happened that first time at the cabin."

Tears rolled down his face as he clung to her. "I told you my boys were well rested."

She laughed through her own tears. "Now we know the secret: no sex for a year, and then bam, pregnant."

He rested a reverent hand on her belly. "If that's what it takes, I hope this guy doesn't mind being an only child, because there's *no way* I'm ever again going without for a year." He held her tightly as he struggled to absorb the news. "Is this why you had the doctor's appointment today?"

"Uh-huh. I've been waking up every morning starving and was feeling some other signs that reminded me of when I was first pregnant with . . . Justin." Her voice had faded to a whisper by the time she said his name. "Just like then, I could tell almost right away."

Brushing the hair back from her face, he asked, "Are you scared, baby?"

Her chin quivered. "Petrified," she said with a brave smile even as her eyes glistened with new tears.

"Me, too," he confessed.

"Pam said everything's fine, and we have to believe it's going to stay that way."

"She's right, of course."

"It's going to be a *long* thirty-nine weeks," she said with a sigh.

"Agonizing."

"But at the end of it, we might just have a baby."

"We *will* have a baby."

"Yes." She toyed with the tiny shirt. "But until we do, this is the only thing I want either of us to buy, okay?"

Remembering the painful dismantling of Justin's nursery, he understood exactly what she was asking of him. He nodded. "Whatever you want."

"I also don't want to tell anyone until I start to show. That way there's no one to tell if, well . . . I don't want to tell anyone."

"That's fine. It'll be our secret until we decide to share it."

"Thank you for understanding." He watched her make a huge effort to pull herself together and not let her fears take over their special evening. "Next on the agenda is more champagne."

"Um, don't hate me for asking, but should you be having that?"

"It's sparkling cider," she said with a smile as she got up to refill their glasses. "I was hoping you wouldn't notice."

"Very clever." He took his glass from her and brought her back down to his lap. "What comes next?"

"New business."

"Finally," he sighed, hooking his hand around her neck to bring her in for a kiss that was gentle, possessive, and very, very thorough.

Chapter 23

RYAN LAY WITH HIS EAR PRESSED TO SUSANNAH'S stomach. "Hello, in there, it's me, Dad. Sorry if we disturbed you, but you're going to have to get used to it. I seem to have trouble keeping my hands off of Mommy, especially lately. Someday you'll understand."

Her fingers combing through his hair, Susannah dissolved into quiet laughter.

"Do us a favor," Ryan continued, "and let us know if there's anything we can do to make your stay more comfortable." He kissed her bellybutton. "Just don't check out without telling us."

"Ry . . ."

He kissed a path to her lips. "Sorry."

She held him close and watched the flickers of light coming from the candles he had carried into the bedroom.

After a long period of contented silence, he said, "I was wondering."

"About?"

"Do you think it's possible Justin suspected we weren't ready for him?"

"What do you mean?" she asked, startled by the question.

"Well, it took us so long to conceive him."

She nodded. "Years."

"But this guy," he said, running his hand over her belly.

"Or gal . . ."

"Or gal. He or she didn't seem quite so reluctant to join our family. Perhaps it's because we're ready for him—or her—and we weren't before. Mommy and Daddy still had some things to figure out." He looked up at her with his heart in his eyes. "Is that dumb?"

"No," she whispered. "Not at all."

"Then we shouldn't have anything to worry about. This little person was meant to be, and Justin was meant to teach us a few things."

Susannah hiccupped as she tried in vain to stem a flood of tears.

Alarmed, Ryan sat up and brought her into his arms. "What, baby? I didn't mean to make you cry."

"You didn't," she said between deep gulping sobs.

"Then what's wrong?"

"You just . . . "

"What, Susie? Tell me. What did I do?"

"What you said . . . It gives his life meaning. He came into our lives to show us what really matters."

Ryan wiped away her tears. "Yes. That's what I meant. It took us a while to get the message, but I think he'd be proud of us now."

"I think so, too."

"I'm sorry I upset you."

"These aren't sad tears."

"No?"

She shook her head. "Thank you," she said, clutching his hand. "For helping me to see it that way."

He leaned his forehead against hers.

"Do you remember when they made us hold him in the delivery room?"

"Yeah," he whispered.

"I didn't want to, but now I'm glad I did."

"So am I. They said it might take a while for us to understand why it was so important."

"It only took two years."

"Are you okay?"

"I'm good. How about you?"

"Never better."

"You're going to have to get used to the tears. Remember the last time?"

He groaned and fell back against the pillow, bringing her with him. "I'd forgotten."

"And the heartburn and the cravings."

"Do I get to rub cocoa butter on your belly again? I liked that part."

"So did I." She dragged a finger lazily over his chest and stomach. "Remember what I craved the most?"

He smiled. "I *sure* do. Lucky for you, I'm retired now and available on a moment's notice to satisfy any and all cravings."

"A moment's notice, huh?"

"Yep." He yawned and stretched. "Are you hungry?"

"No."

"Tired?"

"No."

He glanced over at her and seemed startled by her expression. "What?"

She crooked her finger at him.

When he tilted his head closer to hers, she whispered in his ear.

Shocked, he asked, "*Now?*"

She nodded.

He stared at her.

"You said a moment's notice . . . "

"What *is it* about that outfit?"

She laughed. "Apparently, it came with an attitude."

"Do we get to keep it?"

"The outfit or the attitude?"

"Both."

"Bought and paid for. Now, quit talking and get busy. I'm not getting any younger over here."

"Yes, ma'am."

"*Oh,* I like that," she gasped a moment later. "And *that.*"

"We've turned The Brown Palace into a no-tell motel," Ryan said the next morning as they prepared to leave.

"Why do you say that?"

He picked up the framed newspaper page. "Leaving in the same clothes we wore in, no luggage . . . It's all very seedy."

"I have my luggage." She twirled the Nordstrom bag on her finger. "So you're the only one who's seedy."

"I was lured here under false pretenses."

"You loved it."

Propping the frame on the chair that still held his hat and coat, he took her into his arms. "You're absolutely right. I loved every sinful minute of it. Thank you so much for the most unforgettable night."

She went up on tiptoes to kiss him. "It was completely and entirely my pleasure."

"Do we need to check out?"

"Nah, I paid by the hour," she joked and was rewarded with the dimpled grin she so adored.

"Have you got everything?" he asked.

"I think so."

"No fishnets under the bed or anything else that'll end up in the paper?" He was kidding, but they had learned to be careful.

"Don't worry. I checked."

"Let's go." He held the door for her. "If they only knew what was in that bag of yours . . . "

"See if you can behave until we get out of here, will you?"

In the elevator, he pinned her against the wall and kissed her like he hadn't spent the whole night doing just that.

She giggled as she pushed on his chest. "Stop."

"We're having a baby," he whispered.

"Yes, we are."

"I can't wait."

Laughing softly, she cuffed his jaw. "You'd better find some patience. We've got a long road ahead of us."

A bell chimed to indicate they had reached the lobby where they ran into the doorman Ryan had befriended the night before. "Good morning, Tom."

Tom's face lit up with delight that Ryan had remembered him. "Good morning, Mr. Sanderson, ma'am."

"This is my wife, Susannah."

"Pleased to meet you," Tom said, shaking her hand.

"You, too," Susannah said.

"I wondered if you could do me a favor, Tom," Ryan said.

"Of course. Anything you need."

Ryan pressed his valet ticket and a hundred dollar bill into the astounded man's hand. "Can you bring the Escalade to my house in Cherry Hills when you get through with work?"

"For real?"

Ryan laughed. "Yes, for real." He rattled off the address. "I'd really appreciate it."

"I'd be happy to," Tom stammered.

"Can you get a ride home?"

"No problem."

Ryan shook his hand. "Great. If we're not home, leave the keys in the mailbox."

"I will."

"Thanks again," Ryan said, ushering Susannah to the door with his arm around her.

"What was that all about?" she asked.

"I want to drive you home."

"Oh, for God's sake, Ryan! I can drive myself. What if that kid steals your car?"

"He won't."

"How do you know?"

"He and I are old friends."

She laughed and handed her valet ticket to the attendant. "This is going to be a *very long* thirty-nine weeks if you're going to be doing this kind of stuff all the time."

"What kind of stuff? Driving my wife home?"

She shot him a withering look. "Hovering."

"Loving," he corrected.

"Smothering."

"Adoring."

"Suffocating."

"Protecting."

They suspended the debate when the valet arrived with her silver Mercedes coupe.

Ryan held the passenger door for Susannah and then walked around to the driver's side after stashing the frame in the trunk. "Thanks very much," he said, tipping the valet with a twenty. He stuffed himself into the small car and shifted the seat back as far as it would go but still could've used another foot.

"You need to scale back on the tipping," she said when they had pulled onto Seventeenth Street. "I hate to remind you, but you're unemployed."

"You'll be glad to know we won't be on the bread line any time soon. I found out yesterday that my endorsements are safe despite my retirement."

"Oh, I meant to ask you what they had said."

"Apparently, my Q score is intact," he said, referring to the formula used to determine the value of a persona or image.

Susannah nodded. "They'd be crazy to dump you, especially now when you'll be all over the media for a while. I'll be surprised if there's ever a dip in your Q."

"I should've brought you with me to the meeting. That marketing degree of yours is going to come in handy."

"I hope I get to finish it before the baby arrives."

"You should have plenty of time, right?"

"We'll see how I'm feeling. I was so tired the last time. If it's that bad again, school might have to wait."

"I want you to finish, so we'll do it together. I'll help you study."

"I can just imagine your kind of help."

"Magna cum laude, baby. You'd be lucky to have me, and since it's you, I'll keep my fee very reasonable."

"Something tells me we aren't talking about money."

"More of what you were handing out last night should do the trick."

"Eyes on the road, Ryan."

They arrived home twenty minutes later to find Henry's Toyota parked in the driveway.

"What the hell is he doing here?" Ryan fumed. He leaped from the car but came to a halt when Henry's mother emerged. "Oh . . . "

Susannah got out of her car. "Mrs. Merrill?"

With a nervous glance at Ryan, Henrietta said, "Do you think I could speak to you for a moment, Susannah?"

"Of course. Please come in."

Ryan unlocked the front door and disabled the alarm. He took Susannah's coat and offered to take Henrietta's.

"I'll hang on to it, thank you," she said, appearing to make a huge effort to refrain from looking at him.

"Can I get you something to drink?" he asked.

"No, thank you."

"Come on into the den," Susannah said, making brief eye contact with Ryan.

He squeezed her hand and left her with an encouraging smile.

She led Henrietta into the den. "Are you sure I can't get you anything?"

"You can cut out the social graces, Susannah. We're past that at this point, wouldn't you say?"

Startled, Susannah said, "Yes, I suppose we are. I'm sorry you're upset. I never meant for any of this to happen."

"What *did* you mean to have happen? When you accepted my son's proposal, did you ever have any intention of actually marrying him?"

"Yes," Susannah said softly. "I had every intention of marrying him."

"You've broken his heart—again. For years I've watched you use him as your fallback guy, but I never imagined you'd be capable of something like this." She gestured toward the other room where Ryan had presumably gone.

"I'm sorry Henry's hurt, but there are things about our relationship you don't know."

"There are things *you* don't know. Like, for instance, did you know he left college for a semester after you broke up with him the first time?"

"No," Susannah said, stunned. "I didn't know that. He told me he had an internship . . . "

"He barely left his bedroom for three months. His father and I were despondent over his withdrawal from life. Eventually he pulled himself together, but he never got over what you did to him—until recently, that is. I've never seen him as happy as he was when you two were engaged. He's waited forever for you, Susannah."

"*Don't you see?*" Susannah cried. "While he was waiting for me, he was hoping my marriage would fail! I was nineteen years old. I shouldn't be made to feel responsible for ruining his life because I wasn't ready to commit to my high school boyfriend for a lifetime."

"What about now? Are you responsible this time, Susannah?"

"I deeply regret that I've caused Henry—and you—pain. That was never my intention."

"What was your intention when you sent your *husband* to intimidate my son at his place of business?"

Susannah gasped. "What are you talking about? I never asked Ryan . . ."

Henrietta's round face twisted into a cold smile as she got up to leave. "I wish you the best of luck, Susannah. Apparently you're going to need it. I can show myself out."

After she heard the front door click shut, Susannah sat perfectly still for a long time.

Ryan came into the room holding a sandwich. "Is she gone?" he asked. "Damn, that was awkward, huh?"

"Did you go Henry's office yesterday and hassle him?"

Without blinking an eye, Ryan said, "You're damned right I did."

Chapter 24

"WHY?" SUSANNAH CRIED AS SHE STOOD TO FACE HIM. "I asked you not to do that!"

"No, you said I couldn't kill him. I was very proud of myself for letting him live."

"Why didn't you tell me about it?"

"Because there was no way I was bringing him into that room with us last night, not after you had gone to all that trouble to surprise me." He finished the sandwich with one big bite. "And I didn't want to upset you."

"You didn't tell me because I would've told you not to do it."

"Maybe."

"Why couldn't you have just left it alone?"

His eyes hardened. "He hurt you, Susannah. Did you honestly expect me to let that go? If you did, I guess you don't know me very well."

"I don't expect you to fight my battles for me. You can't be going around intimidating people. It's uncivilized."

"Uncivilized." He took a moment to absorb that. "Right. And what would you call what he did to you? Civilized?"

"Don't be twisting my words all around. You shouldn't have done it."

"Well, I did, and I refuse to apologize for it. I'd do the same thing if I had it to do over again."

"I'm almost afraid to ask, but what exactly *did* you do?"

"I just let him know what would happen if he ever came near you again."

"Care to elaborate?"

He shrugged. "Not really."

"Was the word 'kill' used?"

"Perhaps."

"*Ryan!* You can't be threatening to *kill* people!"

"It's not a threat."

She threw up her hands with frustration and stormed from the room.

Ryan followed her into the kitchen. "Don't be pissed, Susie. It's not worth it. *He's* not worth it."

"You're right, he's not. He's not worth lowering yourself to the level of a common thug. That's exactly what he expects from you."

"Then I'm glad I didn't disappoint him. He *hurt* my wife, and he did it on purpose. He's lucky I didn't have his ass thrown in jail." With his hands on her shoulders, he urged her to look at him. "I needed to take care of this, Susie. Can you please try to understand that?"

She studied his earnest face. "I don't want you doing this kind of stuff. It's beneath you."

"No, it really isn't."

She gasped. "Oh my God." Her hand flew up to cover her mouth. "What you said last night about me marrying down . . . Henry put that idea in your head, didn't he?"

"It doesn't matter."

"*He did!* That rotten son of a bitch!"

Ryan laughed. "Baby, you know it turns me on when you talk like that."

"I can't believe he would say such a thing—especially to a man who can buy and sell him millions of times over."

"Well, I said a few things that might've driven him to it," Ryan conceded.

"What else did he say?"

"Nothing worth repeating."

"Tell me."

"Susie . . ."

"I want to know, Ryan."

He sighed. "Something about all the money in the world not being able to buy class and that he gives us a month, maybe two before I screw it up again. Apparently, he plans to stay in Denver so he can pick up the pieces like he always does."

Enraged, she looked up at him. "I'm sorry you had to hear such ugly things."

"Well, I did start it, so I guess I had it coming." He tugged her tight against him. "Can we please forget about all of this and rewind the clock to when we were having a good day?"

She rested her head on his chest. "I didn't like hearing about it from someone else."

"I'll apologize for that but not the rest."

"I don't want us to have secrets from each other. We've come too far for that."

"I'd never intentionally keep something from you unless I thought it might upset you."

"You don't need to protect me from life, Ryan. I'm not made of glass."

"No, but you're carrying my child and keeping you both safe and happy is the only thing in this world I really care about. So please don't ask me to be anyone other than who I am."

She beat lightly on his chest with her fists. "I want a partner, not a protector."

"Can't I be both?"

"You're enormously exasperating sometimes, do you know that?"

He grinned. "And you love me anyway."

"Don't push your luck, and quit acting like a bully. Since Henry plans to stick around, you'll be running into him from time to time. So you need to try a new tactic. If you ignore him, it'll be much more effective than if you act like you want to beat the crap out of him every time you see him. Our happiness will be the best revenge. He can't touch us unless we let him."

He thought that over for a moment. "I hate to admit you have a point, but you have a point."

She flashed a victorious smile. "Excellent. Now, I have a hair appointment—and *no,* you can*not* come with me."

"But—"

"Ryan, I swear to God, you're going to drive me nuts if you keep this up. Get a hobby, call Bernie, take up golf, find *something* to do."

"What time will you be back?" he asked sullenly.

"Later." He looked so pathetic she reached up to leave him with a kiss that gave him plenty to think about in her absence.

"That wasn't nice," he growled as she walked away from him. "In fact, it was downright *uncivilized!*"

She giggled. "You'll survive."

He was still pouting in the kitchen when she called "love you" on her way out the door. "You, too," he replied, as he contemplated following her. Then he remembered he didn't have a car. "Crap!" His motorcycle was still in the garage, but he never used it in the winter, and he certainly wouldn't risk it with broken ribs that were finally beginning to heal. "*Goddamn it.*"

"Okay," he said to the empty room. "You're officially losing it. She's only going to be gone for a few hours, and nothing's going to happen to her at the hair salon." His gut tightened with anxiety when he thought about the baby and the crazy look he'd seen in Henry's eyes the day before. The combination was enough to fill Ryan with the kind of fear he seldom experienced. The helpless feeling reminded him of his mother being diagnosed with lung cancer at age forty-five after having never smoked a cigarette in her life.

In an effort to pull himself together, he placed calls to Bernie and Darling, but neither of them answered their phones. With nothing else to do, he went into the den to watch Sports Center where he learned the Mavs had officially promoted Todd "Toad" McNeil to starting quarterback.

"That didn't take long," Ryan grumbled. For the first time, he had a tiny twinge of regret over his decision to retire. Feeling like yesterday's news, he watched the coverage of Duke's press conference at which he announced Toad's promotion. Poor Toad still resembled a deer in the headlights as he faced off with the media for the first time as the team's leader.

Ryan watched as much as he could stomach before he flipped through the channels, landing on a special that one of the local channels was running about his own career. "That's better," he said with a grin. But as he relived the glory days at Florida and his tenure with the Mavs, he realized Susie was right. He needed to get a life. Turning off the T.V., he picked up the phone to call his agent. It was time to make a plan. He was still talking to Aaron an hour later when the doorbell rang. Expecting it to be Tom returning his car, Ryan continued his conversation as he swung open the front door.

When he saw who was on his front porch, he said to Aaron, "I'll have to call you back." He clicked off the phone. "What are you doing here?"

Susannah fought the urge to doze as the stylist dried her hair. The action of the brush and the hairdryer was mesmerizing, and after an all-but-sleepless night, she was ready for a nap. But while her body was relaxed, her mind raced. The more she thought about the things Henry had said to Ryan, the angrier she became. To suggest Ryan had married up! What a thing to say! *That must've really hurt him.* He was sensitive about his humble beginnings and fiercely proud of the many sacrifices his mother had made to ensure he had every advantage.

Susannah thought about the mother-in-law she had adored from the first time she met her. Theresa hadn't lived long enough to finish decorating the sprawling house Ryan bought for her in a Dallas suburb. He used his signing bonus—the first real money he'd ever made—to make sure she wouldn't have to work another day in her life. She was diagnosed with cancer just four months later and died soon after. Losing her had been among the most shocking and devastating events in Susannah's life, and for a long time afterward, she had wondered if Ryan would ever recover from the blow. All these years later it was still a raw wound, and just thinking about it made her angrier with Henry for what he had implied to Ryan.

I'm so glad I saw Henry for what he really is before I married him. Susannah was still amazed at the twists and turns her life had taken since Ryan's boots had landed in her foyer nine days earlier. Was it *only* nine days? She chuckled softly and then was swamped with relief that they had gotten back what they had almost lost forever. *Thank you, God, for sending him back to me. Even with all his faults, he's the only man for me.*

While half of her wanted to strangle him for confronting Henry, the other half—the half she would never admit to—was secretly thrilled by what he had done. To have such a strong, protective, and unpredictable man crazy in love with her was exhilarating, to say the least.

She left the salon and did a few last-minute errands in preparation for the ball. On the way home, she checked in with Carol and several of the other vendors, all of whom reported they were ready for tomorrow night's festivities. At this point, Susannah could only hope for the best. Months of planning were coming to fruition, and she had learned from experience that all the worrying in the world wouldn't change the outcome. A few things might go wrong, but she only cared about raising as much money as possible for the hospital. The Mavericks would match whatever they took in, for a grand total that usually hovered around two million dollars.

A car she didn't recognize was parked in the driveway when she got home. Opening the garage door, she discovered Ryan's car had not yet been returned and wondered if they would ever see it again. It was just like him to trust a man he barely knew with something as valuable as his car. She did have to admit, though, his instincts about people were rarely wrong. After all, he had never liked Henry, and in the end he'd been right about him.

She closed the garage door and went into the house through the kitchen, hoping to entice Ryan into joining her for a nap. "Ry?"

"In here," he called from the den.

"Hey, baby, whose car . . . " The words died on her lips when she walked into the den to find her parents and sister waiting for her. "What are you guys doing here?"

"Hello, darling." Her mother stood up to greet Susannah with a warm hug. Grace Freeman was an older version of Susannah, but her hair was short and looked, as it always did, as if she too had just stepped out of the salon.

"Mama," Susannah stammered. "I'm so surprised to see you. Why didn't you tell me you were coming?" She hugged her father. "Hi, Daddy."

"You look beautiful, honey," Dalton Freeman said. He was tall with white hair and bright blue eyes. "But you've had us mighty worried."

"Worried?" Susannah asked, turning to her sister, who made no attempt to hide her dismay.

"Yes, Susannah." Melissa hugged her sister. "Worried."

"I take it you've been talking to Henry."

Melissa glanced at Ryan. "Would you mind giving us a moment alone, Ryan?"

When he would've left the room, Susannah reached for his hand. "He stays. Anything you have to say to me, you can say in front of him."

"This is personal, Susannah," her mother said.

"He's my *husband*. What's personal to me is personal to him."

Ryan squeezed her hand.

"We thought you two were divorcing," Dalton said.

"We're not," Susannah said.

"What about Henry?" Missy cried. "*How can you do this to him?*"

"You know nothing about it, Missy! If you love Henry so much, why don't you marry him?"

"There's no need for that kind of nastiness," Missy said. "You know full well I only want what's best for you."

"If that's the case, then you'll support my marriage to the man *I love*. And for once, you'll butt out of my life and leave us alone."

"Susannah!" Grace said.

"I'm sorry, Mama. I mean no disrespect, but I'm all done trying to justify my marriage to you. If you can't treat my husband with the respect he deserves, then I've got nothing left to say to any of you."

"Be careful, Susannah," Missy warned. "Don't say something you can't take back."

Despite her brave words, Susannah's hands shook with nerves. "What I'm saying is something that should've been said years ago."

Ryan put his arm around her. "Take it easy, baby."

"What happened to your arm?" Grace asked.

Susannah suddenly wished she hadn't taken off the brace. "I sprained my wrist."

"How?" Dalton asked.

"Moving some furniture."

Her mother reached for her hand. "Let me see."

Susannah didn't move fast enough.

Grace gasped. "Are those fingerprints?" She looked up at Ryan with eyes full of contempt.

"Oh, sure." He shook his head with thinly veiled fury. "Naturally, I did it."

"Are you saying you didn't?" Dalton asked.

"That's exactly what I'm saying."

"He didn't do it," Susannah said.

"Well, then who did?" Melissa asked.

Susannah and Ryan exchanged glances.

"Henry did," Susannah said.

Melissa snorted with disbelief. "Do you *seriously* expect us to believe that?"

"Funny you have no problem believing *I'm* capable of it," Ryan said, swearing under his breath.

"Now, Ryan," Dalton said. "No one is saying—"

"Sure you are. I know you think I'm nothing more than a dumb jock, Dalton, but I'm just smart enough to get when I'm being accused of something."

Susannah looped her arm around Ryan's waist. "Henry twisted my arm and sprained my wrist when I ended our engagement. That's the truth whether you choose to believe it or not." She paused, took a breath, and added, "I want you all to leave my home. Right now."

"I don't know what's gotten into you, honey," Dalton said. "But if he's pressuring you—"

"*Daddy!* Will you *listen* to yourself? Ryan is my *husband.* He's not pressuring me to do anything I don't want to do. Either you accept that and him, or there's nothing left for us to say to each other."

"You don't mean that, Susannah," Grace said. "We surprised you by dropping in this way, and it's obvious you're not thinking clearly."

"I meant it, Mama, and I *am* thinking clearly." She stepped back so they could get by her. "Please go now."

"We were hoping to take you to dinner tonight," Dalton said with a smile that had Susannah wondering if he'd heard anything she had said. "You, too, Ryan, of course."

"I'm sorry," Susannah said. "We have plans tonight."

"When we told Henry we were coming for the weekend, he got us tickets to the ball," Missy said. "We'll see you there."

Susannah didn't say another word as her mother and sister brushed by her on their way to the front door. Her chin quivered when her father stopped and placed a kiss on her forehead.

"I love you, honey."

"Bye, Daddy," she whispered.

Ryan closed the door behind them and returned to Susannah. He hugged her so fiercely he lifted her off her feet.

"*Ryan!* Your ribs! Put me down."

"In a minute." But one minute stretched into two and then a third. Finally, he eased her down. "I'm so sorry you had to go through that. I really am. But *damn,* baby, you let them *have* it."

"Did I?" she asked with a shy smile.

"Oh, yeah. You were scary tough."

She rested her hands on his chest. "I'm sorry you had to hear it. I was wishing I'd let you leave the room."

"No, you were right. We have to present a united front." He paused when his voice broke. "You showed me a lot in there just now, Susie."

"Hopefully, you saw how much I love you and how much I want our marriage to work."

"I saw all of that and so much more."

Susannah reached up to kiss him. When she finally released him, his fingers had tunneled into her hair.

"I messed up your pretty hair," he said, dropping soft kisses along her jaw.

She tilted her head to give him better access. "I don't care."

"It smells so good. Mmmm. I love it."

"How long were they here before I got home?"

"About twenty minutes."

She winced. "Were they nice to you?"

"They were okay," he said with a shrug. "They weren't very happy to see me, though. I think they'd been hoping it wasn't true."

"Well, now they know it is."

"They're your family. You can't just cut them off completely—"

With her fingers on his lips, she silenced him. "You're my family. You and the baby."

"I love you, Susie. I've always loved you, but what you did just now, sticking up for me like that . . . I love you more than ever. I don't know what I would've done if you hadn't given me another chance."

She took his hand and headed for the stairs. "I'm so glad you blackmailed me into it."

"Blackmail is such an ugly word."

She laughed.

"Where're we going?" he asked.

"I'd hoped to cajole you into taking a nap with me when I got home."

"What about those plans you told them we had tonight?"

"That was it."

He howled with laughter. "I love it!"

"I had a feeling you would. By the way, no sign of your car yet, huh?"

"He'll be here."

She sat down on the bed. "He's halfway to Vegas by now."

"So little faith." He clucked with disapproval as he knelt down in front of her and removed her shoes. "How's the bambino doing?"

"She's getting hungry."

He raised an eyebrow. "*She?* Is that a hunch or a strike for women's lib?"

"No hunches. Just making sure you're aware of the possibility that *it* might be a *she.*"

"Can you imagine me with a little girl?" he asked as he massaged her feet.

"God help her and any man who ever wants to date her."

The thought made him shudder. "God help *me*. If she's anything like her mother, she'll have me wrapped around her finger in no time flat."

Susannah's stomach growled, which made them laugh.

"All right, I hear you," Ryan said to her belly. "Do you want to go out?"

She shook her head. "Let's order in."

"Sounds good to me."

"Ry?"

"Hmm?"

"It's going to stay like this, right?"

"What is?"

"I just want to pinch myself because I've never been so happy. Even before, when it was really good between us, it wasn't like this. I'm so afraid it won't last."

"Susannah," he sighed. "It's going to last forever."

"Promise?"

He kissed one of her hands and then the other. "I promise."

Chapter 25

SUSANNAH TOOK ONE LAST LOOK IN THE FULL-LENGTH mirror. Her simple black silk gown left one shoulder and most of her back bare, which ruled out a bra. As she moved this way and that to make sure nothing would fall out of the dress, her stomach knotted with tension. Henry would be there tonight, most likely with his parents, her parents, her sister . . .

She wished she could skip the whole thing and spend another quiet night at home with Ryan. If she hadn't been the chairperson of the event, she would've invented a stomach bug to get out of it. After this, she and Ryan were getting off the social merry-go-round for a while. They needed to spend some time together that didn't include regularly running into Henry.

"I just hope he doesn't make a scene tonight," she whispered to her reflection. The charms on her bracelet jingled as she smoothed a hand over the French knot in her hair. "Please let them all just leave us alone."

With one last deep breath for courage, she picked up her faux fur wrap and clutch purse and headed for the stairs.

Ryan waited for her in the foyer. "Wow," he said. "Look at you."

"No, look at *you*," she said, straightening his bow tie. He had gotten a haircut earlier in the day and was even more handsome than usual, especially since the bruises on his face were all but gone. "I love your hair short like that."

He studied her from head to toe. "I'll have to get it cut more often then."

"Is the dress okay?"

"Way, *way* better than okay."

"What?" She squirmed under the heat of his gaze. "You don't like the front, right? Too much showing?"

"I *love* the front, but it needs this," he said, bringing a jeweler's box from behind his back.

"What is it?"

"Open it and find out."

Her heart beat fast with excitement as she nibbled on a polished thumbnail. "You open it."

When he flipped open the box to reveal a huge teardrop diamond pendant, she gasped.

"Oh my God!" she sputtered. "When did you, why did you, I mean . . . " Her eyes filled with tears. "It's beautiful."

He turned her around and fastened the necklace, kissing the back of her neck when he was done. "To answer your questions, I got it today when I went into the city to get my tux at the apartment. As for why," he said, moving around so he was in front of her, "I should hope that'd be obvious." He kissed her lightly. "You're absolutely gorgeous, and the thought of having to share you with the world tonight makes me nuts."

Fingering the pendant, she said, "I wish we didn't have to go."

"We don't *have* to do anything."

"Don't tempt me. We *do* have to go."

He wrapped her shoulders in faux fur. "All right, then. After you, my lady."

When Ryan and Susannah arrived at the Seawall Grand Ballroom at the Denver Center for the Performing Arts, most of the expected five hundred people were already inside the room. At a thousand dollars a plate, the Black and White attracted the cream of Denver society and was among the year's most anticipated events.

Before they walked into the room, Susannah stopped him.

"What's wrong, baby?"

"I need a minute."

He put his hands on her shoulders. "Deep breaths."

"This is our grand debut," she said, looking up at him with a small smile.

"Re-debut."

"Stay close, okay?"

"I'll be like glue."

She reached for his hand. "Why does it feel like we're swimming into a shark tank?"

"Because we are."

"Hey, you guys," Bernie said from behind Ryan.

Ryan kissed Susannah's cheek and turned to greet their friends.

"I saw that you called yesterday," Bernie said to Ryan. "We were at Hayden's soccer game."

Susannah heard them talking but had no idea what they were saying. With a critical eye, she checked the yellow and purple sheers suspended from the ceiling over tables covered with the Mavericks' colors.

Decorative lighting cast a warm glow and managed to make the huge room seem almost intimate. There were a wide variety of black and white gowns and an even wider variety of gems. Susannah reached up to touch her new pendant and was relieved to find it right where it belonged.

Unfortunately, her colleagues on the committee reported things were progressing perfectly, and nothing needed her immediate attention. She had no choice but to withstand the inquisitive looks and downright stares directed at her and Ryan. The back of her neck tingled, which was the only warning she got that Henry was nearby.

Out of the corner of her eye, she saw him introduce his parents to some people just inside the door. He wore the big grin of a man who hadn't a care in the world, but when one of the women he was talking to leaned in to whisper something in his ear, Henry sobered and nodded. It didn't take much to deduce that she had expressed her sympathies about Henry's broken engagement.

Susannah tuned back into the conversation Ryan was having with the evening's master of ceremonies, Mavericks' Coach Duke Simmons, and his wife Abigail.

"Are you ready, sweetheart?" Duke asked Susannah.

"As ready as I ever am."

Duke offered his arm.

"I'll see you in a few," Susannah said to Ryan.

He leaned down to kiss her. "Knock 'em dead, baby."

"Don't get lost," she said over her shoulder as Duke led her to the stage.

"I'll be right here."

At the front of the room, Duke left Susannah by the stairs to the stage when he went up to the dais.

"Good evening, ladies and gentlemen," Duke said, silencing the crowd. "On behalf of the Denver Mavericks, it's my great honor to welcome you to the Sixteenth Annual Black and White Ball. I can't tell you how much we appreciate you braving the cold tonight to support our favorite cause, Children's Hospital. This has been an extraordinary year for the Mavericks." He was interrupted by thunderous applause. "And most of my team is here tonight," he said, gesturing to a group of tables in the front of the room.

Susannah chuckled as the guys, wearing a wide variety of tuxedo concoctions, hammed it up to the enthusiastic applause.

"I know I speak for everyone in the Mavericks organization," Duke continued, "when I thank you for your support during the season and throughout the year at events such as this where we try to give something back to the best city in America." He paused for another round of applause. "Now, I'm just here to keep things moving. The real star of the evening, as you well know, is a member of the Mavericks family who needs no introduction in this town. It gives me great pleasure to welcome my dear friend and the chairperson of the Black and White Ball for the last seven years, Susannah Sanderson."

As she climbed the stairs to the stage, the resounding applause embarrassed her, but the hooting and hollering from the players was amusing.

Duke kissed her cheek and left the stage.

While she waited for the players to settle down, she scanned the room. She found Henry watching her with an intense expression on his face, and she quickly moved on. Next to him, his parents were doing their best not to look at her. Susannah's parents and sister were sitting at Henry's table as was Betsy James, who met Susannah's gaze with a satisfied smirk. *What the hell is she doing there? He knows how much I despise that woman. Why would he let her sit at his table? Maybe it's because he knows I despise her, and he's trying to rattle me. Well, it's working.*

Tearing her eyes off Betsy James, Susannah stepped to the microphone. "Thank you, Duke, and thank you all for that warm welcome." The players whistled and hooted some more. They laughed when she said, "Easy, boys." Among other friends, Susannah was comforted to see her divorce attorney at one of the front tables, as well as her caterer friend Carol, who had apparently turned over the event to her staff, since she was dressed in formal attire. The one person Susannah couldn't locate was Ryan. *Where did he go?*

"If you all could take your seats, I have just a few things to mention before dinner is served." She gave a boilerplate welcome on behalf of her committee, the hospital, and the team. Gesturing to the back of the room, she talked about the silent auction and urged attendees to be as generous as possible.

"In addition to the items outlined in your program, Ryan has provided a signed and dated football. He seems to think there might be some interest because of what happened this week, but I'm skeptical." A ripple of laughter went through the crowd.

"Now, I have to live with him," she said in a conspiratorial whisper. "So it would really help me out if someone could pony up a few bucks for that ball." This time applause accompanied their laughter. "If you could also appear to scuffle over it a little bit, well, that would help, too." She smiled at their enthusiastic reaction, but her eyes were drawn to Henry's table where he shared a laugh with Betsy James. *Ugh! Of all people!* "Thank you so much for coming. I'll leave you with this video the folks from Children's Hospital asked us to show to give you an idea of what you're supporting. Enjoy your evening."

Ryan appeared at the bottom of the stairs as Susannah left the stage. When he kissed her, his teammates cheered. He escorted her to their table where Duke and Abigail were sitting with the event's honorary chairman, Chet Logler, and his wife Martha.

Ryan held Susannah's chair for her. "Very funny up there, Mrs. Sanderson."

"Got to keep that ego of yours in check," Susannah said with a saucy smile.

He leaned down to whisper, "As only you can do."

Susannah gasped and grabbed the place card next to hers that said, "Henry Merrill."

"What's that?" Ryan asked when he sat down next to her.

"Nothing."

Reaching for her hand, he unrolled it. "Well, someone didn't get the word, did they?" He tore the card into pieces and tossed it under the table. "No worries, baby."

"That should've been taken care of," Susannah said with annoyance.

"I wouldn't put it past Henry to have gotten here early to swap out the cards." Ryan kissed her hand. "Forget about it, okay?"

She nodded and looked over at Henry's table. "What's he up to with *that* woman?"

Ryan's eyes narrowed. "That's a very good question. An odd pairing, to say the least."

When she glanced at Ryan and saw his eyes fixated on Henry's table, her stomach knotted. The rumors about Ryan and Betsy James had nearly driven Susannah mad, and they had been the final straw for their struggling marriage. She reached for his hand under the table. "What're you thinking about?"

He smiled, but there were no dimples, and his eyes were hard. "Dinner. What are we having?"

Hours later, Susannah was dancing with Ryan when her father tapped him on the shoulder.

"Do you mind if I cut in for a minute, Ryan?"

Ryan glanced down at Susannah, and she nodded. "Don't run away with my girl, Dalton."

"I won't."

With an encouraging smile for Susannah, Ryan left them.

"You're breathtaking," Dalton said as he led her around the dance floor.

"Thank you, Daddy."

"This is a very impressive event you've put together, honey. I'm glad we finally got to attend one of them."

"I am, too, especially since this'll probably be my last year as chair."

"Why's that?"

"Well, with Ryan retiring and leaving the team, they'll probably want one of the other wives to take over."

"I was surprised to hear he's retiring."

"I would've told you before it was in the papers if I thought y'all would've cared."

"I don't know what makes you think we don't care."

"Could be the way you've treated him all these years."

"Susannah . . . "

"Daddy, can I ask you something?"

"Sure you can."

"Do you care at all that I love him? Really, really love him?"

Dalton softened. "Of course I do. In fact, I told your mother and sister just this afternoon that it's time for us to let you live your own life and make your own mistakes."

"Being with Ryan isn't a mistake. Being without him was."

"All I want is for you to be happy."

"If that's what you want, then you have to accept Ryan. He loves me so much. What more can you ask for in a son-in-law?"

"Not much, I suppose," Dalton conceded.

Henry and Betsy danced up next to Susannah and her father.

"Hello, Susannah," Henry said with a mild smile. "Another great success. Congratulations."

"Thank you," she said, going to great pains to avoid making eye contact with Betsy James, who wore her auburn hair in a sleek pageboy. Her plunging white gown offset a deep tan and showcased a spectacular pair of surgically enhanced breasts.

"Henry, I'd like to have a word with you," Dalton said. To Betsy, he added, "Would you please excuse us for a moment?"

Startled, Betsy said, "Certainly." With a perplexed glance at Henry, she left the dance floor.

Dalton kept a hold of Susannah's hand as he led her and Henry to a quiet corner.

"You don't need me, do you, Daddy? I want to go find Ryan."

"This will only take a moment, Susannah." He turned to Henry. "I want to ask you a question, and I'd like a truthful answer, son."

"Of course, Dalton," Henry said with a charming smile. "What can I do for you?"

Dalton raised Susannah's wrist, which was still bruised and swollen. "Did you do this to my daughter?"

"Daddy!" Susannah struggled against the light grip her father had on her hand. "Don't."

"I asked you a question, Henry."

"We were talking," Henry stuttered, "and she was going to leave before I had a chance to tell her—"

"*Did you do this to her?*"

"It was an accident," Henry blurted out, his ears flaming with color.

Dalton's jaw shifted, hardening his usually amiable face.

Susannah was both mortified by the confrontation and fascinated to see a side of her father that was new to her.

"I'm disappointed in you, Henry," Dalton said in a measured tone. "At the very least, I believe you owe my little girl an apology."

Henry finally looked at Susannah, but there was contempt in his eyes. "How about what she owes me?"

"She doesn't owe you a damned thing," Dalton growled. "I'm waiting."

"I'm sorry."

Susannah cast her eyes down.

"Steer clear of her, do you hear me?"

"Yes," Henry said, his Southern breeding forcing him to add a reluctant "sir" before he walked away.

"Daddy," Susannah said, stepping into his embrace. "You didn't have to do that."

"Yes, I did, and when I get a chance, I'll apologize to Ryan. I was wrong to infer that he'd do such a thing to you. He may not have been husband of the year, but he never laid a hand on you as far as I knew."

"He didn't. He wouldn't."

Dalton kissed his daughter's forehead. "I love you, Susannah, my sweet girl."

"I love you, too.

Susannah lifted her head off her father's shoulder to find Ryan having an intense conversation with Betsy James in the back of the room. Her hands were on his chest, and she appeared to be pleading with him. He took her by the shoulders as he replied to whatever she had said to him. Susannah felt her stomach clench with nausea when she realized everyone in the room was watching her husband have a passionate moment with the woman most of them had once believed to be his mistress.

Breaking free of her father's arms, Susannah crossed the room. She felt her control slipping through her fingers, and as she marched over to Ryan, the room around them disappeared. A red haze blurred out everything except Ryan and Betsy. Touching.

With his back to her, Ryan didn't see her coming.

"Susannah," Carol said, reaching out to try to stop her.

Susannah ignored her friend and kept moving, the roar in her head escalating with every step she took.

"Get your hands off my husband," Susannah snarled.

Startled by her sudden appearance, Ryan cried, "Susie!" He pulled his hands from Betsy's shoulders like he'd been scalded.

When Betsy didn't immediately remove her hands from Ryan's chest, Susannah shoved her.

Betsy recovered and took a swing at Susannah, sending a gasp through the room.

Ryan moved fast to put himself between them and grimaced when Betsy's fist made contact with his ribs.

"*Get away from him!*" Susannah shrieked, flailing against the hold Ryan had on her arms, which was the only thing that kept her from hitting Betsy.

"*Susannah!*" her sister exclaimed. "You're making a spectacle of yourself."

"Shut up, Missy!"

When Ryan tried to lead Susannah away, she pushed at him. "Don't *touch* me," she snapped. "I can't believe you'd even *talk* to her in front of everyone, let alone touch her!"

"I wasn't talking to her! She was talking to *me*."

"*I saw you with my own eyes!*" Susannah knew she was creating a scene that would keep tongues wagging forever, but she didn't care. That he'd put his hands on that woman and let her touch him had sent Susannah right over the edge.

His eyes grew dark with anger. "You saw *nothing*."

She burst into tears. "You're a liar! Everything they said about the two of you was true. *You lied to me!* Once again you've ruined *everything!*"

Ryan bent down, scooped her up, and made for the door.

Struggling against him, she pounded on his back. "*Put me down!*" Before they turned the corner, she caught a last glimpse of the cream of Denver society watching with astounded expressions on their faces as her enraged husband hauled the star of the evening from the ballroom. The last thing she saw was Henry's victorious smile.

Chapter 26

RYAN CARRIED HER ALL THE WAY TO THE PARKING GARAGE where he finally put her down, shed his tuxedo jacket, and wrapped it around her.

Bernie and Dalton were right behind them.

"Ryan!" Bernie called. "Wait a minute."

"Not now, Bern."

Susannah stood in stunned silence as Ryan opened the passenger door and urged her inside the Escalade.

Bernie put himself between the door and the car so Ryan couldn't close the door. "Take a breath, Ry," he said with a hand on Ryan's heaving chest.

"I don't want a breath. I want to leave, so please get out of the way."

"Not so fast," Dalton said, pushing past Bernie to lean into the car. "Do you not want to go with him, Susannah?" He brushed back the hair that had sprung loose from her French knot. "Because all you have to do is say so, and I'll get you out of there."

"This is between me and my wife, Dalton," Ryan snapped. "You need to butt out."

"I'm not leaving my daughter with you if it's not where she wants to be."

Susannah shivered from the cold and wept quietly, not at all sure *where* she wanted to be right then.

Bernie squeezed in beside Dalton and bent over to talk to Susannah. "Susie, honey, I know you're upset. But you need to give Ryan the opportunity to explain what was going on in there. It's not what you think."

"I know what I saw."

"And I'm sure it looked really bad, but you need to hear him out."

"I'm tired of hearing him out, and I'm tired of his lies."

Ryan exploded. "*I've never lied to you!*"

Bernie took a firm hold of her hand. "We're friends, aren't we, Susie? Good friends?"

A sob hiccupped through her as she nodded.

"Do you trust me?" Bernie asked.

She nodded again.

"Then please go with him, and let him explain. Will you do that for me? I give you my word that everything he's going to tell you is true."

Susannah studied him for a long moment before she whispered, "Okay."

Bernie kissed her cheek. "It's all going to be fine. I promise." He straightened and turned to Ryan.

"Thank you," Ryan said.

Bernie hugged him. "Keep your cool."

Ryan nodded. "Dalton, Bernie will tell you what's going on. Will one of you please get Susannah's coat and purse?" He handed the coat check ticket to Bernie.

"Of course," Bernie said.

Dalton leaned into the car to kiss Susannah. "We're at the Inverness. If you need me, call my cell phone, and I'll come get you. I don't care if it's the middle of the night."

"Thank you, Daddy."

Dalton closed the car door.

Ryan got in and started the car. Before he shifted into reverse, he looked over at her with such fury that she burrowed deeper into the big tuxedo jacket.

He didn't say a word during the drive home.

When they arrived, he came around and lifted her out of the car.

"What are you doing? I can walk! Put me down."

"Be quiet, Susannah," he said as he carried her inside and deposited her in the den. "Don't move." He turned around and went back out the front door.

A moment later she heard the car door close, and he came inside carrying a piece of paper, which he handed to her.

Her hand trembled when she reached out to take it from him. "What's this?"

"Read it."

Susannah unfolded the paper to discover some sort of form. She saw his typewritten name and Betsy's with legal mumbo jumbo typed below the names. "I don't understand . . . "

"It's a restraining order."

Startled, Susannah looked up at him. "She's got a *restraining order* against you?"

"*No!*" he growled. "*I* have one against *her!*"

"Why?"

Like a caged tiger, he paced the room. "At first it was a nuisance. She seemed to be everywhere I was. She'd show up at practice, at appearances, in restaurants. If I was there, she was, too. I never paid much attention to it, because there are always so many people around us. I lumped her into the groupie category and went on with my life. But then I found out she was telling people we were seeing each other. This wasn't long after we lost Justin, and everyone knew we were having a hard time." He ran a hand through his hair. "Anyway, I went to see her to tell her to stop spreading lies about me. That turned out to be a big mistake."

"Why?" Susannah asked in a small voice.

"Because she secretly videotaped our discussion and threatened to send the tape to you unless I had sex with her. I panicked, because the tape would prove I'd been in her apartment. You and I were on real shaky ground at that time, and I was pretty sure some of the rumors she'd started had reached you by then."

"They had."

"Anyway, I refused to sleep with her, and she went nuts. She was totally crazy, hitting me, scratching at my face. It was insane."

"You told me you got those scratches at practice."

"What was I supposed to say?" His eyes were hard and dispassionate. "You know, though, I realized something tonight. When you said I'd ruined everything—*again*— that was the same thing you said when you threw me out. You heard something about me and her and just assumed I was having an affair with her, didn't you?"

"I heard a lot of things."

"*But you never asked me!* You never came right out and said, 'Are you sleeping with her, Ryan?'" By now he was shouting. "Because if you had, I would've told you the same thing then that I'll tell you now: No, I am *not* sleeping with her. I haven't slept with her or *anyone else* since the day I met *you!*"

"Things had gotten so bad between us," she whispered. "We were hardly speaking to each other. Everyone was saying—"

"We'd been married for almost *nine years,* Susannah. Didn't you owe me more than to believe a bunch of rumors?"

"We hadn't had sex in months. I thought—"

"*You thought wrong!*" he roared. "I couldn't get rid of her! I found her naked in my car after practice one day. That's when I told Bernie what'd been going on, and he was all over me to call the cops about protection. I laughed at that. I mean six-foot-four, two-twenty Ryan Sanderson seeking protection from a *woman?* I was more afraid of the ridicule from the other guys than I was of her." His laugh was bitter. "Turns out I should've listened to Bernie."

Susannah was almost afraid to ask. "Why? What happened?"

"After you and I separated, she really ramped up her game. She was popping up every day rather than a couple of times a week. Then, my apartment in the city was broken into and ransacked."

Susannah gasped. "Oh my God."

"I knew it was her because every photo of you and us together had been shredded."

"She should be in jail!"

"They arrested her and charged her with breaking and entering."

"Why wasn't it in the paper?"

"The team used its clout to keep it out of the press. I was terrified it would get back to you. I figured you would think we'd had a lover's quarrel or something. I didn't want you to know anything about it because I was still hopeful we might get back together. I knew you'd think the worst if you heard my name and hers mentioned in the same sentence."

As Susannah sat down on the sofa, she felt sick to realize she had done exactly that tonight, even after all the progress they'd made over the last ten days.

"The judge put her on probation and issued the restraining order. What you *think* you saw tonight was me reminding her she can't be within a thousand feet of me. I was giving her ten minutes to leave, or I was going to call the cops."

"You were touching her . . . "

"*I was trying to get rid of her!* For Christ's sakes, Susannah! After everything we've been through, do you honestly think I'd risk it all with a piece of shit like her?"

Susannah was filled with shame as tears rolled down her face. "I'm so sorry, Ry. I just assumed—"

"I *know* what you assumed. Most of Denver knows what you assumed."

Hurt radiated from him like an infection that threatened to destroy them both.

"I just saw you with her, touching her, letting her touch you, and I lost it."

"I know. I was there."

"I'll bet Henry had something to do with it," Susannah said, remembering the smile she'd seen on his face.

"I'm sure he put her up to confronting me. They both knew I wouldn't call the cops or make a scene with you there if I could avoid it."

"Instead *I* made the scene."

"And it was a doozy," he said, but there was no humor in the statement. He reached up to take off his bow tie and release the top button of his shirt.

"You should've told me all of this."

"You're probably right. If I had, then I could've dealt privately with your accusations rather than having to withstand them in front of my teammates and just about everyone else we know."

She winced. "I'm so sorry for what I said."

"So am I. When we were at the cabin, I swore to you, I *swore* I've never lied to you and I've never cheated on you. Yet, in spite of everything we've shared over the last week, you saw me with her and automatically thought the worst. That hurts, Susannah."

"I know, and I'm sorry. I wish there was something I could say or do to take it all back."

"I need you to have faith in me. I need you to believe me when I say I love you, that I've been faithful to you, that there's no one else for me but you. I can't be fighting these battles for the rest of my life. I just don't have it in me."

She stood up and went to him. With her arms around his waist, she said, "I do believe you, and I *do* have faith in you. I'm sorry I doubted you, even for a second."

"A second is all it takes to undermine everything we've worked so hard to put back together. Not to mention it gives people like Henry and Betsy and your sister such satisfaction to see us brawling."

"I know, and I'm so sorry, Ry." She broke down into deep sobs. "I'm sorry."

He put his arms around her and held her close to him, but his embrace was stiff rather than welcoming. "You must be getting tired, and we have court in the morning."

"What are we going to tell the judge?" she asked.

"What do you mean?"

She rolled her lip between her teeth and wiped at the tears that remained on her face. "After what happened tonight, I'd understand if you wanted to go forward with the divorce."

He closed his eyes and sighed. "I don't want a divorce, Susannah. That's the last thing I want. We have a baby on the way. Have you forgotten that?"

"Of course I haven't. But I don't want you to stay with me just because of the baby."

"I'm not," he said, but she wasn't convinced. "Go on up to bed. You need to get some rest."

"Are you coming?"

"In a while."

She reached up to kiss him. "I love you, and I'm so sorry about what happened tonight. I'd give anything to be able to go back to when you were giving me this beautiful pendant."

"Me, too."

Susannah left him and went upstairs where she moved robotically through the motions of getting changed, washing off her makeup, and freeing what was left of the knot in her hair. She took off the pendant and held it in her hand for a long time before she put it away in her jewelry box. When she got in bed, she was hit by a new wave of helpless sobs. The image of Ryan's wounded face was more than she could bear, and she cried until she thought she'd be sick. She had embarrassed him in front of the most important people in his life and accused him of such terrible things, only to learn he had been victimized by that horrible woman. Susannah shuddered when she recalled the dreadful scene at the ball.

"He's never going to forgive me for this," she whispered to the dark, empty room. "And I can't say I blame him."

She lay there reliving the evening's events for a long time until she drifted into a restless sleep. Dreaming of pretty babies and football games, she awoke with a start when the faces of the babies began to disappear. Her heart beat hard as she looked over and found the other side of the bed empty. The bedside clock read three twenty.

Susannah got up, reached for her robe, tied it tightly around her, and went downstairs. Still wearing most of his tuxedo, Ryan was asleep on the sofa with his arm hooked over his head. Her heart hurt at the sight of his handsome face, soft with sleep. She squatted down next to him and caressed his cheek.

"Ry?" she whispered.

He didn't stir.

She removed several of the onyx studs from his tuxedo shirt. Pressing her lips to his chest, she said, "Ryan."

"Yeah?"

She looked up at him and saw the exact moment when he remembered what happened earlier. "Come to bed with me." Clutching his hand, she added, "I need you."

After an endless moment during which Susannah feared he would say no, he let her help him up from the sofa and lead him upstairs.

She removed the rest of the studs and eased the shirt off his shoulders. When she reached for his pants, he turned away from her, went into the bathroom, and closed the door.

Susannah got in bed and waited for him.

Ten minutes had passed when he came out wearing only his boxers and slipped under the covers. He stayed on the far side of the bed, so she moved closer to him.

With her hand on his belly, she kissed his chest.

He trembled ever so slightly.

Encouraged by his reaction, she slid her hand down.

He stopped her. "Don't, Susie."

"Let me love you, Ry."

"Not now."

Her eyes burned with tears. "It might help."

"No, it won't."

The first thing Susannah noticed when she awoke at eight fifteen the next morning was that she had her pillow all to herself. The discovery was devastating. With his back to her, Ryan slept as far from her as he could get in the big bed. The gulf between them was wide, and she wondered if they would be able to bridge it a second time. She was studying his broad, muscular back trying to figure out what to do when the phone rang. Wondering who would be calling so early, she reached for the extension.

"Hello?"

"Susannah?"

Her heart sank and her stomach clenched. "What do you want, Henry?"

"I was just checking to make sure you're all right."

"I'm wonderful. Why wouldn't I be?"

Her reply seemed to throw him. "But," he stammered. "Last night, you were so upset . . . "

"Oh, that," she said with a light chuckle. "That was just a silly misunderstanding. Ryan explained everything, and we had a good laugh over it." She squealed into the phone. "Ryan, *quit* that!"

"I wonder if that's what Betsy says, too," Henry said sharply.

Susannah saw red but kept her tone light and chatty. "Since we both know she can't come within a thousand feet of Ryan, I doubt she says much of anything to him. I really appreciate your oh-so-concerned phone call, Henry, but my husband and I are still in bed. It really is *much* too early to be calling here. We don't get up until we absolutely have to."

"You're a bitch, Susannah," he fumed. "I'm glad I realized that before I shackled myself to you for a lifetime."

"And you're a manipulative weasel. Thanks for showing me once again that going back to my husband was the smartest thing I've ever done. Don't call me again." She turned off the phone and returned it to the cradle on the table. When she looked over at Ryan and found him watching her with amusement in his eyes, her heart lifted with hope.

"An Academy Award-winning performance," he said.

"He deserved nothing less."

Ryan extended his hand to her.

Her hand met his halfway across the big bed, and he laced his fingers through hers.

They lay there looking at each other for a long moment.

Giving her hand a little tug, he brought her closer to him. "What exactly was I doing while you were on the phone?"

With a coy shrug, she said, "Oh, I don't know. Maybe you were kissing me right here?" She pointed to her neck.

He replaced her finger with his lips. "Here?"

"Yes," she sighed. "Right there."

He caressed her breast through the silky fabric of her nightgown.

"Ry—"

"Don't say anything."

"But I want you to know—"

He stopped her with a deep, soulful kiss.

Tearing her lips free, she said, "That I love you."

"And I love you," he said as he rolled her under him and eased her nightgown up to her waist.

Her final thought before she ceased to think at all? *Thank you so much for calling, Henry.*

Chapter 27

HAND-IN-HAND, SUSANNAH AND RYAN SCRAMBLED UP THE courthouse stairs.

"We're going to be late, and he's going to let us have it," she said.

"I tried to tell you that when you wouldn't get your butt out of bed."

"You wouldn't *let me* out!"

"We've got thirty seconds."

"Move it!"

Breathless, they arrived at the judge's outer office at exactly eleven o'clock.

"His Honor and your attorneys are waiting for you in chambers, Mr. and Mrs. Sanderson," the judge's clerk said with a dour frown. "Go on in."

Ryan ushered Susannah in ahead of him.

"Mr. and Mrs. Sanderson," Judge Prescott Tohler said. "How nice of you to join us."

"Your Honor," Ryan said with a nod for his attorney.

"You two have given me more gray hairs than anyone has in a long time."

Ryan held a chair for Susannah as they exchanged perplexed glances.

"First, you get me all excited with this." The judge referred to the newspaper coverage of Ryan's retirement. He read, "'At the press conference, Sanderson also announced the couple recently reconciled.' Oh, that did my old heart good! To think maybe the six months I'd given you had made a difference . . . " He shook his head with satisfaction, but his smile quickly faded. "And then, today when I'm looking forward to hearing *all* about how right I was, I almost choked on my Honey Nut Cheerios when I saw this." He held up the morning's society page featuring a huge picture of Ryan hauling a furious Susannah out of the Black and White ball.

Susannah gasped. "Oh, no . . . "

"Oh, yes, Mrs. Sanderson. Oh, yes." With a deep sigh he sat back in his chair. "You two disappoint me."

Ryan got busy brushing some imaginary lint from his suit pants.

"Do you have any idea how many kids in this city look up to you as some sort of hero, Mr. Sanderson?"

"Yes," Ryan said through gritted teeth. "I'm acutely aware of it."

"Then how can you justify fighting with your wife in public like this?"

"Your Honor," Susannah said. "It wasn't his fault. It was mine. I totally overreacted to something." She glanced at Ryan who was fixated on the window behind the judge. His face was flushed with anger, which sent a burst of nervous energy through her. "Ryan was just trying to get me out of there before I made it worse."

"And you've gotten to the bottom of this misunderstanding?" the judge asked.

Susannah reached for Ryan's hand. "Yes, we have."

Ryan nodded in agreement.

The judged rested his elbows on his desk and leaned forward. "Are you at all curious as to why I've handled your divorce somewhat unconventionally?"

At that, both attorneys perked up.

"We have something in common, you and I," the judge said.

"We do?" Susannah asked, glancing at Ryan.

The judge nodded. "I, too, lost a son." Pausing for a moment, he added, "My son was sixteen years old when he was hit by a car crossing a street he'd crossed a hundred times before. And as devastating as it was to lose him so suddenly, I can't imagine how much worse it would've been to never have known him at all."

When she was swamped with tears, Susannah looked down at her lap.

Ryan squeezed her hand.

"We lost our boy nineteen years ago," the judge continued. "And for a very long time afterward, I thought I was going to lose my wife, too. We just couldn't seem to get back on track. It took years—*years*—for us to laugh together again."

"I'm sorry for your loss," Susannah said in a whisper.

"And I'm sorry for yours." He shifted his eyes to focus on Ryan. "I've followed your career, Mr. Sanderson, from the time you and your pretty young wife landed here in Denver, and I've admired your grace under pressure. You two always seemed to be so happy together—at least that was what you showed the public. So I was saddened to hear of your loss a few years back and even sadder to find your names on my docket a short time after that. Because I know better than most what you'd been through and how long it can take to get a marriage back on track after a loss like the one you'd suffered, I couldn't help but wonder if you were acting in haste. That's why I insisted on the six-month waiting period, among other things."

"You were right, your Honor," Susannah said. "I acted too hastily."

"Mr. Sanderson, do you feel the same way?"

Ryan's expression was impassive when he said, "Yes, I do."

"Are you sure?" the judge asked him. "I need to be certain. My bag of tricks is empty. I'd already decided if you two came in here today and told me you still wanted the divorce, I was going to grant it."

"I don't want a divorce," Ryan said.

"Neither do I," Susannah said.

The judge studied them for a long moment before he said, "All right then. The petition is hereby withdrawn. I hope I won't see your names on my docket again."

"You won't," Susannah assured him.

The judge shook hands with both of them. "Good luck to you."

"Thank you," Susannah said. "You stopped us from making a huge mistake."

"I just had a feeling about you two," he said. His clerk called him into court a minute later.

While Susannah received a hug from Diane, she watched Ryan shake hands and exchange a few quiet words with his attorney.

"Are you sure everything's all right, Susannah?" Diane asked.

"I'm positive. I know I made quite a scene last night—"

"Oh, please. That was the most excitement we've had in this town in years. I wanted to stand up and cheer when you shoved that rotten bitch Betsy James."

"I'm still mortified that I acted that way."

"If that woman had had her hands on *my* husband, I would've done the same thing. Most of the women there would agree with me. So don't worry about it."

With another hesitant glance at Ryan, Susannah added, "I'm hoping we can put the whole thing behind us."

"I'll be wishing for all good things for you both, Susannah. You deserve it."

"Thank you for that and for everything else over the last year." Susannah took a deep breath. "So how'd we do last night? My abrupt departure caused me to miss the best part—the grand total."

"$2.1 million."

"Wow," Susannah gasped. "That's two hundred thousand better than we've ever done."

"Ryan's ball put us right over the top. We got two hundred ten thousand for it—by far the most we've ever gotten for a silent auction item."

"Oh, boy," Susannah said with a chuckle. "That'll go right to his head."

Diane smiled. "In this case, it's warranted."

"Susannah, are you ready?" Ryan asked.

With one last quick hug for Diane, Susannah left with Ryan.

In the parking lot, he held the car door for her.

Before she got in, she asked, "Where do we go from here, Ry?"

"Um, home?"

"That's not what I mean."

"I don't know, Susie. I guess we'll just do the best we can."

"I want more than that. I want what we had before I lost my mind last night. I want to go back to before my father cut in on us."

Ryan looped a hand over the top of the car door and dropped his head. "I do, too."

Susannah cradled his head against her chest. "I just wish I knew what to do," she said. "I want to fix this, but I don't know how." During the course of their meeting with the judge she'd realized the closeness they had shared that morning wasn't going to be enough on its own to undo the damage she had done to their fragile union.

He brought his eyes up to meet hers. "Let's just take it one step at a time. First, we go home."

"What's second?"

He shrugged. "Since I missed my big chance to unload you in there, I guess we'll cross that bridge when we come to it."

She smiled. "Thank you."

"For?"

"Not unloading me. I wouldn't have blamed you if you had."

"Nah, I'm stuck with you. One way or the other, we'll get through this, darlin'. The way I see it, we've been through worse, right?"

"We certainly have. But I hurt you, Ry. I hurt *us*."

"Yeah, you did, but I'm a big boy, and I'll get over it. Eventually."

"Then I'll just wait."

"Fair enough."

Susannah moved the curtain aside to watch the snow and was startled by how fast it was accumulating. A streetlight illuminated the blustery sheets of snow as her stomach knotted with worry. *Where is he? Just a few days ago, he was driving me nuts with his hovering. Now, I have no idea where he is or when he'll be home.*

She sighed and turned to once again inspect the table she had set for them. Dinner was ready, and she had spent the last hour resisting the overwhelming urge to call him. She didn't want him to think she was checking up on him. *God, I hate this. Everything is so stilted and weird between us.*

The lights flickered as she wandered into the den to toss another log onto the fire, wanting to keep it going in case they lost power. She turned on the T.V., figuring if he'd been in an accident it would make the news. Thirty minutes and no mention of him later, she heard the garage door open and breathed a deep sigh of relief. She went into the kitchen and was tending to the asparagus when he came in from the garage, bringing a blast of cold air with him.

"Hey." He took off his boots, Stetson, and leather coat in the mudroom. "The roads are a mess. Sorry I'm so late."

"It's okay."

"Did you try to call?"

"No."

"Oh, good. I was afraid you were worried. My phone is dead. I just took it off the charger this morning, so it must need a new battery."

"I'll get you one tomorrow if you want."

"If you have time." His nose was cold when he kissed her cheek. "Something smells amazing. What'd you make?"

"Lamb."

"Mmmm, my favorite."

"I know."

"Want me to set the table?"

"Already did it," she said, gesturing toward the dining room.

He peeked into the room. "Wow, Grandma Sally's china and everything. What's the occasion?"

She shrugged. "No occasion."

After Susannah had lit the candles on the table and poured him a glass of wine, they sat down to eat. "How is it?" she asked.

"Fabulous. Your cooking was number two on the list of things I missed the most about you when we were separated."

Amused, she took a sip of her ice water. "Do I need to ask what number one was?"

He shot her a withering look that made her laugh. "I feel bad drinking wine in front of you."

"Go right ahead. It doesn't appeal to me at the moment."

He looked at her with concern. "Are you feeling sick?"

"Kind of queasy today," she said, pushing the food around on her plate. She wasn't sure if it was the pregnancy or the tension between them that was causing it.

"Did you call Pam?"

She shook her head. "It's normal."

"You didn't have it before, with Justin."

"I think I got lucky."

"Are you sure you're okay?"

Touched by his genuine concern, she squeezed his arm. "I'm fine. What were you up to today?"

His expression changed to one of distaste. "I had a meeting at the T.V. station."

"I gather it didn't go well?"

He shrugged. "I hate going in there. They treat me like I'm an idiot."

"What do you mean?"

"They kind of talk down to me like I'm too dumb to understand the business side of the station. It's irritating."

"You *own* the place. Shouldn't they be sucking up to you?"

"You would think."

"That makes me mad."

He chuckled. "Me, too. I think I'm going to find an asshole who wants to buy a T.V. station."

Susannah laughed. "That would serve them right. Don't forget—you're Ryan Sanderson. You can do—or *not* do—anything you want. Let your management people run the station, and don't bother yourself with it."

"Good point. I was just trying to show some interest. Anyway, how was your day?"

"Kind of quiet." She didn't think he needed to hear she had spent most of the day on the phone canceling what was left of her wedding to Henry. "But I got a few more calls from people who were thrilled I gave Betsy

James the what-for at the ball. You'll also be glad to know they loved the way you picked me up and took me out of there. They found it very sexy."

His dimpled grin lit up his face.

"That went straight to your fat head, didn't it?"

"Of course it did. I guess all this approval means we can safely show our faces in polite society again."

"Let's not get ahead of ourselves. I still say we lay low until someone else causes a bigger scandal than I did."

"Good plan."

"I talked to my mother today, too. She actually asked about you."

"*Get out of here,*" he said, shocked.

"I'm not kidding," she said, appreciating his reaction. She was desperate to do anything she could to please him. "She really did."

"Well, it's *something.* I'll take it."

The lights flickered again.

"We might be in for another night in front of the fire," she said.

"That'd be fine with me."

Her smile was small and sad as she remembered the night they had slept by the fire at the cabin—and most likely conceived the child she was carrying.

He brushed his thumb over her hand. "Why so sad, baby? We're doing all right, aren't we?"

She shrugged. "I guess. But I feel like we're trying too hard. Even when we're doing what we always did, *it* is in the room with us."

"At least we're trying."

"I wish I had something to blackmail you with," she said.

He laughed. "What do you mean?"

"Well, when you were in my shoes—groveling to right some terrible wrongs—you had my wedding with Henry to hold over my head. You had a way to force me to deal with you. I don't have anything like that."

His eyes softened as he brought her hand to his lips. "You really have no idea what you have over me, do you?"

He was right, she had no idea.

"Everything, Susie. *You.* That's what you could threaten to take away from me."

"So if I tell you I'm going to leave that'll scare you into getting over what I did to you?"

"Maybe."

She stood up.

"Where are you going?"

"To pack."

He tossed his head back and laughed as he reached out to bring her onto his lap. "You're not going anywhere."

Her eyes filled. "I want you back, Ry."

"I'm right here, baby."

"But you're *not.*"

"Yes, I am."

"I wanted to call you. When you were late, I *was* worried. I was worried sick, actually, but I was afraid to call you."

"*Why?* That's crazy. You can call me any time you want to. You know that."

"I didn't want you to think I was checking up on you."

"Susie." He gave her a playful little shake. "I *want* you checking up on me. It shows me you love me."

"I was afraid it would also show you . . . "

"What?"

"That I don't trust you." She took a deep breath. "I guess it doesn't matter because your phone was dead anyway."

The lights flickered again, but this time the power went out, leaving them with only the candlelight.

"Susannah, baby, listen to me." He turned her chin so she was looking at him. "If you're worried, or scared, or nauseous, or lonely, *call* me. I don't care where I am or what I'm doing, I'll always want to talk to you. And I promise I won't ever think you're checking up on me. Deal?"

Touched, she shook the hand he held out to her. "Deal."

"Feel better?"

She nodded and tipped her head to touch her lips to his. What she had meant to be a quick kiss took a passionate turn when he wove his fingers into her hair and dragged his tongue over her bottom lip.

After several long, hot kisses, he stood up to carry her into the den where he settled her on the sofa and stretched out next to her.

She wrapped her arms around his neck, wanting to resume the kiss.

"Susie," he whispered against her lips. "I love you so much. Don't go to the trouble of blackmailing me, okay? You can have whatever you want."

"The only thing I want is you—all of you."

"You have me."

"Good, because I'm having a craving."

He raised an amused eyebrow. "Anything I can help with?"

She nodded. "In fact, you're the only one who *can* help."

"This sounds serious."

"It's a matter of life and death," she said, unbuttoning his shirt. "Are you up to the task?"

He flexed his hips, pushing his erection into the V of her legs. "What do you think?"

She giggled. "It seems you're well prepared for this mission."

He was still laughing when he captured her mouth in a kiss that was both passionate and reassuring.

In that moment, she finally began to believe they were going to be okay.

Chapter 28

SUSANNAH STOOD IN THE MIDDLE OF THE EMPTY YELLOW room and opened her heart to the storm of emotions that came with venturing in there for the first time since they lost Justin. If she closed her eyes, she could still picture the nursery she had so lovingly put together for him with yellow ducks and gingham curtains. Tears spilled down her cheeks, but she did nothing to stop them, knowing they were a necessary part of this final act of saying goodbye to the son she had lost.

For two long years, his place had remained sealed off from her home and her heart, but someday soon another baby would come home to this room. That baby *would* come home. She felt it with a certainty she couldn't explain and didn't question.

Fear had blossomed into hope over the last two weeks. And tonight, on the eve of what would have been her wedding to Henry, she was filled with the peace she had craved and finally found with Ryan. She was right where she belonged with his child thriving inside of her, waiting to be born to two parents who wanted him—or her—more than they wanted anything else.

Clutched in her hand was the tiny Mavericks jersey she had bought for the baby. She had come in here tonight to find a place to put it until it was needed. Squatting down in front of the window, she raised the lid on the built-in seat and tucked the jersey away inside. She closed the seat and rested her cheek against it, as if to seal the deal she had made with fate. If she bought only that one thing, maybe, just maybe . . .

"Susie? What are you doing, baby?" Ryan asked from the doorway.

She wiped her face and turned to him with a smile. "Just putting something away. Did you get all your football stuff unpacked?"

He came in to help her up. "Right back where it belongs."

"There's no escaping now," she joked. "Your bachelor pad is history."

Leaning in to kiss her, he said, "Good riddance. Are you sure you're okay?"

She nodded. "I haven't been in here since . . . "

"Never?"

"No."

He held her for a long, quiet moment. "I have a present for you."

"You do?" She frisked him. "Where?"

He laughed and led her from the room. "Downstairs."

"I heard you playing earlier," she said as she closed the door behind her. "Was that Enrique Iglesias?" She made a face. "Not your usual thing."

"There's a funny story behind that," he said with a grin as they went down the stairs. "After we beat Atlanta, we were partying in the hotel bar and this lounge lizard type was performing. He did *Hero,* and the whole team sang along at the top of their lungs like idiots. The guy was thrilled. I really think he had no idea we were making fun of him. So over the next week, I learned the song and played it for the guys on the plane after the Houston game. They went nuts, and it sort of became our anthem this season."

"That's hilarious."

"There's another reason why I learned it."

"What's that?"

He led her into the den. "If I tell you, you can't tell the guys," he said in all seriousness.

"I won't," she said, mimicking his grave expression. "I promise."

"You know how he says she takes his breath away?"

Susannah nodded.

"Well, that reminded me of you," he said with a shy smile. "Because you take my breath away."

"Ry . . . That's so sweet. Will you play it for me?"

"After you open your present," he said, gesturing to a small, flat package on the coffee table.

She picked it up and shook it. "What is it?"

"Open it," he said with exasperation.

"Remind you of anyone you know?"

"Susannah . . . "

She tore off the paper and found plane tickets and a brochure for a resort in Barbados. "Oh, Ry, this is fabulous! It's just what we need."

"There's more. Flip it open."

Inside was an engraved card that said, "A Renewal: Ryan & Susannah Sanderson, Sunset on March 21."

"I thought it would be cool to renew our vows on the beach, just the two of us, before your summer semester starts and before the baby comes."

"You set this all up?" she asked, astounded.

He nodded. "I think it's important we do it, don't you?"

"Yes," she said, reaching for him. "It's really important. Thank you for arranging it."

"Is it okay that it'll just be us? I mean, if you want to invite your family—"

"No. It should be just us." She rested against his chest. "Thank you, Ry."

He brushed his lips over her hair. "You're welcome."

Shifting so she could see him, she added, "Not just for this. For coming back, for taking a stand, for fighting for us, for being the guy I need you to be. For all of it."

"If you'd told me the night I first came home that one day you'd be thanking me for it . . . "

She chuckled softly. "I shouldn't tell you this, but . . . "

"What?"

"I can't."

He tickled her, making her squeal with laughter. "Tell me," he said, threatening to tickle her some more.

"Okay, okay." She took a deep breath. "I was secretly thrilled to see you."

He laughed. "Must have been *very* secretly, because you could've fooled me."

"Oh, don't get me wrong. I was mad at you, too. It was just like you to pull something like that."

"I believe you just thanked me for pulling 'something like that.'"

"Shut up."

He grinned. "Make me."

"I thought you were going to play for me."

"You really want to hear that song?"

She nodded.

"You seriously can't *ever* tell the guys. They'll abuse the shit out of me if they think I used it to score with you."

"Are you?" she asked, raising an eyebrow.

He reached for his guitar. "What?"

"Using it to score with me?"

"Well, *yeah.* Why else would I sing such a fruity song?"

She laughed until there were tears in her eyes. "Don't worry. Your secret will be safe with me."

"Don't look at me, or I'll laugh," he said as he played the first few notes.

Susannah was surprised when her eyes filled as she listened to him. Both his guitar playing and his singing were amazing.

The doorbell rang.

"Hold that thought," Ryan said, leaning over to kiss her before he got up.

He swung open the door to find two men in suits on the front porch.

"Good evening, Mr. Sanderson," the older of the two said as they flashed their badges. "I'm Detective Cooper, and this is my partner, Detective Ortiz. May we come in for a minute?"

Startled, Ryan stepped aside to admit them. "What can I do for you?"

Susannah came out of the den and stopped short when she saw the two men. "What's going on?"

"This is my wife, Susannah."

"Ma'am," Cooper said before he turned back to Ryan. "Is there somewhere we could speak privately?"

Ryan put his arm around Susannah. "Right here is fine."

The cops exchanged glances.

"Do you know a Misty Carmichael?" Ortiz asked.

"No, should I?" Ryan asked.

"She claims to know you."

"I've never heard that name before in my life. Have you, Susie?"

"No," Susannah said. "What's this all about?"

"We were contacted earlier today by Ms. Carmichael's father. His daughter, who's six months pregnant, has named you as the baby's father."

Ryan gasped. "*What?*"

Susannah recoiled in shock.

Ryan tightened his grip on her.

"We'd like you to come downtown with us to sort this out," Cooper said.

"There's nothing to sort out!" Ryan cried. "I don't know her! And if there's a woman claiming I fathered her child, why are you guys involved?"

"She's sixteen years old," Ortiz said.

"Oh my God," Susannah whispered. "Oh, God."

"Am I being charged with something?" Ryan asked as his cheeks flushed with distress.

"Not at this time," Cooper said. "Right now, we're asking you to cooperate with our investigation by coming with us."

"I don't see why we can't sort it out right here."

"Normally, we'd do our best to accommodate you, Mr. Sanderson. We're well aware of your standing in this community. However, Mr. Carmichael is a good friend of the mayor's, and we've been instructed to handle this by the book."

"Great," Ryan said, his jaw clenched with tension. He turned to Susannah. "Call Chuck, and tell him to meet me at the station."

She snapped out of her daze and nodded. "I'll be right behind you."

"Stay here, Susie. I'll be right back when they find out I had nothing to do with this."

"I can't just sit here! You can't ask me to do that."

"I don't want you anywhere near this."

Something about his expression filled her with fear, which must have shown on her face, because he looked away from her.

"Mr. Sanderson?" Cooper said. "Grab a coat."

They escorted him—thankfully without handcuffs—from the house a minute later. Susannah was paralyzed as she watched them go. The car pulled out of the driveway and was out of sight before she forced herself to move, feeling like she was wading through quicksand. Her hands shook as she rifled through the papers on Ryan's desk and finally found the home phone number for the attorney he had told her to call.

"Are you *kidding* me?" Chuck exclaimed when Susannah explained what had happened.

"I wish I was."

"And he's never met this girl?"

"He said he's never even heard of her."

"Do you believe him?"

"Yes, but the cops—they seemed pretty sure they had the right guy. I can't imagine they'd go so far as to come here and pick him up, especially in light of who he is, if they didn't have some kind of evidence against him, right?"

"Susannah, listen to me. This is a girl in crisis. Everything she says and does will be suspect at this point. Don't panic, and don't think the worst until we know more."

Susannah took a deep breath. "Okay. Can you get over there right away?"

"Absolutely. I'm also going to call one of my partners who specializes in criminal law, just in case we need him."

"Do you really think that's necessary?"

"It will be if they charge him with statutory rape."

She gasped. "*They can't do that!*"

"Let's just wait and see what happens. I'm leaving right now."

"I'm leaving, too. I'll see you there."

Susannah's mind raced as she drove to the police station, which teemed with people that Friday night. After fifteen minutes in line, she was told to have a seat and someone would be with her as soon as possible. A tense thirty minutes passed before an officer came to find her.

"Mrs. Sanderson?"

Susannah leaped to her feet.

"Right this way."

She followed him through a winding maze of hallways to a room where Ryan conferred with his attorney.

Ryan stood up when she came in. "Susie! I told you not to come."

His distress was so palpable that anxiety rippled through her.

"What's going on?" Susannah asked as she took the seat next to Ryan and reached for his hand. "What are they saying?"

"Apparently," Chuck said, "this girl, Misty, had refused to name the baby's father until yesterday."

"But how could she name *you?*" Susannah asked Ryan. "You said you've never met her, right?"

"Yes," he said through gritted teeth.

"Are you sure, Ry? You meet so many people . . . "

His eyes were cold as he took back his hand. "I'm positive. I've never met her, and I've *certainly* never *slept* with a sixteen-year-old!"

"That's not what I meant!"

Ryan turned back to Chuck. "What are we waiting for?"

"They're talking to her again. They should be back soon."

They waited in silence for twenty long minutes until the door opened and the detectives came in.

"Mrs. Sanderson, we're going to need you to wait outside."

"Why?" Ryan asked. "If I'm not under arrest and not being charged with anything, why can't she stay?"

The detectives exchanged glances.

"All right," Cooper said. "She can stay. For now."

"Ms. Carmichael said she met you on the evening of September twenty-ninth after one of your games," Ortiz said. "There was a party somewhere downtown. She couldn't recall the exact location, just that there were a lot of people, including other members of your team. She said you bought her several drinks, you danced with her, and then invited her back to your place at . . . " He consulted his notebook and rattled off the address of Ryan's apartment in the city. "Where you had sexual relations."

Susannah stiffened as she listened to the detective's monotone account.

"She's lying," Ryan said first to the cops and then again to Susannah.

"You're going to have to do a little better than that, Mr. Sanderson," Ortiz said.

"No problem." Ryan's eyes flashed with anger. "On September twenty-ninth we played the New England Patriots. We lost twenty-four to twenty-one. I remember that date because after the game I had dinner with my father for the first time in thirty years."

The detectives were clearly taken aback by this news.

"Do you have a phone number where we can reach him to confirm this?"

"I don't know it by heart. We aren't exactly in touch. His name is David Sanderson, and he lives in the San Francisco area. I'm not sure where."

"What restaurant did you go to?"

"Sullivan's," Ryan said, referring to the downtown steakhouse.

"Who paid?"

"I did."

"Cash?"

Ryan thought for a second and then shook his head. "AmEx."

"Where did you go after dinner?" Ortiz asked.

"I was upset."

Susannah reached for his hand and was startled when he shook her off.

"Why were you upset?" Cooper asked.

"Because all he wanted was money—a half million dollars, to be precise."

"Did you give it to him?"

Ryan nodded. "I can get you the canceled check to prove it."

"Did he say what the money was for?"

"Gambling debts. After I left him I drove over to the house in Cherry Hills. My wife and I were estranged at the time. I sat outside for a long time. I wanted to talk to her, but . . . "

"So you didn't go in?"

Ryan shook his head. "I didn't think I'd be welcome. Eventually I went home."

"To your place in the city?"

Ryan nodded.

"Did you see or talk to anyone in the building?"

He thought about that. "Not that I can recall, but it was more than six months ago. The one thing I know for sure is I didn't have sex with this Misty Carmichael or anyone else for that matter."

"He's told me this before," Susannah said in a voice that sounded high and almost hysterical, even to her. "This whole thing about seeing his father and the money and coming over to the house afterwards. He told me this a month ago after we got back together."

"Give us a chance to confirm what you've told us," Cooper said. "We'll be back."

"This is good," Chuck said with an enthusiastic grin. "This is really good."

But one look at Ryan told Susannah it wasn't good. It wasn't good at all.

Chapter 29

RYAN FIXATED ON A FADED POSTER-SIZED PICTURE OF the Rocky Mountains but didn't say a word while one hour stretched into two as they waited for the detectives to return.

"I need to use the restroom," Susannah finally said, and Chuck showed her where it was.

She was washing her hands when the door opened and a pretty young girl came in. Only her pregnant belly gave her away as the girl who was trying to turn their lives upside down. Her long blond hair was in a ponytail, and her blue eyes were red from crying. Susannah was startled to realize the girl was a younger version of herself. She could have been her sister or her daughter.

"Why are you doing this?" Susannah asked her. "My husband has never met you, let alone slept with you."

"Please excuse me," she whispered. "I need to use the bathroom."

"*You're lying!* I don't know what you hope to gain from this, but you're not going to destroy his life—our life. I won't let you."

The girl began to weep. "Please . . . "

A female police officer came in to check on the girl. "Mrs. Sanderson, please be on your way."

"I just want some answers," Susannah pleaded.

The cop gestured to the door, the warning clear in her expression.

With one last pointed look at the girl, Susannah left the bathroom. "I saw her—Misty Carmichael," she said to Ryan and Chuck when she returned to the interrogation room. "She looks just like me."

"What do you mean?" Ryan asked.

"Just what I said. She could be me fifteen years ago."

"What the *hell?*"

Chuck shook his head. "This whole thing stinks to high heaven."

By the time the detectives finally returned an hour later, it was after one in the morning.

"I'm afraid we owe you an apology, Mr. Sanderson."

Ryan's sigh of relief was audible. "I *told* you she was lying."

"Did she say *why?*" Susannah asked.

"She was hired to say Mr. Sanderson fathered her child. However, she wasn't counting on *her* father bringing the police into it."

"*Hired?*" Ryan roared. "By who?"

Ortiz consulted his notebook. "A Henry Merrill and a Betsy James. Do you know these people?"

Susannah, who had been pacing the small room, sat down hard when her legs gave out under her.

"Yes," Ryan snarled. "We know them."

"And do you know why they'd want to do something like this to you?"

"I know exactly why." He told the cops about Henry's history with Susannah and the restraining order he had out on Betsy. "That should be easy enough for you to confirm," he said, barely managing to contain his hostility.

"We have people running their names through the system right now."

"Please tell me they're going to be charged with something substantial," Chuck said.

"They've both been arrested and are on their way in right now to face numerous charges. We're still sorting out the details, but apparently Ms. James knew Ms. Carmichael's family and somehow discovered the girl was hiding a pregnancy."

"So who's the father?" Ryan asked.

"Ms. Carmichael has been seeing a University of Colorado student, whom her parents didn't know about, and he's the baby's father. When Mr. Merrill and Ms. James offered her twenty-five thousand dollars to name you as the baby's father, she saw it as a way for her and the boyfriend to live together. That she closely resembled Mrs. Sanderson was a bonus to them. According to Ms. Carmichael, they figured it'd make sense that you'd be attracted to someone who looked like your estranged wife. Their scheme fell apart because they took a gamble and picked a date when you had a solid alibi, which your father has confirmed, by the way. Eventually, DNA would've exonerated you, but that would've taken a while." He didn't have to add it would've taken just long enough to ruin Ryan's life, which, of course, had been the goal.

Ryan's lips were white, and his cheek pulsed with tension.

"I hope the girl is being charged, too," Chuck said.

"Yes, as a juvenile. Reporting a false crime and defamation."

"Can't you leave her out of it?" Ryan asked. "She's as much a victim in this as I am."

Cooper looked at Ryan with surprise. "Mr. Sanderson, do you have any idea how much trouble you would've been in if we could've made this case?"

"*Of course I do!*" He slapped his hand on the Formica table. "You've given me three hours to sit here and think of nothing else. But she's a kid who was victimized by two people with a thirst for revenge against my wife and me. Leave her out of it."

"I'll pass along your thoughts to the family court judge," Cooper said. "That's the best I can do. You're free to go. I appreciate your cooperation and your patience. I'm sorry again for any inconvenience."

"Is this going to be all over the papers?" Ryan asked.

"We've had several calls from reporters. Unfortunately, it's public information."

"Great," Ryan said. "That's just *great.*"

"You were the victim of a crime, Mr. Sanderson. I'm confident it'll be reported as such."

"Yes, with my name and the words 'statutory rape' in the same sentence," Ryan said with a bitter laugh. "I'm sure that'll do wonders for my reputation not to mention my endorsement deals. Damage done, Detective."

"I'm sorry."

Ryan glanced at Susannah. "Let's go."

Chuck followed them as they navigated the maze to the waiting area, which had all but cleared out in the hours since they had arrived. The doors burst open and four cops came in, escorting Henry and Betsy, who were handcuffed. Henry's coat hung open, and there was a big, wet stain on the front of his pajamas.

Since Ryan and Susannah were blocking their way, the cops had no choice but to stop with their prisoners.

"You stupid son of a bitch," Ryan hissed at Henry, who refused to look at him. "Didn't work out quite like you planned, did it? You just assumed I spent the time I was separated from Susie whoring it up, didn't you? Must've been a big shock to hear I had a rock-solid alibi that had nothing to do with another woman. I've got to give you an A for effort, though. When you go over the edge, you do it spectacularly."

"Fuck you," Henry muttered.

"Ryan, don't," Susannah said, placing her hand on Ryan's back. "He's so not worth it."

Henry's eyes filled when he looked at her. "This is all your fault! You drove me to it by jerking me around for years."

"No, Henry," Susannah said quietly. "You drove yourself to this with your unhealthy obsession with another man's wife."

"Today was supposed to be our *wedding* day, Susannah. You made promises to me, and then you left me for *him,* just like you always do."

"*Ryan,*" Betsy said with a frantic edge to her voice. "I only went along with it because I love you. She doesn't appreciate you. Not like I do."

"Shut up, Betsy," Henry snapped.

"All right, that's enough," one of the cops said. They ushered Henry and Betsy toward central booking.

"*Ryan!*" Betsy cried again before the door closed behind them.

Susannah clutched her stomach when a vicious wave of nausea rippled through her.

"What's wrong?" Ryan asked.

"I think I'm going to be sick."

He hustled her outside into the cold, which was a shock to her system after the stagnant air of the police station.

"Better?" he asked.

"Yeah."

He turned to shake hands with his attorney. "Thanks for everything tonight, Chuck."

"You might want to consider civil charges against them," Chuck said.

Ryan shook his head. "No way. This'll get enough ink without me perpetuating it. I just want it to go away."

"You'll both be called to testify if it goes to trial," he warned them.

"Freaking nightmare," Ryan muttered.

"Take your wife home," Chuck said, his hand on Ryan's shoulder. "She's looking kind of pale. You'll both feel better after you get some sleep."

He left them, and Ryan guided Susannah to the passenger side of her car. They drove home in silence to a house where the lights were still on in the den, his guitar still leaned against the sofa, and the fire had burned down to embers. The house was exactly as they had left it, but everything was different. Altered.

They went up to bed and lay awake for hours, both trying on their own to absorb what had happened, what had nearly happened, and the stunning array of implications.

"Ry?" Susannah finally said as the sun began to peek through the blinds.

"What?"

"Talk to me."

"What do you want me to say?"

"Something."

"Hmmm, how about I'm grateful to be here with you and not in jail? Or, your ex-fiancé did a real number on me? Or how about this? I appreciated your support. Where do you want me to start?"

She sat up to look at him. "What's that supposed to mean? You appreciated my support? I was right there with you the whole time."

He chuckled, but there was an edge to it that set her already frazzled nerves further on edge.

"If you have something to say, just say it."

"You believed it. For an instant, you believed what they were saying about me. I saw it on your face."

"Ryan Sanderson, I don't know what you think you saw, but the only thing I was feeling was shock—the same thing you were feeling."

"No, it was different for me, because I *knew* I hadn't done anything wrong. You weren't so sure."

"*How can you say that to me?* I never thought for *one second* that you fooled around with a teenager!"

He mimicked her tone and her accent when he said, "'Are you sure you don't know her, Ry? You meet so many people.'"

"That was a perfectly honest question! I was just wondering if maybe you *did* know her, and she'd turned something innocent into something more. We both know how that can happen to people like you who're in the public eye. We've *seen* it happen. That's all I was saying." When her stomach churned violently, Susannah bolted for the bathroom and vomited.

Ryan came to the doorway. "Are you all right?"

With her head hanging over the toilet, the whole thing finally hit her, and her sobs echoed through the bathroom.

He wet a face cloth and sat down next to her, drawing her into his arms. Running the cloth over her face and mouth, he wiped away her tears.

"I didn't believe them, Ry," she said between sobs. "I didn't. I believed you. I tried to help you. When I said you'd told me that story about your father before. I tried to help."

"Okay, baby. Let's just forget about it."

She pulled away from him. "Do you believe me?"

"Yeah," he said, bringing her head back to rest on his shoulder.

"I'm so sorry," she sobbed.

"For what?"

"Henry. You tried to warn me he was dangerous, but I never imagined he'd do something like this to you."

"He didn't do it alone," Ryan said bitterly. "He found an able accomplice in psycho bitch. We should've reported him when he sprained your wrist. Maybe *that* would've scared the piss out of him before any of this could've happened."

Susannah chuckled sadly. "I just can't believe . . ."

"What, baby?"

"That they hate us so much just because we're together and we're happy," she whispered. "It's overwhelming."

"Well, they're going to be punished for it."

"So are you. What you said to the detective about your reputation and your endorsements was true. This'll kill your Q."

He shrugged. "I didn't do anything. That's got to count for something."

"The whole ugly mess will be in the paper tomorrow—what happened tonight, Henry, our broken engagement, the restraining order, a rehash of the fight at the ball. All of it."

"Probably."

She shuddered.

Ryan helped her up and leaned against the counter while she brushed her teeth. "Why don't we go to the cabin for a few days until it dies down? We'll just pretend like nothing ever happened."

"Won't running away make us look like we have something to hide?"

He grimaced at the irony. "We've got nothing left to hide, so let's go right now before this thing has time to settle in and infect us with its ugliness. Do you feel up to it?"

"I guess I can be nauseous there as well as here."

He kissed her forehead. "Hurry up. Pack what you need and throw on a coat. We'll sleep when we get there."

On the way to Breckenridge, they made two phone calls despite the early hour—to Bernie and to her parents in Florida. They were all shocked to hear what had transpired and agreed Ryan and Susannah were doing the right thing by going to the cabin.

"Let me know if you need anything, man," Bernie said. "I just can't get over this."

"Believe me, neither can I," Ryan said.

Susannah's parents were flabbergasted.

"It's just *outrageous,*" was Dalton's take. "That Henry would do something so evil and not just to you and Ryan but to that young girl, too."

"I know, Daddy," Susannah said. "I'm still trying to get my head around it."

"We're here for you if you need us, Susannah," her mother said. "We're here for both of you."

"Thank you, Mama. We'll call you in a few days." As she ended the call, it wasn't lost on Susannah that it had taken an evil act on Henry's part for Ryan to finally earn her parents' support. She glanced over at him. "Are you having trouble staying awake?"

He shook his head. "I'll be surprised if I can sleep when we get there. I'm so wired."

Susannah took his hand and rested her head on his shoulder. She must have dozed off because she awoke as he carried her into the cabin. "Hey," she whispered. "That was a quick trip."

"Especially when you slept for most of it."

"Sorry."

"Don't be. It's been a long night." He helped with her coat and tucked her into bed with a kiss. "Go back to sleep."

"Are you coming in?"

"Not yet."

She reached for him. "Stay for a minute. Please?"

He shrugged off his coat and stretched out next to her.

"That's better," she said with a sigh, as she curled up to him.

She fell asleep to the feel of his fingers running through her hair. When she woke up, it was twelve thirty, and she was alone and nauseous. Groaning, she rested her hands on her still-flat abdomen. "Please tell me you're not going to make your Mama sick for months."

Her stomach surged, and she ran from the bed, making it to the toilet just in time. Since there wasn't much left after the last time, she suffered through a wicked bout of dry heaves that left her weak and sweating. She sank to the floor with a whimper.

Ryan stood at his favorite ridge and absorbed the stunning view of the Rocky Mountains, replacing the flat image from the interrogation room poster with the magnificent real thing. His hands had finally stopped shaking, but he hadn't been able to sleep or eat. He still couldn't believe how easy it had been for everything he'd worked so hard for to be seriously threatened.

On his first day at rookie camp, Duke Simmons had taken him aside for a stern lecture about protecting himself from the crazies who followed professional athletes around. It was a lecture Ryan had taken to heart, and he had a strict rule about never being alone in a room with a woman who wasn't his wife. He had broken that rule only once and paid a mighty price for it. In a culture where celebrities were guilty until proven innocent, he had learned that accusations on their own could be destructive enough.

Another piece of advice—this one from his mother in the days just before he signed with the Mavs—kept running through his head: it takes a lifetime of hard work to build a reputation and just a minute of stupidity to lose it. He'd found out in the last twenty-four hours that your reputation could also be stolen from you if someone hates you enough to go to such extremes.

He cringed when he imagined the headlines in the morning's *Denver Post*. Just weeks after he had been hailed as his generation's greatest football player, his fans were reading about statutory rape, restraining orders, and broken engagements. He wondered how many people wouldn't bother to read the whole story and would come away thinking he *had* impregnated a sixteen-year-old while separated from his wife. The whole thing made him sick, and for once he was actually grateful his mother wasn't around. It was also sickening to realize he had to rely on his deadbeat father to provide an alibi. But at least his old man had stepped up for Ryan when he needed him for once, so there was that.

With a deep sigh, he finally allowed himself to think of Susannah and the flash of revulsion he had seen on her face in the minutes before the police had led him from the house. When he needed righteous indignation, she had given him mute shock. He wanted her to scream and yell and tell the cops there was *no way* he could be guilty of these charges. No way. But they had spent fourteen long months apart—fourteen months during which she was well aware that he had been confronted with opportunity every day. So in some deep, private part of her where her insecurities lived, he was certain she *had* believed what the cops were saying, despite her protests to the contrary.

With one last long look at the spectacular view, he turned to walk back to the cabin to check on her. As the snow on the path crunched beneath his feet, he told himself he couldn't let these feelings fester or Henry would succeed in destroying something far more valuable to Ryan than his reputation. He and Susie had worked so hard and come so far—too far to let the hatred of others bring them down. So as he approached the cabin, he made a decision to chalk up her reaction to the shock of the moment and let it go. It might not happen overnight, but he *would* let it go.

Inside, he shed his coat and kicked off his boots before he went into the bedroom to see if she was still asleep. The bed was empty, so he called for her.

"In here," she said from the bathroom.

He found her on the floor crying. "Susie," he said, alarmed. "Baby, what's wrong?"

Sobs hiccupped through her as she said, "I'm bleeding."

Forgetting every thought he'd had at the ridge, he dropped to his knees in front of her and reached for her hands. "Susie, look at me."

She raised her shattered eyes to meet his.

"I need you to listen to me, okay?" Where this calm was coming from, he couldn't say, because what he really wanted to do was bawl right along with her. "Are you listening?"

Fat tears fell from her eyes as she nodded.

"I'm right here, I love you, and everything's going to be fine. We're going to get you to a doctor, and they're going to tell us the baby is just settling in for the ride, okay?"

"I can't," she sobbed. "I can't do this again."

"Susie," he said firmly. "You're a mom now. The baby needs you to be strong. *I* need you to be strong." With his hands under her arms, he helped her up, and then held her close to him. "Can you be strong? For me?"

With her head resting against his chest, she whispered, "There's nothing I wouldn't do for you."

His eyes flooded with tears, and his voice was hoarse with emotion when he said, "Come on, baby. Let's go."

Epilogue

"IT'S A PERFECT DAY FOR FOOTBALL IN THE MILE HIGH City of Denver, Colorado. Welcome to Fox's coverage of the Denver Mavericks' final home game of the regular season. I'm Steve Tate along with Terrell Peterson. Terrell, the Mavs secured a place in the playoffs with last Sunday's spectacular come-from-behind win against Chicago and will end their season with this match-up today against the Kansas City Chiefs. And what a season this has been for the Mavericks, behind first-year Quarterback Todd 'Toad' McNeil, who's done an admirable job of stepping into the formidable shoes left by Ryan Sanderson."

"That's right, Steve," Terrell said. "And today the Mavericks will honor Sanderson, who brought home three Super Bowl trophies during his ten years with the team, by retiring his number."

"While we wait for the ceremony on the field to begin," Steve said, "we're joined by Ryan Sanderson's high school football coach, Jimmy Stevens, who's in the studios of our affiliate KDFW Fox 4 in Dallas. Thanks for joining us, Jimmy."

"It's a pleasure to be with you, but I sure do wish I was there!"

"We should mention Jimmy just had a knee replaced or he'd be here in Denver today," Terrell said.

"You bet your life I would," Jimmy said.

"Tell us what this day means to you as the coach who first saw a potential NFL quarterback in Ryan Sanderson," Steve said.

"Oh, I can't tell you how proud I am of him and everything he's accomplished in his career. Ryan always played with guts and smarts. I see a lot of players with one or the other but few with both. He was such a pleasure to coach, and I'm delighted the Mavericks are honoring him this way."

"And just days after we heard Sanderson has signed a new five-year deal with Nike came this week's news that he'll be taking over for you as coach of the Arlington Colts when you retire next month," Steve said. "Can you tell us how that came about?"

"Well, since Ryan announced his retirement from the Mavs earlier this year, he and I have had several conversations about his interest in coaching at the high-school level."

"Did that come as a surprise to you, Coach?" Terrell asked. "I mean he could do anything he wants in the NFL, on television . . . "

"No, it really didn't surprise me," Jimmy said. "He believes he has something to offer these kids, and I couldn't agree more. I've been contemplating retirement for some time now, with my bum knee and all, and the idea of turning over the reins to Ryan took hold over the last few months. Who better to coach the Colts than a guy who got his start right here in Arlington and went all the way—and did it with so much style and class."

"Well said, Coach," Steve said. "Thanks for sharing your thoughts with us. It looks like they're ready on the field, so we'll turn it over to Darren Murphy who's with Mavericks' owner Chet Logler. Darren?"

"Thank you, Steve. Chet, before we get started, let me ask if you thought you'd see your team back in the play-offs again this year—the first year in a decade without Ryan Sanderson calling the plays."

"No," Chet said bluntly. "I didn't expect it at all, but as we've seen all season, Toad McNeil wasn't just sitting on the sidelines collecting dust the last few years. He was watching Ryan, taking notes, and mentally preparing himself to do exactly what he's done for us all season. He learned from the very best."

"Thanks, Chet," Darren said. "I'll turn the microphone over to you."

"Good afternoon, Mavericks, fans!" Chet said to applause. "I'm Chet Logler, and it's my pleasure to preside over this very special day in the history of the reigning world champion Denver Mavericks! Today we honor the greatest player ever to wear the Mavericks' purple and yellow."

The crowd went wild.

Ryan and Susannah waited in the tunnel by the forty-yard line while Chet gave a quick overview of Ryan's many accomplishments as a Maverick.

She brushed her hands over his Mavericks' jersey. "You look great."

He tipped back his Stetson and leaned in to kiss her. "So do you." Wiggling his eyebrows, he added, "You know I love it when you wear my jersey."

"It covers all my baby fat."

"You are *not* fat! You're gorgeous. And since my number is being retired, maybe you could retire tonight wearing just my number, hmmm?"

She rolled her eyes. "Two more weeks until you're back in the saddle, cowboy."

"I'm *never* going to make it," he groaned.

They fell silent when Chet said, "Ladies and gentleman, please give a warm welcome to the last man to ever wear Mavericks' number eighteen—Ryan Sanderson, accompanied by his wife, Susannah."

Susannah looked up at Ryan. "Ready?"

He nodded and adjusted his Stetson. "Let's do this thing."

Holding hands, they emerged from the tunnel to thunderous applause that lasted for almost ten minutes. Ryan and Susannah waved to the crowd while his former teammates stood on sideline benches and cheered.

As Ryan stepped to the microphone, Bernie came out of the tunnel and handed a purple and yellow bundle to Susannah.

"Thank you so much," Ryan said as he took off his hat and waved again to the fans. He took a full minute to gaze at the capacity crowd, as if to drink it all in one final time.

"On a day a lot like this one, but under much different circumstances," Ryan said, "Lou Gehrig stood before his hometown crowd in New York and declared himself to be the luckiest man on the face of the earth." Ryan paused, cleared the emotion from his throat, and said, "Thanks to all of you, that distinction surely belongs to me today."

The crowd replied with another enthusiastic round of applause.

"I was blessed to play this game with some of the finest people I've ever had the privilege to know." He gestured to his teammates as he said, "Everyone in the Mavericks organization, from Chet Logler to Duke Simmons to all my teammates and coaches to Tony in the locker room, and all the folks who work behind the scenes—you made my stay here in Denver the greatest ten years of my life. But it was you, the fans, who made coming to work every Sunday such a pleasure. You stood by me through the good times as well as the not-so-good times, and I'll never forget you."

As the crowd responded to him, Ryan swiped at his eyes and reached out to bring Susannah closer to him.

"I'm also blessed to be joined today by my wife, Susannah, and our one-month-old daughter, Hope Theresa Sanderson."

After the fans had expressed their boisterous love for Susannah and the baby, Ryan said, "It's certainly no secret that Susie and I have had our struggles and our challenges, but her love and support have sustained me. There's no way I'd be here right now if I hadn't had her to remind me every day of what's really important in this life. Now, you've heard this week that we're moving to Texas, but I want to assure you we're keeping our place in Breckenridge, so you won't be getting rid of us entirely." With his hand over his heart, Ryan concluded by saying, "No matter where I am or what I'm doing, I will *always* be the Denver Mavericks' biggest fan—and the biggest fan of the Mavericks' fans. Thank you all so very, very much for this overwhelming honor."

Dealing with her own flood of tears, Susannah smiled up at him as he wiped his face and absorbed the deafening roar of the standing ovation.

Chet returned to the microphone. "At this time, please direct your attention to above the Mavericks' end zone where eighteen becomes just the third number in franchise history to be retired. Ryan, you're joining number four, Johnny Palmer, and number twelve, George Urban, as a legend among legends." He handed Ryan an elaborate plaque to commemorate the moment. "Congratulations."

"Thank you, Chet," Ryan said, accepting the award with a hug for his former boss.

The crowd grew silent as Ryan's number made the slow climb into history. Just as it reached its destination to the right of the purple number twelve, Ryan's teammates, led by Marcus Darlington, broke into an off-key but loud and enthusiastic chorus of *Hero.*

Ryan looked down at Susannah, and they burst into laughter.

With their daughter between them, he leaned in to kiss her before he wrapped his arms around his girls. They had everything they'd ever dreamed of—and then some.

Acknowledgments

AS A LIFELONG BOSTON RED SOX FAN, WRITING A FOOTBALL book wasn't in my plan. So when my muse showed up one day toting Ryan Sanderson—every inch the NFL quarterback—I did what any self-respecting baseball girl would do and turned to the football people in my life for guidance. Thank you to my brother, George Sullivan, for helping me flesh out Ryan's career and stats; my husband, Dan Force, for tolerating my presence *and* my questions during the 2006 NFL season; and my friend, Julie Cupp, for filling in some missing details while resisting the urge to razz me about venturing into *her* sport. Joy Morgan answered all my Denver questions, and Gator fan Debby Boree helped with the Gainesville details. I appreciate their assistance. Thank you also to my eagle-eyed copy editors, Lisa Ridder and Paula DelBonis-Platt, for cleaning me up and keeping me sane. To all those who read, critiqued, cheered, and prayed from the sidelines, you know who you are, and you have my undying love and gratitude for not allowing me to give up. To my editor, Deb Werksman, thank you for making the dream of a lifetime come true. And finally, to my daily reader, plot coach, and coffee tawk compadre, Christina Camara, I simply couldn't have done any of it without you. The wrist twist is all yours, babe.

About the Author

Marie Force has been a writer and editor for more than twenty years. She lives in Rhode Island with her husband, two children, and a dog named Consuela. Visit her online at www.mariesullivanforce.com or via email at mforce@cox.net. Marie would be happy to call into your romance book club meeting or attend a New England area meeting. Contact her by email to arrange an appearance.